Death and Sweet Temptations

AN ALEX BAIN STORY

KRISTEN COAR

CHAPTER I

A cautious dawn blushed across the Chicago skyline, its light a timid witness to the night's transgressions. In the hush of Evanston's sleeping streets, a lone silhouette emerged, dark against the awakening hues of morning. The outline, distinctly feminine, was disrupted by the unmistakable jut of a sword hilt from her back.

She moved with practiced ease, despite the weight of exhaustion and the duffle digging into her shoulder. Behind her, footprints left vague imprints of something dark on the pavement.

Not her blood. Not her mess to clean—her roommate Argo would handle that when he got up.

At her doorstep, Alex Bain's form cut a stark contrast against the quiet suburb. Her shadow stretched long, contorted by the muted pastels of dawn, pooling at the base of weathered brick.

The air hung still, as if offering a silent benediction.

She inhaled deeply—October crispness laced with damp earth, decaying leaves, the distant hush of Lake Michigan. A neighbor's fireplace whispered woodsmoke into the morning, nearly erasing the lingering metallic tang of blood still clinging to her senses.

For a second, she let it.

Her eyes closed, and a stray dance of wind brushed her face with an unexpected heat, reminding her that it had been unseasonably warm this year.

Her breath wavered as she opened her eyes. The tension in her ribs loosened—but only just—as her fingers brushed the doorknob. Cool metal met her skin. She hesitated.

The relief tried to creep in, the kind that came after surviving another night on Chicago's streets. She should have felt it, let the exhale be final. Instead, something coiled tight inside her refused to let go.

The door creaked open. Then she saw it. The tear in her sleeve.

Her grip tightened. Adrenaline, muted but still simmering beneath the exhaustion, surged back to the surface.

The deep slash through her leather jacket ran clean across the forearm, stopping just short of flesh.

Alex stared. The phantom heat of the strike ghosted over her skin. Too close. Way too close.

A pulse kicked at the base of her throat.

Unable to look away, recent memories cleaved through the fog of her fatigue, as sharp and insistent as the blade that had drawn blood from her target.

Earlier that night.

The zoo, usually filled with laughter and overpriced popcorn, had transformed into a bleak stage for their grim pursuit under the cover of darkness.

"Did you get the bastard?" Izzie's voice cut through the darkness, sharp with urgency. The two women had been hunting together for years; Izzie knew what Alex could do.

Alex flexed her fingers around the Twins, the short swords resting easy in her hands. Her jaw tensed. "No. Not fatally. He got away."

As the night dragged on, the unsettling awareness of being watched gnawed at her nerves—not by people, but by the silent, captive audience of animals in their nighttime enclosures.

"Do you know where he went?" Izzie asked, hovering beside a pen.

Alex didn't answer immediately. Instead, she lifted one of her swords, dragging her tongue across the edge, tasting, seeking the unique signature of the monster's blood.

Metallic tang. Cold. Tainted with hunger.

Her pulse thrummed in her chest, ancient and knowing, and an invisible thread yanked at her senses, pulling her toward the rogue's fading trail.

"Gotcha," she said, already moving.

Izzie fell into step beside her, her gun raised, but Alex barely registered the sound of her partner's boots crunching against gravel. Her focus had narrowed to a razor-thin edge, every sense reaching for the prey ahead.

The vampire was faster than she expected. Even wounded, he tore through the zoo's winding paths, slipping between benches and empty food stands, the wind howling around him. But he was leaving pieces behind.

It wouldn't outpace them for long. The rogue was bleeding, slowing, his desperation staining the path ahead in frantic drops of crimson. Alex pushed harder, the hunt thrumming in her veins, her senses tunneling in on the fading trail.

Then—an abrupt turn. A dead end.

The bear enclosure.

The air reeked of old fur and damp concrete as the monster whirled to face them, chest heaving, wild eyes darting between Alex and Izzie.

He was young. Too young to have pulled off the kind of murders he had. Someone had taught him. Someone had turned him loose. But that wasn't her problem right now.

"You're done," Alex said, drawing the Twins.

The vampire snarled, baring bloodstained teeth. His shoulders coiled, muscles bunching—

Then he lunged.

But Alex moved faster.

Her swords flashed in the dim light, slicing through the space where his claws had been an instant before. Two fresh gashes split across the monster's chest, dark and wet. It staggered back, coughing up blood in a spray of crimson, its ragged breaths tearing through the silence.

For a fleeting second, she wondered if that was enough.

Then it snarled, and the fight exploded into a violent, breathless storm. Claws slashed through the air; steel met flesh, and bodies collided in the tight space.

The vampire was strong, but not trained—wild and erratic, lashing out with desperate, swinging claws. But Alex was calculated, her every move honed from years of hunting and sword training. Unless he got very lucky, there was only one way this could end.

From the corner of her eye, Alex saw Izzie, her stance wide, gun raised and ready. Alex feinted left, baiting the rogue into exposing his flank to her partner.

Thunder cracked the night apart.

Izzie's bullet slammed into the vampire's shoulder, snapping his body sideways. Not a kill shot. But enough.

Alex moved with the opening. She surged forward, one blade slicing across his gut, the other aiming higher.

Too slow.

The rogue lashed out wildly, his claws raking through the air—through Alex. Pain flared white-hot across her arm.

The force of the blow sent her stumbling, her sleeve splitting open, leather parting like paper, but the wound was shallow and already healing.

"Alex!" Izzie was already moving, already firing.

The rogue staggered, bleeding, snarling.

Recovering her balance, she sidestepped the monster, her blades flashing up. Steel met flesh, and a severed head hit the ground.

Then dust as the zoo fell silent once more and the wind carried what was left of him out into the night.

Alex exhaled. Fire still roared in her veins, drowning out the distant city noise beyond the enclosure.

"You good?" Izzie asked, her voice even, but her gaze flicked to Alex's arm.

Alex followed her line of sight. The deep gash in her sleeve gaped open, revealing the scraped skin beneath. A fraction slower, and...

She clenched her fists. "Yeah. I'm fine."

Izzie didn't press, but Alex could feel her watching.

It was finally over.

Present

For weeks, Alex had hunted the rogue vampire that had been terrorizing the forgotten corners of Lincoln Park. The predator had preyed on the city's most vulnerable—homeless drifters who wouldn't be missed, lured beneath the North Avenue Bridge and drained slowly over agonizing days. Unremarkably, it had managed to evade the attention of official law enforcement, staying beneath the radar of the police while leaving a trail of death in its wake.

By the time she and Izzie had finally caught up to him, the body count was already too high. A shudder traced down her spine, tightening her shoulders. If Izzie hadn't put the pieces together... She swallowed, jaw clenching. It could have been worse. Much worse.

Sergeant Isabella "Izzie" Bliss had once led the Special Investigations Squad, a division handling the kind of crimes no one wanted to admit existed—especially the ones involving the supernatural. Too outspoken and too damn good at her job, she'd made enemies in the department, costing her rank and resources. But that hadn't stopped her. Izzie was relentless, still hunting the monsters the city ignored, and Alex trusted her more than anyone to have her back. Dangerous work for a human—especially one who was getting on in years—but Izzie never backed down, and that was what made her the best.

"Is it over?" A deep voice echoed through the entrance, drawing her from her reverie.

Alex barely looked up as Argo padded into view, his stout body casting an exaggerated shadow in the dim light.

"Yeah," she sighed. "But not before he ripped out his last victim's throat. A final 'fuck you' to the world, I suppose."

She tossed her hunting kit into the bin near the door, then knelt to unzip her steel-toed boots. The leather was scuffed, the steel plating dented—yet another reminder that she'd let the vampire get too close, hit too hard.

"You did everything you could, boss. You know that."

Alex was silent as she peeled off her ruined jacket, the blood-splattered Nirvana T-shirt, and sword holsters. With an unconscious growl, she flung them into the laundry bin, a little harder than necessary. Tiny droplets of blood spattered the off-white wall behind it.

"Damn it," she muttered. "Whatever. I'll clean it later."

Argo trotted closer, nudging her calf with his wet nose. The warmth of his fur against her bare skin was grounding, but not enough to shake the weight sitting on her chest.

"Argo, it doesn't matter. She's still dead."

The corgi tilted his head, ears twitching. Then, with deliberate mischief, he crouched low, fixing her with his most devastating puppy-eyed stare.

Alex groaned. "Oh, no. Don't even try it."

Argo snorted, then went for the kill.

He spun in tight, dizzying circles, his fluffy corgi butt wiggling with expert-level precision. Once, twice, until the sheer absurdity of it cracked through her walls.

"Oh my god, not fair," she grumbled, scrubbing a hand down her face.

She kneeled and wrapped her arms around him, burying her face in the thick fur at his neck. He smelled like fresh laundry and a little like the expensive salmon treats he liked.

Her chest loosened—just a little. "Okay, okay. You win. You're too cute to be too serious for too long. I bow to your superior disposition."

Argo huffed in triumph, tail wagging like a metronome. "You know what your real problem is, boss?"

"I swear to God, if you say 'stress relief,' I will—"

"You need to get laid."

Alex shoved him off her lap.

"Argo!"

"What? I'm just saying a little action would do you some good. And I don't mean another one-night stand. I mean actually making love. The kind with feelings and aftercare and—"

"I will throw you in the lake."

"You won't. You love me too much."

Alex stood up and grabbed a throw pillow from the couch

and launched it at him. Argo dodged like a trained assassin and hopped onto the coffee table, smirking like an absolute menace.

"It's just basic logic, Boss. If I wasn't stuck taking care of you, I'd have a girlfriend by now. Meanwhile, you haven't had a real relationship since—"

"Not happening. And who says you're stuck?! You're lucky I keep you around."

"Fine, fine." He stretched luxuriously before hopping back down. "But I reserve the right to say 'I told you so' when you inevitably crash and burn from sexual frustration."

Alex rolled her eyes and stood. "I'll keep that in mind, oh wise and sexually enlightened corgi."

She yawned and stretched, her muscles aching from more than just the fight.

"All right, then. Time to get ready, I suppose," she said. "It's an important day at work." Somebody had to pay the bills, after all, and buying new body armor every couple of weeks wasn't cheap.

She stood up, giving Argo one last pat on the head, and began walking to the shower connected to her small bedroom. "Do you mind getting breakfast and the morning papers ready?"

"Sure thing, boss. Take your time. I assume bacon and eggs are on the menu after that battle?"

"Yeah, that'd be great, thanks," she said from the bedroom doorway, peeling off her tight black yoga pants, using the frame for balance.

"And the latest on sugar abroad, plus any company emails that came in earlier this morning?" Argo inquired.

She groaned. "Crap, I had forgotten about that during the hunt." She shrugged off the rest of her clothes with a sigh. "Thanks, dude. You take good care of me."

"Of course, boss. The trade is fair, and besides, you've

grown on me. Either way, how would you afford the premium salmon treats and regular grooming visits if you lost your job?"

"Too true, you stinker." She chuckled to herself, closing the door behind her.

By the time the shower water was hot enough to scald away the night's grime, Alex's mind had already drifted back to the rogue vampire.

For weeks, she had assumed he was a lone predator, another young bloodsucker who lost control and went feral. It happened more often than people realized. But now? Now, she wasn't so sure. He was too sloppy, too reckless. It was almost as if he'd been let loose on purpose.

Alex let the water run longer than usual, the steady stream drumming against her skin as her racing heart gradually slowed, each drop washing away the lingering anxiety and guilt from the night's adventure.

She'd figure it out later. Because if someone had set that thing loose on Chicago... then the hunt wasn't over. Not by a long shot.

CHAPTER 2

Alex turned off the water, the final streams cascading down her back before retreating into silence. Steam curled around her, thick and slow, clinging to the intricate mosaic beneath her feet—a phoenix rising from golden embers, its fiery plumage awash in reds, oranges, and molten gold. The tiles glistened under the dim bathroom lighting, each droplet refracting light like embers catching fire.

She let the warmth linger for a breath longer, the remnants of scalding water still kneading the tension from her muscles. The multiple shower heads—angled jets and a heavy rainfall cascade from above—had worked their magic, unraveling the tight coil of stress wound deep in her bones. This space had been designed for indulgence, and for the briefest moment, she'd allowed herself to enjoy it.

Finally, she stepped back, reaching for a plush amethyst towel as the cooler air pressed against her damp skin like a whisper of reality creeping back in.

Pausing, she glanced at her reflection in the wide mirror. At first glance, she appeared to be a woman in her early thirties, her height commanding but not imposing.

Alex wasn't sure what people saw when they looked at her. A sleek corporate shark in designer heels? A predator wearing human skin? Maybe both. Her cerulean eyes, cool and unreadable, had learned to reveal only what she allowed. Her hair—sun-kissed blonde, still damp—clung to her shoulders like a ghost of the night before. Strong, sharp, composed. Always composed.

"Who are you? What are you?" she whispered to her reflection. They were questions she asked herself almost every day. Alex Bain and dhampir had never felt like fully satisfactory answers to her.

She sighed when no revelatory answers came, then abandoned the mirror to make her way into the closet.

"Time to get ready for the day job," she mumbled, thankful her dhampiric nature or whatever it was allowed her to function with little to no sleep.

Given the significance of the day, she felt compelled to wear a slightly more formal outfit. Falling back on what she knew and trusted, she shimmied into a sleek, knee-length grey sheath dress, which complemented her eyes. She paired it with a set of graceful black Louboutin pumps. Radically high and fashionable heels were her other indulgence. They also made convenient weapons when needed.

Having adorned her corporate armor, she smoothly exited the bedroom and headed to the kitchen, where the tempting aroma of bacon and eggs filled the entire house.

"Smells delicious, buddy!" she said, taking a deep sniff.

"Of course." Argo's voice rang out from his fluffy, round Tempur-Pedic cushion nestled beneath the small dining table off the kitchen. "Looking sharp!"

Though she was reluctant to admit it, his enthusiastic compliment was nice to hear. "Thanks, buddy."

As she noticed the neatly printed reports and emails arranged on the table next to the breakfast spread, she wondered, for the thousandth time, how the clever corgi imp managed it all. She had never witnessed his process; he always took care of these things while she was elsewhere, and her attempts to catch him in the act had always been in vain.

As if reading her mind, Argo popped his head out from under the table. With a sly grin on his goofy canine face, he teased, "If you knew my infernal secrets, the magic wouldn't work."

Raising her arms in mock defeat, she said, "All right, all right, you win. Again. But don't expect any of my bacon."

"What? Why?" he sputtered, paws scrambling on the hardwood floor.

"Too late, buddy. That delicious greasy meat ship has sailed," she teased him right back, her heels clicking across the floor, before taking a seat at the table.

It was already seven in the morning, leaving her with thirty minutes to fuel up while delving into the stack of reports Argo had left out for her. With a strip of bacon in one hand, she couldn't help but grimace as she read about the deteriorating sugar situation south of the border.

"Damn it, Argo, did you see this?" She gestured toward the corgi with her bacon. "Half of their crop is ruined."

Argo whined before she tossed him the remaining piece of her bacon slice. He swallowed, no need for chewing, then chimed in. "Yeah, boss. That's going to be tough. Let's hope those fancy-pants consultants you're bringing in have some tricks up their sleeves."

Her grip on the coffee cup tightened as she finished reading the reports. She could take down a vampire, but she still wasn't sure how the hell to fight a commodity market bleeding out beneath her hands. Maybe if sugar suppliers could be dealt with at sword point, this would be easier.

She reached for another strip of bacon, then continued, "I don't know how our P&L will handle such a massive surge in raw material costs. Those consultants better come through for us. We're certainly shelling out enough for their expertise."

WITH THE DOOR LOCKED BEHIND HER, ALEX STEPPED INTO the world of the living—where crises came in spreadsheets, not body counts. Where battles were fought with strategy decks instead of steel. It was an illusion, but a necessary one. Because beneath the boardroom polish and the neatly organized supply reports, the darkness inside her never truly slept. It coiled just under her skin, waiting for a crack in the façade.

As the city began to wake up and bustle in earnest, Alex Bain checked her leather messenger bag one last time. Her laptop and all the paperwork for her day job were nestled inside.

The walk to the Evanston Metra pickup was brisk, the transition from summer to fall well underway. The station was a quaint, red-bricked building standing nestled amidst a backdrop of lush greenery, adorned with flowering planters and hanging baskets that added a splash of orange and yellow to the surroundings. Dodging the passengers milling about on the platform with practiced ease, she boarded the UPN as it came to a stop along the tracks.

Settling into her seat by the window, with the rhythmic clatter of the wheels on the tracks a familiar soundtrack, she delved into her bag and located the reports to review again. Being well-prepared for the meeting with the Blackstone

Group was essential. She had been looking forward to this day, to kicking off the project that could shape the future of Sweet Temptations and her career there.

As she arrived at the office, she was greeted by a buzz of activity. After a quick hello to everyone, she settled into her office chair, fired up her computer, and began double-checking her schedule. She hadn't made it far before Lainie, her dedicated category manager for Sweeteners, walked in with a slightly flushed look on her face. Alex swiveled in her chair, groaning internally. She knew this was coming.

"Morning, Alex," Lainie greeted, her voice faltering slightly.

"Morning, Lainie. What's up?"

The woman took a deep breath. "Alex, I swear I checked the numbers three times, but this drought? It's gutting us. Our suppliers are already knocking down my inbox, and I have a very real fear they're about to start setting things on fire."

Alex nodded, not surprised. "Not totally unexpected, given the recent weather. Thanks for staying on top of it. Let me know If you need help managing the suppliers."

Lainie sighed. "I'll get right on setting up those meetings, try to get ahead of it."

"Thanks. Also, please work with Finance to prepare a cost impact analysis for the plants in Ecuador," Alex asked, chewing the edge of her pen in thought. "We know someone's going to ask the question."

"I'll get to work on it right away. We'll come up with a solid strategy to navigate through it."

Alex watched Lainie leave the office, her mind already churning with plans and ideas on how to handle the situation. As if today wasn't already going to test her skills, leadership, and resolve, this sugar situation would add an extra layer of stress to an already high-stakes day.

Glancing at her watch, she noted that it was time. Smiling, she stood up and smoothed the front of her dress, then walked out of her office, shoulders back and chin held high. Whatever the day threw at her—rising costs, supply chain nightmares, bloodthirsty consultants—it couldn't be worse than last night. Probably.

ALEX BAIN, VICE PRESIDENT OF SUPPLY AT SWEET Temptations Cakes, stood poised in the company's modern, yet cozy lobby. Behind the big, comfy leather chairs sitting nonchalantly in front of the elevator doors, shelves of the company's delicious products lined the walls. They were always filled with the latest confectionery innovations and on display for visitors and employees alike who might want a tasty afternoon snack or a take-home goody bag.

Twirling a Signature Truffle between her fingers, she eagerly awaited the arrival of the Blackstone team. She had lobbied the company's board to bring them in to help resolve the persistent supply chain issues, and it would be an understatement to say her career was relying on their success. Over the last two years, sugar and other key ingredients had become harder and harder to find consistently. She needed a way to improve the flexibility of her supply chain.

The Blackstone Group would hopefully help her team do that.

Lost in thought, Alex barely heard the elevator ding open. The first visitor emerged, a seasoned gentleman clad in the typical consultant uniform—blue suit, crisp white shirt, sans tie. Following him was another consultant, looking barely out of college, likely the team's analyst. He matched the wardrobe choice of his older colleague, except for the fashionable black

TUMI backpack strapped to his shoulders. Neither paid much attention to their surroundings. They certainly didn't notice Alex waiting for them.

As expected, they were all men. They probably assumed "Alex Bain, VP of Supply" was a man, too. The supply chain industry wasn't exactly known for its diversity, and she had long since stopped being surprised by the oversight. Still, it never failed to irritate her.

And then, as if to break the monotony of their arrival, a final man emerged. He was assisting one of the elderly office administrators, gallantly helping her balance an unwieldy stack of candy samples as they stepped out of the elevator together. It was a surprising and thoughtful gesture, immediately setting him apart from the other two.

The newcomer had an air of quiet confidence as he joined his colleagues. Alex's gaze flicked over him—lean, athletic, the kind of build that came from years of movement rather than just gym sessions. His gray slacks fit too well for corporate-issued wear, hinting at powerful legs beneath.

Probably soccer, she thought absently before a rush of heat prickled at the back of her neck. *What the hell is wrong with me?*

But she couldn't look away. Dark, wavy locks framed a sharp, handsome face. The barest hint of an afternoon shadow added a masculine grilse to already striking features, accentuating a strong jawline and severe cheekbones. Everything about him was controlled—except his eyes. Deep brown, assessing, but filled with something wild.

When those deep brown eyes finally found her leaning casually against the far wall—trying like hell to will away the heat threatening to creep up her cheeks—he gave a subtle nod and a friendly wave of recognition.

He'd done his research and knew who to look for.

Her pulse kicked harder as he closed the distance. Professionalism. Focus.

But the air between them told a different story—something unspoken, charged, just beneath the surface. It was a pull she neither understood nor cared to acknowledge despite the way it curled around her. Ridiculous. Inconvenient. Unacceptable

Closing the distance, the man extended his hand towards Alex. His grip was warm and assured, with a quiet confidence wrapped in restrained strength. As their palms met, a flicker of heat curled low in her stomach, sharp enough to make her inhale just a little too quickly.

Get it together, Bain, she hissed internally.

"You must be Alex, VP of Supply." He smiled, his brown eyes twinkling. "I'm Lucas DaChama, your Engagement Manager. We're eager to get started."

Alex cleared her throat. "Alex Bain. We're eager to have your expertise on board." She could have sworn she detected a glimmer of mutual appreciation in Lucas's eyes. Did he also feel the magnetic pull that was affecting her? If so, he hid it well, but she could see the way his gaze lingered just a fraction longer than necessary as he held her hand in his before he politely nodded.

Breaking the tension, the older gentleman extended his hand with a genial smile. "Rory Davenport, Managing Director. It's great to meet you in person finally."

The younger consultant bounced slightly on the balls of his feet. "Jake Dean, Analyst. Just show me the data," he declared, grinning like this was the most exciting part of his day.

Alex arched a brow, her lips twitching despite herself. "Straight to the point. I like it."

The exchange pulled some of the lingering tension from the air, shifting the mood from stiff professionalism to something easier, lighter.

"Alex. Nice to meet you all." She shook both their hands before continuing, "All right! Time to get to work. We have a lot of problems and not a lot of time to solve them."

As Alex ushered them into the vibrant, high-tech workplace of Sweet Temptations, her chest filled with pride, and she couldn't resist giving them the company line. "Welcome to the heart of Sweet Temptations, where innovation and imagination blend to create chocolate magic."

A quick glance over her shoulder caught Lucas's attention, and she found a mirrored flash of mischief staring right back at her. That look unsettled her more than she cared to admit. The intrigue curled deeper, insistent, impossible to ignore.

Was her carefully curated life about to face a different kind of temptation—one that had nothing to do with cake?

CHAPTER 3

THAT NIGHT, Alex decided to channel any pent-up energy from meeting the consultants into patrolling the moonlit streets of Chicago. She mostly hoped for a quiet evening, but a rebellious part of her itched for something—anything—to distract her from those dark brown eyes.

Maybe she'd even find some clue as to who set up that last vampire. That was logical. Productive. Not reckless. Izzie was tied up with her mundane patrol duties for the CPD, and she wouldn't approve of Alex going solo, but Alex felt a surge of confidence. It wasn't like she was hunting anything. Just keeping an eye out. Keeping busy. Keeping herself from thinking too much.

Right, she reasoned with a sarcastic snort.

Alex chose to roam close to her old haunts, the familiar neighborhood near Northwestern University. The area, normally buzzing with academic pursuits by day, transformed at night, especially near the fraternity houses. Tonight was no exception. As she passed a particularly raucous party, the loud music spilled into the streets, mingling with the shouts and giggles of young, pretty, intoxicated students. Alex knew all too well that these places drew more than just party crashers.

Alex found an elevated spot near the end of the street, which offered a clear view of the festivities. She settled in, her posture still, her awareness sharpening as she watched over the unsuspecting students. Quietly, she nudged open the door deep in her subconscious that held her dark heritage at bay. As the hungry power trickled in, she felt all her senses heighten and expand beyond her like greedy tendrils looking for prey. Ignoring the impulse to take down her own meal, she scanned the crowd, her gaze flitting from person to person, searching for the tell-tale signs of a predator. Body language, a peculiar glint in the eye, reactions from those around them, abnormal body temperatures, even specific scents—many signals could betray a preternatural creature to those who knew how to look and had the perception to see them.

After many hours, as the first subtle hints of dawn warmed the horizon, perhaps an hour away, everything remained calm. *That's a good thing, woman,* she chastised herself silently. But the itch under her skin hadn't settled. That familiar, restless unease told her she'd missed something, even if she didn't know what. She blew a stray strand of hair from her face, exhaling. One more pass, then home.

She was just about to lock up her inner monster when the hairs on the back of her neck lifted. Not a sound, not a movement, but something had shifted. Her gut clenched. Predatory instinct kicked in, sharpening her focus as she scanned the quiet street.

There. She spotted what had caught her attention. A young woman with long, curly brown hair was propped up by a shorter man beside her. At first glance, he appeared completely normal, but then Alex saw it again—a glint of red in his eyes as they caught the streetlight. She tensed, her instincts screaming.

The girl's head lolled to the side, revealing her unconscious state. The man—likely a vampire, Alex guessed from his hurried movements and the nearing dawn—was attempting to drag her off to some hidden lair while the cover of darkness still protected him.

Not tonight, she thought grimly. Alex slipped into the shadows, her movements a silent, swift blur as she darted down the street. *Close enough.* She stepped out from a side street to abruptly materialize right in front of the unsuspecting pair.

"Hey there! Need some help?" she slurred. "I'm headed back toward the dorms, too." She didn't exactly pass for a college girl these days, but she hoped the vampire's focus on his late-night snack would play to her advantage.

"We're fine," he growled, shifting the girl's limp body to his other shoulder. "Go home before you get hurt."

"Oh whoa, whoa, whoa, friend." Alex swayed, raising one hand in a conciliatory gesture while her other hand discreetly reached behind her back for the long knife sheathed there. "Just trying to help. I guess I'll just be on my way then."

She turned as if to leave, clumsily pretending to pirouette, then stumbled directly into them. Flailing her arms dramatically, she collided into them—hard. The vampire growled, his grip tightening on the girl. For a split second, it felt like he wouldn't let go. Then the momentum broke, and the girl tumbled free, spinning into a nearby bush.

"Ah! Fuck!" Alex cursed, now grappling with the "man" who was attempting to seize her instead. "Sorry about that, friend!" She finally wrenched free from his grasp.

The vampire hunched before her, and she could see the beginnings of fangs starting to descend over his lips. With the girl still unconscious on the ground, a fight wasn't just "far from ideal"—it was dangerous. One wrong move and the girl would be collateral. Alex clenched her jaw. *Think fast, Bain.*

Taking a risk, she turned her back on it, pointing toward the eastern sky where the sun would soon rise. "Ah! Look! The sun is coming up," she exclaimed, glancing over her shoulder to see its reaction. He was now peering nervously in the same direction, momentarily distracted by the ruse.

"Don't you just love a good sunrise!" She turned around to him. "Hey! Do you want to watch it with me?"

"I will find you, slut," it hissed, then disappeared down the street.

As soon as the vampire was out of sight, Alex rushed to the bush where the girl had landed. She found her groaning softly, wiping at her mouth where a slight blue residue shimmered.

"Hi there. I'm Alex." She crouched next to her. "How are you feeling?"

The girl groaned again, struggling to get onto her feet. Alex winced, noticing the scratches and cuts marring her skin from the tumble into the bush. Offering her hand, she said, "Can I help you get home? What's your name?"

The girl pinched her nose, then pressed a palm to her forehead. "Goddamn, my head hurts. I didn't think hangovers were supposed to hit until the next day. What's up with that?"

"Dang, that sucks. I totally know what you mean," Alex replied, pulling the girl to her feet. She didn't actually know what she meant—Alex had never experienced a hangover, probably thanks to her supernatural metabolism—but empathizing seemed the right approach. "Hey, can I help you get back to your dorm?"

"Yeah," the girl answered, rubbing her arms against the chill. "Uh, thank you. I'm Brittany. Uh, was there a guy with me?"

"Hi, Brittany." She pulled off her leather jacket and handed it to the shivering girl. "No, sorry. It was just you. I was heading to the bus stop when I saw you fall into the bush there."

"Well, that's embarrassing," Brittany admitted with a lopsided smile. She then leaned her head onto Alex's shoulder and wrapped an arm around her waist for balance. "You know, Alex, you're the best. I'm so glad I met you."

"Don't worry about it, kid." Alex smiled back, her voice soothing as she began to guide them both toward the distant lights of the campus. "I remember my days here."

They walked in comfortable silence, Alex supporting Brittany all the way to her dormitory. After the dorm door closed securely behind the girl, Alex let out a relieved sigh. *I did good tonight*, she thought. But as she turned away, a flicker of unease settled in her ribs. That blue shimmer on Brittany's lips? Alex would bet her next paycheck that wasn't from a cocktail.

CHAPTER 4

AFTER THE HIGH of saving the girl, Alex was pleasantly surprised to find the next couple of days relatively quiet. At Sweet Temptations Cakes, Alex worked closely with Lainie, refining their strategy for managing the sugar challenges. Meanwhile, the Blackstone consultants had, for the most part, secluded themselves in their private project room. They appeared engrossed in the heaps of data that her team had gathered.

Occasionally, Jack would emerge from the room seeking clarifications on various analyses or requesting deeper dives into specific areas. Lucas, too, made brief appearances, pulling aside each of her commodity leads for in-depth interviews, but otherwise left her alone.

These were only a few moments when Alex encountered the handsome engagement manager, yet with each passing day, his presence grew more and more palpable. By Wednesday afternoon it was as if she could pinpoint his location within the building unconsciously.

You're going crazy; it's just been too long since you got any.

He's not that hot. Get it together! She clenched her fist around the pen in her hand, trying to focus on the spreadsheet in front of her.

Their exchanges had been entirely professional, but Alex couldn't help but feel that Lucas was experiencing it, too. She could have sworn he occasionally stole glances at her when he thought she wasn't looking unless that was a figment of her imagination, as well.

Overall, though, things were chill. With no active investigation or any leads on zoo vampire, she spent another night at Northwestern trying to track down the vampire she'd run into before and check on Brittany. *He was probably just a newbie testing the boundaries,* she told herself for the tenth time when she didn't find him or Brittany. His maker probably reigned him in after she sent him scurrying. For the most part, the vamps in Chicago stayed in their lane, sticking to consensual blood-sharing relationships. Her and Izzie made sure of it.

Still, it made her uneasy that she hadn't identified him and made sure he wouldn't continue the stalking habit. Unfortunately, though, there wasn't much she could do until a body dropped. Even Argo's cooking hadn't been able to completely distract her. Last night's dinner was a wild concoction of chicken, rice, and cheese, all expertly blended and somehow magically baked together into a delectable fusion of flavors and textures. It was as if Argo had taken the essence of comfort food and elevated it to an entirely new level, turning a simple combination of ingredients into a mouthwatering masterpiece. How the infernal corgi managed to operate an oven without thumbs was a mystery that had stopped bothering her years ago, and she just went with it these days.

Alex was chuckling to herself at a mental image of Argo whining for a piece of the chicken he'd just prepared. "Come on, boss! Just one piece!" she mimicked under her breath when a sudden knock at the door jolted her from her reverie.

"You coming to the team building thing?" Lainie asked, peeking in. "I don't want to be the only woman."

"Team building?"

"Oh! Don't tell me you forgot!" Lainie pouted. "STC vs. the Consultants. The soccer game?"

"Crap!" Alex pinched the bridge of her nose. "Look, soccer's not really my thing anymore, anyway."

"No way! I thought you played in college."

"I played in a drunken rec league with a bunch of witches."

"Witches?" Lainie's eyebrows shot up.

"Oh, you know. We were called the Witches, like the name of the team," Alex quickly corrected, a wistful smile flickering across her face as she recalled the truth. They had indeed been witches, and using their light telekinetic powers, they had never lost a game.

"So, then you're coming." Lainie clapped her hands. "You're definitely coming. I know you keep a spare set of gym clothes somewhere in here."

"Oh my god, fine, fine. I'm coming," Alex conceded, turning back to her spreadsheets.

"Now, boss lady."

"Shit, okay. I'm coming." Alex rose from her chair and reached into a large desk drawer, pulling out a gym bag.

By the time she and Lainie arrived at the high school field near the office, everyone was already out kicking balls and warming up.

"Come on! We're late!" Lainie practically dragged Alex the rest of the way.

"The girls are here!" someone yelled from the sideline, waving yellow beanies—those lightweight, on-the-verge-of-tattering scrimmage colors.

Alex jogged the rest of the way, joining her boss, the Chief Operations Officer at Sweet Temptations, in their side's eighteen-yard box. "Hey, boss," Alex said, raising her fist for a light bump.

Steve rolled his eyes. She knew he hated being called anyone's boss. Then he looked down at her feet. "Sneakers? Really, Alex? We actually want to win here, you know."

She shrugged. "It was all I had."

"If you say so. Just tell me you know how to kick a ball. You and Lainie have to play the whole game since we only have two of you. I don't want Operations to be the weakest link. The IT folks are here for crying out loud."

"I'll be fine," she said, rolling a nearby ball onto her foot, balancing it there for a second, then popping it into the air before executing a perfect volley kick, sending it flying into the net. "Besides, Jim from IT played semi-pro for a couple of years."

"Well damn." Steve's brow shot up. "I wonder if Jim from IT can do that."

Alex had always loved soccer, though she never really played on a team until she felt confident in controlling the dark wellspring within her. Instead, she spent hours in whatever abandoned parking lot or field she could find, juggling and kicking the ball when she wasn't at the dojo practicing her sword forms. By the time she was in college and felt she could play with others without putting them in danger, the only option was a rec league with a bunch of witches, but she loved it all the same.

"Who's on the Consultant team, anyway?" she asked, refocusing on the present. She knew the Blackstone Group was only a small part of a broader consulting team supporting international expansion for Sweet Temptations. And she doubted they'd be here since they just started.

"Hmmm," her boss hummed. "The usual PMO crowd. They hardly do anything anyway."

"Don't let them hear you say that." Alex chuckled.

"And the new acquisition integration gals," Steve continued. "And I think two of your guys are here, too."

"My guys?" Alex asked, a flicker of renegade hope lighting her eyes at the possibility it might be Lucas.

"Yeah, not sure which ones, though. Just saw BG on the roster."

"Cool, well, I guess we'll find out."

She was about to take another kick at the goal when a sharp whistle blew, cutting off any further conversation.

"Game time!" their Chief Financial Officer yelled from the sideline. "Get over here so I can tell you your positions."

"Somebody's extra bossy today," Steve grumbled before jogging with Alex to the sideline where their team gathered.

Two minutes later, Alex found herself on the other side of the field, taking the left wing. Her role was basically to sprint up and down the field at breakneck speeds, hoping someone would send the ball her way.

When the game kicked off, she quickly settled into the flow, observing the other team from her position on the far side of the field. Despite the organized chaos of twenty-one other moving bodies around her, her gaze immediately fell to the opponent's center midfielder. She couldn't look away.

She watched him read the play in front of him and step in the way of a pass from her team, taking control of the ball with impressive speed and agility. Watching him dribble through two of her players while directing Jake in front of him for a pass nearly took her breath away. *He's good,* she thought.

As if sensing her attention, Lucas looked over to her, drifting slightly in her direction. And it was all the distraction

Steve needed to hit him with a big defensive tackle, sending the smaller man flying.

Alex winced as Lucas landed hard on the ground, and Steve took off with the ball in the opposite direction.

"Alex!" her boss hollered. "To the corner!"

Shit! That's my cue. Then she took off at a sprint down the line. She guessed Steve would launch a long ball to the corner any second.

She was fast, faster than anyone on the turf by far, and it took a second for her to realize that the little door was cracked open again, and she was pulling a trickle of that dark power to fuel her muscles.

Reign it in, bitch! She tired to ease her pace while still tracking the flight of the ball coming her way.

By the time the ball reached the corner, Alex was already waiting for it. She expertly trapped it on her chest, sending it straight to her feet, then arced it back through the air toward where Jim from IT was barreling into the penalty box. The computer guy shifted his position only slightly to catch the incoming cross perfectly on his head, redirecting it past the Consultants' goalie and into the back of their net.

"Goal!" Steve came charging first toward Jim for a double-fisted high-five and then Alex. "Eat it, Consultants!"

The referee blew the whistle, signaling them all back to starting positions. "Holy shit, Alex," Steve said, clapping her on the back as they walked to the center line.

"Thanks," she said, still trying to tamp down the adrenaline coursing through her veins. "Your pass made it easy."

"Yeah, whatever, just be ready for the next one." He then bumped her fist and retreated to his position.

She was moving back to the far left when she saw Lucas moving to his side from the spot where Steve had clocked him.

"Holy crap, Alex." He broke into a broad grin that sent her stomach fluttering. "You never mentioned you played before."

"What's it got to do with the project?" She shrugged, trying to play it cool, even though her heart was racing—probably from that last sprint. *Yeah, right.*

"Besides," she continued, "you never mentioned it either, and wow, you can really play."

"Alex," he said, his smile broadening even further, if that was possible. "I am Brazilian. Of course, I play futebol." Then he winked at her and ran back to his spot in the middle of the field.

That asshole. Her cheeks burned—definitely from exertion, not because he'd just turned a simple sentence into sin with that damn accent. Nope. Not hot. Not at all. She needed a drink.

The game progressed more or less like that for the next hour. Alex ran up and down the line crossing balls to the center, while Lucas controlled the center of the field for the opposing team. There were only a few minutes left, and the Consultants were up by one.

"Brazil! Go mark Supply!" the Consultant's goalie yelled across the field, preparing to punt the ball. "We just have to hold them for a little longer!"

Lucas nodded and switched out with Alex's counterpart on the other team. He faced her, then turned to the goalie to track the flight of his kick.

As the ball arced toward them, Alex and Lucas converged, both intent on taking control. They leaped at the same time, but as she jumped, Alex's sneakers slipped on the dewy grass, causing her to falter and miss her step. Lucas seized the moment, his body brushing against hers as he darted away with the ball at his feet.

"Fuck!" she cursed, watching him take off toward her goal

and getting immediately distracted by the sight of his shorts stretching over his ass with each stride. "Fuck!"

Luckily, Jake missed the shot from Lucas's pass, and they prepared for the goal kick.

"Nice try, Supply." Lucas smirked in her direction.

As Alex's keeper lined up the kick, she could tell it was coming her way. She squared off with Lucas, both jockeying for position as the ball sailed through the air again. As they pushed and shoved, trying to gain the upper hand, Alex felt the undeniable draw of his hard muscles beneath the shirt she found herself clutching.

In the heat of the moment, Alex let her hand graze his abdomen in the space just above his shorts, catching his gaze just long enough to see a flicker of surprise.

"Ha!" She used the momentary lapse to her advantage, pivoting with her hip to propel him aside, settling the ball at her feet before taking off at a dash down the line. Careful to manage her speed and not appear too supernatural, she sensed Lucas right behind her, his heavy footsteps and labored breaths filling the air. She could almost hear his heart pounding, mirroring the frantic pace of her own.

Approaching the baseline, Alex wound up for her shot, aiming to send the ball flying back to Jim. Just as her foot connected, Lucas crashed into her, knocking them both to the ground. A sharp inhale, the burn of friction, the press of solid muscle—then they tumbled, rolling in a tangled mess of limbs. When the world finally stopped spinning, he was on top of her, hips pressing her into the grass, heat radiating between them in the breathless pause that followed.

They both craned their necks to watch her pass sail directly to where she wanted it to go as Jim leaped high above the defenders to head it into the net one last time. While the pitch exploded in cheers and roars, Lucas turned back to face her, and the world around them screeched to a halt. Her mind whirled at all the things they could do from this position as her eyes locked with his.

Abruptly, Lucas shook his head, causing his raven hair to fall across his face. He then jumped back and off her, extending a hand to help her up. "Nice cross, Alex."

She took his hand, feeling the rough, callused edges of his fingers and the strength in his grip. *God, I want those hands all over me.* She startled at the thought. *Where did that come from?*

"Thanks," she coughed out, quickly pulling her hand back as she got to her feet. "You almost got me."

She could have sworn his eyes darkened at her words, a single corner of his mouth pulling up in a half-smile. "I'll get you next time, Supply."

Before she could respond, as if she'd have anything intelligible to say to that, the whistle blew, signaling the end of the game.

CHAPTER 5

IT HAD BEEN a full day since the supposed team-building exercise, and Alex was two seconds away from stabbing her own hand with a pen just to distract herself. Her body hummed with a restless energy she couldn't shake, and if she spent another minute sitting still, she was going to explode. A good workout. That's what she needed. Something to sweat it out—before she did something embarrassing in front of her coworkers.

And drinks with Izzie. Lots of drinks with Izzie. The woman always knew how to get Alex out of her head and back down to earth.

Concealed in the privacy of her bedroom, she took a moment to savor the familiar surroundings, her eyes roving across the space, appreciating the carefully chosen elements that made it uniquely hers.

Her red-bladed katana was mounted above her bed, and while it looked decorative, it served a purely functional purpose. Even though she didn't often sleep, she kept "Talon" close on hand whenever she did, in case any of the monsters she hunted decided to turn the tables and hunt her instead.

She turned away to change into her workout clothes—a set of form-fitting leggings and a moisture-wicking sports top. Ready to go, her eyes fell once more on Talon. The weapon called to her as it shimmered with a deadly elegance, the shiny blade sparkling against a polished black hilt adorned with intricate dragon engravings.

Since the day a mysterious legal firm delivered Talon to her on her sixteenth birthday—no explanation, no sender, just a polished black case and a name scrawled on the paperwork—Alex had devoted herself to mastering the ancient art of swordsmanship. It was the one thing that was undeniably hers in a world where everything else felt temporary, slipping through her fingers like smoke.

She remembered taking the sword down to a local dojo, where the old owner, Sir Jiraiyai, reluctantly agreed to teach her. In exchange for cleaning the building and performing odd jobs, the old sage imparted his wisdom and expertise. Over the years, she had learned the invaluable skills of emotional control and how to wield a sword with precision. Jiraiyai's teachings helped her temper the simmering rage that always lurked beneath the surface of her mind.

With the katana in hand, she descended into the basement, her private training space. There, Alex took a moment to stretch, her muscles elongating and preparing for the rigorous exercises ahead. She thought about what forms she wanted to practice, then decided to let Talon lead her, flowing according to its soundless rhythms, a dance in the shadows.

The room was soon filled with the rhythmic swish of the blade slicing through the air. Each technique and strike was executed with speed and power guided by elegance. The mat beneath her feet absorbed her sweat, causing it to glisten like tiny stars in the dim light.

As she flowed through each form, her muscles tightened and released in perfect rhythm, the controlled movements stoking a slow, steady heat that spread through her limbs.

Usually, practicing the forms helped her clear her mind, but today, something was different. In the midst of her practice, a flash of Lucas DaChama invaded her thoughts. It was as though he had entered her refuge, an intruder in her private world of discipline. In her mind's eye, she imagined their bodies shifting together in both combat and a different kind of dance.

Her movements grew more intense, mirroring the growing strain within her, the quickened pace of her breathing, and the flush of heat on her skin. Somehow, the martial art forms had transformed into a seductive tango where each step drew them closer together.

As the line between fantasy and reality blurred, she envisioned sweeping his legs out from under him, sending him sprawling. Then, in a surge of raw impulse, she followed him down, straddling his torso, her thighs tightening around his waist as she hovered just above him.

She could almost feel his breath, heavy and labored, beneath her as she rocked on top of him, and her restraint fell away. Heat bloomed across her cheeks, anticipation coiling tight in her core as a slow, insistent pressure built between her thighs—the unmistakable pull of release drawing near.

She sensed his firmness, hardening and pulsating with her, and her body moved up and down, up and down, no longer under her control. The pleasure continued to intensify, building until that final sweet release washed over her.

Then, with a jolt, she snapped out of the trance, her surroundings returning to the solitude of her basement. She was alone, blissfully alone.

"What in the literal actual fuck was that?" she asked the sword, not expecting an answer.

Wiping the cold sweat from her brow, she caught her breath and gathered her composure, taking a few more minutes of forms and deep breathing before re-sheathing Talon. The predictable movements calmed her racing mind, allowing her to regain control of her body.

Herself again, she looked down at her watch. "Shoot! How long have I been down here?" It was almost time to meet Izzie. "Thank God!" she said and began ascending the steps from the basement.

"Boss?" She found Argo waiting for her at the top, his tail wagging in excitement. It must also be time for his dinner.

"Hey, buddy," she said, ruffling his fur affectionately. "You must be hungry, huh? What do you want for dinner tonight?"

Argo's ears perked up, and he tilted his head to the side as if contemplating the options.

"Chicken and rice it is," she said, and Argo barked in agreement, pretending to be an average dog for the moment. He did that sometimes when Alex was overwhelmed and needed to feel normal. With dinner settled, she began to change into more casual attire.

Drinks with Izzie couldn't come soon enough. She was more than just a friend—really, the only one who truly mattered. She had a way of cutting through life's chaos, balancing the heavy with the light, never letting Alex spiral too deep or take herself too seriously.

Tonight, Izzie wanted to meet at their usual watering hole. It was the same bar where she had first found Alex ten years ago during her freshman year at Northwestern.

Tucked away in the heart of Evanston, hidden from the prying eyes of the uninitiated, stood a mysterious and age-old establishment known as The Other Tabard Inn. The bar's origins were shrouded in secrecy, lost in the annals of time, and few dared to question how long it had truly been there. Only those connected to the supernatural community in Chicago and a select few outsiders like Izzie were even privy to its existence.

The Other Tabard Inn was where the mystical mingled with the mundane, a safe place for creatures of the night and those who walked the line.

Its facade was unremarkable, appearing as an unassuming speakeasy from a bygone era. Its entrance was hidden behind an inconspicuous alleyway door. You had to know exactly where to look to find it.

The Other Tabard Inn catered to a diverse clientele that included various supernatural entities who often preferred to remain anonymous, each seeking solace in their own way. The bartender, a cryptic figure known as Finn, was rumored to have been there since the bar's inception, and his knowledge of extraordinary libations and craft beer was unparalleled.

"Hey! Alex! Over here!" Izzie's enthusiastic call cut through the ambient noise as Alex walked through the heavy wooden door of the bar.

Alex flashed a warm smile and made her way to their regular booth tucked in the cozy corner. With a casual flick of her fingers, she signaled Finn for her usual drink. He nodded in acknowledgment, already preparing her order.

Sergeant Izzie Bliss exuded striking confidence, even seated. Though modest in height, her curvaceous frame carried the quiet strength of her Hispanic heritage. When loose, her long brown curls spilled down her back, a stark contrast to the polished bun she typically wore on duty. Piercing green eyes, framed by expressive brows, held a weariness that not even her natural vibrancy could fully erase—the weight of too many years on the force.

As Alex settled into the plush booth across from Izzie, she noticed a few curious glances from other patrons. Some still got squirmy around her friend, especially when she was in uniform. The folks in The Other Tabard Inn typically avoided the police at all costs, and Izzie, even as their unofficial peacekeeper, had never been able to completely put them at ease.

"Sorry I'm a bit late."

Izzie waved off the apology with a dismissive flick of her hand. "No worries, hun. I just got here myself."

Finn placed a glass of deep red wine in front of Alex, her preferred choice. She nodded her thanks before taking a slow sip, savoring the rich flavor.

Izzie leaned back in the booth, swirling her beer with a smirk. "You're acting weird."

Alex lifted a brow. "Weird how?"

"Weird like someone who's got a thing for someone and is trying real damn hard to pretend they don't." Izzie's green eyes gleamed with mischief. "I mean, look at you—dragging me out for drinks on a random weeknight? You never need liquid courage unless you're about to do something stupid or deny something obvious. So, spill."

Alex nearly choked on her wine. "What? Who?"

Izzie's laugh was pure delight. "Oh, come on. You tell me." She pointed her bottle at Alex. "Because if it's not a guy, then I gotta assume you've developed feelings for spreadsheets, and I refuse to believe even you are that far gone."

"There may be a consultant," she mumbled, cheeks turning red.

"It's about time someone piqued your interest in the romance department. You're always so focused on work and hunting."

"It's complicated, Izz. I brought him in, and I can't afford to be anything less than 100% focused with the amount of money on the table."

Izzie leaned in closer, her voice reassuring. "Hun, life is too short to worry about corporate expectations. If you like the guy, why not go for it? You deserve some happiness."

Alex felt a weight lift off her shoulders, the pressure slowly dissolving. "You're right. But not on this one. At least until after the project is over."

Izzie grinned and playfully bumped her fist against Alex's. "That's the spirit! Now I need details. What's he like? Any steamy elevator moments?"

"I don't know what sort of harlequin workplace drama novels you've been reading." She snorted.

Izzie rolled her eyes.

"Fine!" Alex shared a bit about meeting the man and the final cross on the soccer field. Talking with Izzie about him made it seem less daunting, more normal, just a regular, everyday crush. She could totally handle that.

As the conversation flowed, Izzie's expression turned more serious. "Oh, by the way, I heard something unsettling. There was a murder last night, Alex."

Alex's laughter faded. "A murder?"

Izzie lowered her voice. "It happened south of my place. It's still unclear, but something about it doesn't feel right. I hope it's nothing, but you know how things can get. Be prepared, just in case."

Alex nodded, her mind already shifting into her other persona, the one she kept hidden during the day. "I will. You know I'm always ready."

"I know, hun," Izzie said with a slight downturn of her lips.

Then she smiled, turning the mood like only she could do. "But for now, it's nothing. Just focus on that smoking hot man at Sweet Temptations."

Amidst the cozy ambiance of The Other Tabard Inn, as the two friends sipped their drinks and shared stories, Alex's mind wandered back to the vivid memory of how they met. Whether it was the buzz from the wine or her already frayed emotions, she felt compelled to revisit the past.

"Do you remember," Alex began, her thoughts nostalgic, "in college when I first met you? Izzie Bliss, Sergeant of the Special Investigations team." She paused, taking a sip of her drink. "It all started with those mysterious deaths near OTI."

Izzie leaned forward.

"I was just leaving from a post-study session get-together with a couple would be witches, underage and worried about getting caught drinking," Alex continued. "I had a scholarship to maintain, you know."

She could still feel the weight of the fear that had gripped her that night as she walked out into the alleyway. The memory of the creep who had been hitting on her in the bar and how he had followed her out.

"He attacked me," Alex recounted, her voice dropped lower. "He was unlike anything I'd ever seen—stronger, faster. His face practically rippled with darkness."

She could still recall every detail with startling clarity—standing in the alley, digging through her purse for her keys, when a slow, rasping exhale brushed the back of her neck. The stench had hit her first—rot and blood, thick and cloying—coiling around her like a whispered warning before she even had time to turn.

"You will be delicious, young thing." The voice behind the putrid breath hissed in her ear. "Will you scream for me?"

The sheer terror of that moment when her life hung in the balance was like nothing she had ever experienced. In her panic, it felt like her body was tearing itself apart, even though the assailant hadn't actually done anything to hurt her yet.

When he attacked, trying to pin her to the hard brick wall of the building, she had somehow managed to hold him off. Maybe it had been her sword training or the self-defense classes she'd taken at school. She didn't really remember the details, only the feelings and the uncontrollable anger and need to rip her attacker into tiny, wet pieces. However she had managed it, the next thing she saw was him on the ground, scrambling to get to his feet just as Izzie arrived on the scene.

"You closed the distance and shot him, point-blank, in the head and the heart with your big old Glock."

As she spoke, the striking images of that night played before her eyes like a movie reel. The man who had attacked her lay motionless on the ground by her feet, blood and brain leaking out. Then, out of nowhere, he had disintegrated into a light pile of grey dust. His threat ended in the wind of a light breeze.

"I felt it then." Her voice trembled. "That rage, that hunger, buried deep within me."

Izzie later described her eyes, usually clear and blue, flashing black, and how her canines had elongated into fangs. It had been a terrifying awakening for both of them.

"Izzie," she whispered, her voice breaking, "you drew your gun on me when you saw me like that."

Alex knew that Izzie had initially seen a threat in Alex's transformation. But then, she noticed the clear tears streaming from Alex's eyes and realized the heavy breathing was sobs, not menacing growls.

"I helped you calm down," Izzie said. "I explained that you had just been attacked by a vampire."

Alex remembered how Izzie had paused after that revelation in the alley, then continued explaining.

"I said, 'I'm so sorry, hun, vampires exist. They prey on the weak and vulnerable in human society.'"

Alex nodded, caught in the memory, her eyes glistening

with unshed tears. That night had revealed more to Alex than just the existence of vampires.

"But you're not a vampire, are you, hun?" Izzie asked. *"I saw you walk into the bar with the sun still shining bright."*

Alex shrugged but said nothing more, eyes still wide in shock.

She now knew that Izzie had heard legends of half-vampire dhampirs in a recent case but had never encountered one in person before. Nobody still living had.

"I've heard of dhampirs," Izzie mused, lowering her gun, *"half-human and half-vampire."*

Alex trembled in confusion before her.

"Most legends," Izzie continued, *"agree that dhampirs are created when a pregnant woman is turned into a vampire, and the baby is born before the transformation can be completed."*

The question of her own identity had always been a black hole to Alex. She had always felt different—faster, stronger, and prone to bursts of violence and temper. But she had never known exactly why.

"Um, no offense, but you looked pretty scary there for a second. And you're not a vampire." She hesitated. *"Do you think you might be a dhampir, hun?"*

Izzie's conjecture that night had made sense. And with it, she felt stabilized for the first time in her life. She had always been a freak, never sleeping, always angry, and passed from one temporary home to the next. She'd been in more fights as a kid than she could remember.

Growing up in the foster system had left only emptiness where a lot of knowledge should have been. Now, gleaning this piece of potential information, even though it turned her world upside down, opened a door in Alex she hadn't known existed.

Realizing there was a reason for what she was—and that her unnatural abilities could serve a purpose—had given her direction, a cause. It set her on a path of retribution and justice, not just for herself but for victims like her mother, those who had no one to protect them. And from that night forward, it was a path she had walked alongside Sergeant Bliss.

"You weren't scared of me," Alex said to Izzie.

Izzie took another swig of her drink, some local beer. "Of course not, hun. I'd seen worse than you at that point."

Alex chuckled and tipped her head in Izzie's direction.

"You clearly had potential. And a bone to pick with the monsters." Izzie paused. "You just needed someone to explain it to you."

From there, Izzie took Alex under her wing, guiding her through the intricate and perilous world of the supernatural. Her knowledge, though limited to what she'd learned on the force, was enough to set Alex on the path to becoming the city's sharpest weapon against the non-human predators lurking in the shadows.

"Thanks." Alex's eyes met Izzie's. She knew her life could have taken a different, darker turn without her friend's guidance and support.

Walking home under the faint glow of streetlights, Alex felt a sense of calm wash over her. The weight of her recent experiences and encounters seemed lighter now, and she looked forward to getting a few hours of sleep before diving back into the corporate world the next day.

She was sure she could handle whatever shenanigans Lucas DaChama threw her way. But as she stepped into the night, the unease in her chest whispered otherwise.

CHAPTER 6

THE COMMUTE TO WORK the following morning was relatively calm. The weather helped. It was still in that pleasant in-between temperature—chilly but not so cold your buns freeze. Feeling more grounded than she had all week after seeing Izzie the previous night, Alex felt confident in her ability to do the job and manage her emotions. She would actually have to talk with Lucas today. It was the last day of their evaluation, and he would need to present his findings and recommendations to her. She wasn't at all nervous about this impending encounter. Definitely not nervous.

Busy convincing herself that she wasn't worried about seeing and talking to Lucas, Alex didn't even notice when she accidentally bumped into another person trying to squeeze into the same turnstile door to the building, equally lost in thought. They both looked up simultaneously, murmuring embarrassed apologies, when recognition hit like a blow to the head.

"Oh! Alex. Sorry about that. Please go first," Lucas insisted, eyes still wide in surprise, while his handsome cheeks blushed faintly.

"Uh. Sure. Sorry. Thanks," Alex responded as she hurried through the door, her words fumbling out like a silly junior high school girl facing her crush. *God damn it, you're a professional. Get it together, Alex, you silly twat!*

As they made their way toward the elevator, gone were the high-powered business executives, their standard professionalism overwhelmed by an uneasy and awkward atmosphere that hung between them. They exchanged forced smiles and a few polite words about the upcoming meeting. Lucas mentioned that he was excited to share his team's findings, and Alex agreed, her voice a touch too high-pitched.

Finally, they reached the elevator, sitting wide open and completely empty. Alex went in first, and then it was just the two of them, standing uncomfortably, fidgeting, and avoiding eye contact above all else. *Well, at least it's not just me,* Alex thought, on the verge of hysterical laughter at the ridiculousness of the situation.

Then, just as the elevator doors were about to close, they saw another person rushing toward them, trying to make it inside. Without exchanging a word, both Alex and Lucas instinctively reached to hold the door open, their eyes meeting briefly in silent agreement. They didn't want to be stuck alone together in the elevator. But the newcomer waved them off at the last minute, grumpily groping through his pockets.

"Crap! I forgot my cell phone. Go on without me. I need to go back to the car," he said, stepping away.

Alex watched in silence as the elevator doors slowly closed. They were alone.

With a soft, almost imperceptible thud, Alex found herself standing mere inches away from the man. The confined space seemed to amplify the crackling tension that had been building between them over the past week. She could feel his warmth, his magnetic presence, pulling at her like an irresistible force.

When their eyes met, it was like what happened on the pitch but bigger; everything else ceased to exist. They may as well have been suspended in time, bound together by an invisible thread of longing. The hum of the elevator's ascent was the only sound that reached her ears.

Lucas took a step closer, and Alex's breath hitched. His cologne—a rich blend of dark spices—enveloped her senses.

As their fingers brushed against each other, a jolt of fire coursed through her veins. Alex could feel her heart racing, the rhythm of desire pounding in her chest. She wanted nothing more than to close the remaining distance, to bridge the gap between them. But doubt held her in place. Doubt that this was really happening. Doubt that she could trust her own emotions. And definitely doubt that closing the gap would be a good idea, at all.

Lucas's gaze never left hers as his lips, full and inviting, drew ever nearer to her own. The anticipation was a sweet torture, a slow burn that threatened to consume her.

With a whispered sigh, Lucas's hand found its way to her cheek, his thumb tracing the curve of her jaw. Alex's eyelids fluttered closed, surrendering to the inevitable. His touch was searing, igniting an inferno that blazed through her like a wildfire, destroying any lingering doubt.

Their mouths clashed together, Lucas's lips moving hungrily against hers as if he had been starving for this very moment, yearning for it. It tasted of unspoken cravings and hidden fantasies, a shockwave of sensation that left them both gasping for air.

Alex barely registered a small burst of power or magic around them as time seemed to stand still, and then quickly forgot about it, lost in this man. All that remained was the intoxicating taste of his greedy lips, and his searching hands driving her mad, impossible to resist.

But like all stolen moments of enchantment, it couldn't last forever. The elevator's magic, a fleeting portal to a realm of suppressed desire, was slipping away faster than she dared to admit. With one final chime, they reluctantly tore themselves apart, hastily adjusting their disheveled hair and clothing to a semblance of order.

Waiting for the unavoidable, Alex found herself in a momentary daze. Her heart still thundered in her chest, her breaths echoing in ragged bursts. When she looked at Lucas, he seemed equally disjointed, pressing his hands down the front of his shirt, trying to smooth out the wrinkles she had made with her clenching fingers.

Alex finally broke the silence, her voice soft, almost a whisper. "Lucas..."

His eyes met hers, flickering with yearning. "Alex."

At least I wasn't crazy. The attraction between them was mutual and undeniable, but she knew they had to regain their composure before stepping out into the bustling lobby of Sweet Temptations. Slowly, she pulled away, and with an almost imperceptible pop, time once again resumed its steady press forward.

When the elevator doors finally slid open with a soft *whoosh*, revealing the company's vibrant activity, people rushing here and there, always late to the next meeting, they both took a step forward, returning to the business realm. The scent of chocolate and sugar hung in the air, a constant reminder of the world they were about to re-enter.

Alex led the way, her stride purposeful and confident. Lucas followed closely behind, his eyes still smoldering with fervent want but hidden beneath a veneer of calm detachment. They had shared a secret moment, a stolen kiss that had ignited a fire between them. Would it change everything? Hell, Alex wasn't even sure if she hadn't just hallucinated the passionate exchange as she had in her basement the previous night. Was it just an office fantasy released without warning after months of solitude and celibacy?

She tripped a little on the carpet at that last thought, stumbling to regain balance before she completely fell on her face and humiliated herself in front of the entire staff. But before she could finish her ungainly descent to the ground, Lucas was at her side, using both hands to steady her at the elbow.

"You okay?" he asked quietly, helping her regain her footing while her cheeks flushed with embarrassment. Alex was not used to being clumsy in any environment. She could bound effortlessly through the urban sprawl, vaulting cars or fences and dodging thrown knives or surprise punches, all with the grace of a great feline hunter. She glared back at the offending carpet, Lucas still holding her arm in support, not believing such a trivial challenge had tripped her up.

"I'm fine, thanks," she replied curtly, brushing off his assistance with a quick swipe of her hand.

Catching his gaze before resuming her walk to her desk, she noticed his questioning expression, a mix of concern, confusion, and something else that hinted that their elevator encounter had likely been all too real.

Despite the drama unfolding in Alex's mind, the employees in the lobby went about their business, oblivious to the heated charge that seemed to linger around Alex and Lucas. She greeted colleagues on her path to her office, stopping briefly for quick discussions on the day's tasks and challenges. All the while, she was acutely aware of the invisible string that pulled tautly between her and the consultant walking next to her.

As they neared Alex's office, she cast Lucas a business-like smile. "Please, have a seat. Let's dive right into it."

Lucas nodded, ignoring any hint of a double entendre, and selected a chair across from her desk. Though the layer of formality had seamlessly settled back into place, the memory of their fervent kiss still clung to her lips.

"All right," Alex began, her tone direct and poised. "You've had a week to evaluate our operations. What's your assessment?"

He nodded once more, his attention momentarily drawn to the backpack he had placed on the floor beside his chair.

"No, no." She shook her head in dismissal. "I don't want another PowerPoint presentation. Just talk to me."

A warm smile graced his features as he complied, returning the backpack to its spot on the floor and leaning forward. "Of course. Whatever suits your preference."

It was a simple statement, an earnest response to her request, yet it stirred a maelstrom of emotions within Alex. It felt as though he spoke two distinct languages—one meant for the VP of Supply conducting a formal meeting and another reserved for the man who had exchanged a passionate kiss with her within the confines of the elevator just minutes before.

Thankfully, despite the heat, the meeting that followed was focused and productive, with both Alex and Lucas staying on topic. They discussed the intricacies of Sweet Temptations' supply chain issues, just two operations experts putting their heads together to solve complex problems.

"Well, your initial thoughts on the state of things and what to do about it were spot on," Lucas started.

Alex nodded. "I'm glad you think so. It's clear that volatility, especially in weather-dependent raw materials like sugar and corn syrup, is becoming a significant challenge. We need to enhance our supply chain flexibility."

Lucas leaned forward. "Exactly right. Sweet Temptations must diversify its supply base even more than it already has.

Investing in better demand forecasting and data analytics to optimize your inventory management would be wise. You should also strengthen and formalize your collaboration with key suppliers and improve transparency in quality requirements and non-conformances."

Alex agreed, her pen poised to take notes. "Those are crucial steps, but you're not telling me anything I don't already know. How can Blackstone assist us in implementing these changes quickly and getting business support for the investments we need to make?"

Lucas leaned back. "We can play a pivotal role in helping you maneuver the political landscape and cross-departmental priorities, enabling you to get things done faster and more effectively, especially considering you're still fairly new in the role. We'll also provide change management guidance and training for our team."

Alex smiled, feeling a sense of relief. "Despite the consultant mumbo jumbo, that sounds promising, Lucas. I think we can continue working together. What are our immediate next steps, and what support do you need from me?"

Throughout the meeting, the tension between their official roles and their intimate connection continued to simmer beneath the surface—a secret they both harbored within the heart of Sweet Temptations, and Alex wondered if they'd be able to keep it from boiling over, especially throughout an extended engagement.

As tempting as it would be to succumb to her desires, she knew the consequences of such an affair in the corporate world would be bad for both of them. Alex had staked her career on bringing in these consultants to resolve Sweet Temptations' supply chain issues, a multi-million-dollar investment that carried the weight of the company's future success. Fraternizing with one of them would be a breach of professionalism that could jeopardize everything she had worked for here.

For Lucas, the world of corporate consulting demanded unwavering discretion and ethical conduct. Entangling himself in a romantic relationship with an active client would not only tarnish his reputation but also endanger the integrity of their collaboration.

It was a secret they would have to guard zealously, whether they ever acted on their longings again or not, lest it unravel the very fabric of their careers.

As the meeting concluded, Lucas rose from his seat. "Thank you for your time, Alex. I believe we can make significant improvements to your supply chain."

Alex nodded, her voice steady. "I look forward to working with you, Lucas."

They exchanged a final, lingering look before he turned to leave her office, heading to the consultants' working room. Then, just as he was about to leave, he turned back and asked, "This may sound weird, but you don't by chance know how to use a sword, do you?"

"What?" Alex asked, startled. *Why on earth would he ask that?*

"It's nothing." He waved her off. "Just a weird dream, or daydream. Have a good weekend."

"Yeah, um, you, too," she mumbled, thinking back to her own recent daydream. *Weird, indeed.*

Though she wanted to deny it, she suspected that the kiss in the elevator had changed something. The prospect of turning away from what lay ahead seemed increasingly remote, leaving her with a choice she couldn't ignore if she wanted to stay with a job and a company she genuinely liked.

CHAPTER 7

THE REST OF THE DAY at Sweet Temptations was filled with trivial and mundane tasks and meetings, wrapping up another successful week of sharing delight in every bite. By the end, Alex was ready to head home and enjoy what she hoped would be a relaxing and hassle-free weekend. She needed to recharge after being on edge all week. And while it would embarrass her to no end, she couldn't wait to meet up with Izzie again and tell her all about the elevator encounter.

"Hey, boss!" Argo greeted her at the door, his entire rear end wiggling in time with his tail. It was quite possibly the first time the lethargic little imp had roused himself since she'd left that morning.

Alex dropped her bag to the floor and playfully bent down to ruffle his furry ears, exactly as he preferred. She chuckled. "Hey, buddy!"

Argo's face lit up with a goofy grin, his tongue lolling out the side of his mouth while his right hind leg scratched wildly behind his neck, seemingly of its own volition.

"And how was your day?" she asked.

He continued grinning and scratching, panting out, "Good, the usual routine. Did you finally do something about that Lucas guy?"

Alex took a step back in surprise at this abrupt change from their typical post-work banter. "Ha, ha. What?"

Argo stopped scratching and fixed her with an intense gaze. It didn't take long for his eyes to light up with a mischievous glint, and he said, "Oh, I see. You did do something!"

"What? No! Absolutely not," Alex stammered, then darted into the kitchen, calling back over her shoulder, "That would be unprofessional, you turd!"

"It's about damn time!" Argo hollered after her, his claws skittering on the floor as he attempted an abrupt about-face to follow her into the kitchen.

She must have been more distracted than she thought because when she looked up again, she saw she wasn't alone in her house. Izzie was sitting at her kitchen table, completely engrossed in a pile of papers and large glossy photos scattered before her.

Alex immediately sobered. There was only one reason Izzie would be in her house without notice. There must have been another murder.

Instead of interrupting the police sergeant, Alex walked over to her little Nespresso machine, popped in a pod, and set it to run. As the smell of fresh coffee wafted through the room, Izzie finally looked up from the case files, giving Alex a wan smile.

"Thanks, hun," she said, her shoulders slumped in exhaustion as she reached for the cup of black energy.

Due to her tendency to rock the boat and challenge the status quo, Izzie had found herself on the wrong side of certain influential figures within the police hierarchy. As a result, she had been reassigned to a less glamorous role, primarily dealing with low-priority traffic-related incidents.

Despite her less prominent position, Izzie had maintained an extensive network of informants and allies who had kept her apprised of any potentially "hinky" situations in the city. These well-placed contacts respected her self-appointed position as Peacekeeper and her dedication to providing justice for all, regardless of their supernatural or human nature. When it came to the more obscure and otherworldly cases, Izzie remained a trusted ally, mentor, and source of information for Alex throughout the long years they'd been working together.

With the coffee in hand, Izzie launched into the grim details of this new case, her eyes fixed on the scattered files and photos before her. "Another murder last night, Alex. Same pattern as the first."

"Why is it always young women with the monsters, Izzie? You'd think they'd try something new every once in a while."

Izzie continued clinically, "Found at the end of the Navy Pier, clothes removed, with this symbol burned into her abdomen."

Izzie reached into her pile of photos and pulled one out. It was a close-up of the woman's stomach with a stylized icon burned into her skin. Sharp and angular lines resembled a combination of two triangles, bases facing each other, one end pointed toward the woman's head and the other toward her legs.

"The geeks at the CPD don't think it was made with a branding iron."

"Do you think it was magic?" Alex asked quietly. The possibility of a murder involving magic would be bad.

"I've seen similar wounds in past cases, but none of them quite match what we're seeing now," Izzie replied, pressing her lips together. "Plus, most of her blood was taken, though we couldn't find any wound or bite to indicate how it was done."

"Vampires would be a lot more straightforward than dealing with magic users, but the thought of them teaming up... that would be distastrous," Alex said.

Izzie nodded in agreement. "All we can really say now, though, is that more murders seem likely given the MO so far. You should take a look at the latest scene and see if you spot anything we might have missed, but need to leave now if we want to get there before they clean it." Alex nodded in agreement and went to her room to change out of her work attire.

When she emerged, she was dressed in dark, form-fitting clothing from head to toe, a far cry from her daytime corporate attire. On her feet, she wore freshly cleaned black steel-toed combat boots that would muffle her footsteps while protecting her feet from the heavy claws she sometimes encountered.

She pulled a dark scarf up over the lower part of her face, concealing her identity and adding an extra layer of protection. Her hair, usually hanging loose behind her, was now tied back and secured under a dark ball cap, allowing for better visibility and preventing it from getting in her way during crucial moments.

As they prepared to leave, Argo made sure she had some food, leaving a sandwich on the kitchen island for her to grab on her way out.

He looked up at her with those irresistible puppy eyes. "Hey, be careful, boss. I've got a bad feeling about this."

"Always," she replied, winking at him before hurrying through the door. Izzie had already packed up all her files and was halfway down the driveway, tapping her foot impatiently.

"How's that corgi making a sandwich anyway?" Izzie jumped into the driver side of Alex's beat-up old blue jeep.

Alex grinned. "Sometimes, it's best not to ask questions you don't want the answer to."

"Sure enough," Izzie grumbled, then took off down the nearby side street.

When they arrived at the crime scene on the Navy Pier, most of the police and forensic personnel had already packed up. Only one younger officer was left guarding the perimeter.

"Hey, Joe," Izzie greeted him.

He tipped his hat and gave her a nervous look, eyes occasionally darting to Alex. "One of yours, Sarge?" He fidgeted, eyes darting away, indicating the empty pier behind him. "You know I'm not supposed to let you into active crime scenes."

"Yeah, but you're going to, aren't you?" Izzie replied.

He sighed. "Yeah, somebody has to deal with the weird, and this was definitely weird."

"Thanks, Joe. You've got a good head on your shoulders." Izzie gave the young officer one of her signature smiles and walked in with Alex.

As they approached the white chalk outline on the ground, Alex noticed the red oily splatters and the evidence markers scattered here and there. But as they got closer, her focus drifted, and she felt an eerie sense of déjà vu. Slowing down, she discreetly surveyed her surroundings. That's when she saw a faint shimmering at the end of the pier, beyond the boundaries of the crime scene. She subtly nudged Izzie and motioned to the spot with a nod. "You see anything there?"

Izzie squinted. "No, nothing. What is it?"

"Don't know. Something somewhat shimmery and blurred in one spot."

"Could it be a veil?" Izzie whispered, suggesting a magic trick used to hide one's location or appearance. Yet, when Alex looked again, the shimmering illusion had already disappeared.

"Damn, we missed it," she muttered. "If that was the murderer, though, at least we know something about them."

"Yes, but now we also know we're in for a marathon, not a sprint, if we're after a magic user." Izzie frowned. They both knew that magic users were exceptionally hard to track down and arrest. Unlike vampires, they couldn't just execute them. They were usually humans and, therefore, not technically, literally monsters.

"Fuck." Alex sighed. "This is going to be a tough one."

They finished examining the scene without learning much more and headed back to the Jeep. Once inside, Izzie poked Alex in the ribs. "Don't think I didn't hear that weird little dog talking when you first got home earlier. What happened with Lucas? Dish!"

Alex rolled her eyes, closing the door behind her. "Oh my god, you can't possibly be asking about my romantic life after leaving a murder scene?"

Izzie grinned. "So, you do have a romantic life! Come on, hun, give me something bright and shiny after the day and night I've had."

Alex relented with a relaxed smile as Izzie started the ignition. "Fine, but promise not to make fun of me!"

She proceeded to describe the steamy elevator moment with Lucas. Izzie listened intently, her grin spreading wider with every word. By the end of the short story, she was practically clapping her hands on the steering wheel in glee.

"You go, girl!" she exclaimed, reaching her fist to Alex, demanding a bump. "He sounds hot as fuck!"

Alex somewhat sheepishly obliged the fist bump, exploding her fingers out with a shy swoosh. "But we can't do anything about it, so it doesn't matter."

"Sounds like you're trying to convince yourself here, not me, hun. Either way, it sounds lovely."

"Um, thanks, Izzie," Alex said, shifting her weight in the jeep uncomfortably, watching the passing streetlights through the window.

Back in Evanston, Izzie put the Jeep in park in the small side driveway next to the house. Alex had seen her friend's police cruiser across the street and knew Izzie would head straight home once they got out.

Instead of the expected tired goodbye, though, Izzie's voice turned serious. "But, hey, maybe it's just that I'm always on the lookout for weird. You know how I am. But are you sure he's full-on mundane? Not something on the magic side of the house?"

Alex looked over at Izzie, puzzled. "Huh? He's just a consultant. Sexy as hell, but not anything weird. Why do you ask?"

"Oh, I'm sure it's nothing," she answered, patting Alex's hand reassuringly. "I've just never seen you like this, all flustered."

"What? No, it's not that bad," Alex said, blushing again. She grabbed her bag, dismissing Izzie's concerns, and finally pushed herself off the seat.

"If you say so, but it's not like Sweet Temptations doesn't already have at least one weirdo running around its hallowed chocolate halls, playing at being a boss lady during the day."

"Izzie, that's not fair. I really like this job. I'm not playing at anything. And besides, why would a magic user pretend to be a consultant? There are so many better ways to make money with those skills."

Izzie raised her hands in resignation, backing off the topic. "Fine, fine. I'm sure you're right, and I'm happy for you. Now, go get some rest. Who knows where this investigation will take us."

CHAPTER 8

"BOSS! BOSS!" Argo's short yelps yelled from the top of the basement stairs. "Your phone's ringing. It won't stop, and I'm trying to get some beauty sleep up here, you know."

Her mouth tightened at Argo's interruption. She hoped the phone would stop on its own and he'd shut the fuck up. Alex had finally gotten around to meditating, an exercise she tried to get to at least every other day to help maintain her focus and emotional control both in and out of the office. This last week, though, she'd been too distracted to dedicate the time.

She heard a faint buzz of her phone going off again, and Argo's whining intensified. "Come on, boss! I'm trying to sleep. You know I need at least twenty hours a day."

"Oh my god, fine! I'm coming," she growled, uncrossing her legs and pushing herself up to standing.

She stomped up the stairs, glaring at Argo as she passed by him into the kitchen to retrieve her phone. It had started ringing again. "Who the heck would be calling me this early, over and over again? Izzie would just show up if there were something important."

Phone in hand, she saw the caller ID flashing its irritating light across the screen, outlining the name of her boss.

"Huh?" She frowned, turning the phone to Argo. "What do you think he wants?"

Argo trotted up to her. "I dunno, some kind of chocolate emergency?"

She chuckled. "Oh, you mean like an urgent crisis where all the chocolate in the world suddenly turns into vegetables overnight, and Sweet Temptations needs a miracle to save the day?"

Argo's eyes widened, and he barked. "Exactly! Or maybe a chocolate fountain overflowed in the break room, and they need someone with your expertise to dive in and save it!"

Alex snorted, then said, "Well, I better take this call and see if it's a chocolate catastrophe or something else entirely."

"Good morning, boss. What's up?" she said into the phone.

"What? Oh, Alex, there you are. Haven't I told you one hundred times not to call me boss?" he answered, displaying his usual pleasant annoyance at Alex.

"Sorry, Steve. I was working out. What's going on? Did a supplier blow up or something?"

"You are lucky I appreciate your cheek, Alex," Steve responded. "No, a supplier did not blow up. But apparently, the Family wants to see you in Munich, ASAP."

"What? Why on earth would they care about what I'm doing?" She sat down in her chair, startled.

"Boss! What's going on? You getting fired?" Argo asked from under the table. "How will we afford treats?"

She leaned out a leg to kick at him and focused on what Steve was saying.

"Well, apparently, your proposal with the Blackstone

Group made the rounds yesterday evening after you sent it to Stefan and me for final approval. Now the Family wants to see you in person. They were impressed and want to test the opportunity to bring a similar project to the EU arm of the business."

"That kind of sounds like good news," Alex replied. "Or am I missing something?"

"Oh! Yes, it's very good news. Great work." He hesitated. "It's just that Stefan heard from his counterpart, the EU CEO, that the Patriarch himself made the request. Though I'm sure it's nothing to be worried about."

Mr. Von Mistelweig, the enigmatic head of the billionaire business family, was a figure shrouded in mystery. He was hardly ever seen and rarely involved himself in the business's day-to-day operations. His presence was more like a shadowy legend, whispered about in hushed tones among the Sweet Temptations staff. Alex realized that she didn't even know his first name.

"Huh, well, that's interesting. But doesn't really change much. When do they want me out there?"

"Your flight has been booked for tomorrow. You'll fly out of O'Hare on the red-eye, business class, of course, and present your proposal Monday afternoon in Munich."

"Um, what? That's tomorrow. I'm not sure if I can leave right now," she said, reluctant to go after seeing the latest murder scene.

"Can't be helped. The Family and the Patriarch get what they want, when they want it."

"Dang it. Well, okay. Let me see if I can get a dog sitter. It might be hard on such short notice."

"Alex, look, you need to make it happen. This is one of those things that will make or break you at Sweet Temptations," Steve insisted.

"All right, all right, I'll figure it out," she relented. "Will you be coming as well?"

"I'd love to come, but no, I need to be in California for Project Goober," he answered. "But you won't be on your own. The consultants will be going, too."

"Ah, sure, okay. Which ones?" Alex asked, suddenly nervous.

"Hmmm, let me check my notes," Steve said, while Alex practically held her breath in anticipation, her toe unconsciously tapping under the table. She wasn't even sure what she hoped to hear, but her heart started pounding in her chest, waiting for Steve to answer.

"Ah, all right, here it is. It looks like Rory, the Managing Director, will be going."

"Oh! Great. He will be very helpful," Alex answered in an exhale of relief. The thought of spending so much one-on-one time traveling with Lucas had nearly sent her into a panic.

"Oh, hold on, wait a minute. The other one will be going too. Lucas, I think his name is. He was that center fielder, right?"

Alex froze, sweat forming on her forehead. "Uh, yeah, well, great. The more, the merrier," she replied through clenched teeth.

"Steve! We were supposed to leave twenty minutes ago! You are NOT supposed to be working on the weekend." She heard a strong feminine voice through the phone while she was still trying to wrangle her spinning thoughts into coherent words.

"Coming, Cher!" Steve called in response. "Alex, I've got to go now. Just make sure you're on that plane and ready to present Monday. I'm counting on you." He then abruptly hung up, leaving Alex staring at her darkened phone in apprehension, and maybe just the tiniest bit of excitement.

Later that afternoon, after packing her bags, Alex picked up her phone to make the call she had been dreading. She dialed Izzie's number and waited anxiously for her friend to answer.

After a few rings, Izzie's voice came through the line, sounding tired but concerned. "Hey, Alex. Some of us need sleep, you know? What's up?"

Alex took a deep breath, knowing that Izzie wouldn't be thrilled about what she was about to say. "I have to go to Munich for a business trip. It's last minute, and I'll be leaving tomorrow."

There was a pause on the other end of the line before Izzie sighed. "A trip? Right now? With the murders going on?"

Alex nodded even though Izzie couldn't see her. "I know, I know, the timing sucks. But it's a big deal. I won't get all supply chainy on you, because I know you love that, but I can't really say no."

Alex knew that Izzie knew how important it was for her to have some semblance of a normal life. It helped her stay grounded and human when other instincts threatened to overwhelm her.

Izzie's voice softened with understanding. "I know, Alex. You've got to do what you've got to do. We've been dealing with supernatural crimes in Chicago long before you showed up, and we can handle things for a day or two without you."

"Thanks, Izzie. I really appreciate your support. I wish this trip didn't come at such a bad time."

"Of course, hun." She paused. "So, will you be going alone, or is there someone special joining you on this glamorous adventure?"

"Actually, Lucas will be going, too. The consultants are probably salivating over the opportunity to sell Sweet Temptations more business."

Izzie let out a low whistle. "Well, well, well, Alex. A business trip with the handsome colleague? This is starting to sound more interesting by the minute."

Alex rolled her eyes. "It's not going to be like that, Izzie. We're just colleagues, nothing more." Even Alex wasn't sure she believed that, though.

Izzie chuckled. "Sure, sure. Well, good luck with your presentation, Alex. You'll knock 'em dead, I'm sure."

"Thanks, Izzie. Take care of things here in Chicago. I'll be back before you know it."

Izzie wished her friend safe travels before exchanging their goodbyes, and Alex hung up the phone with a combination of anticipation and reluctance, wondering what the days ahead would bring.

CHAPTER 9

THE NEXT MORNING, Alex went through her regular routine before heading to the airport. If she spent any extra time in the mirror fine-tuning her make-up, she wasn't about to admit it to anyone, including herself.

"Hey, boss! You left out enough food and treats for me, yeah?" Argo called from her bed. He was lying languorously across her plush blankets and silky pillows, licking his paws with fierce attention to detail.

"Of course, buddy. There's plenty of water, too, and the doggy door is open in the backyard. You should be fine," Alex answered, smacking her lips together, blending the soft pink shade of gloss across them.

"All ready!" she said to her reflection. "You're going to kill it tomorrow! And if Lucas happens to think you look nice, too, well, all the better."

"Of course, I'll be fine," Argo interrupted her little pep talk. "I just worry about you not being able to give me any belly rubs for two whole days. Will you be okay?"

She breezed into the bedroom and gave him a rough rub on the head, squishing his soft ears left and right. "I don't know how, but I suppose I'll just have to suffer through it," she quipped and gave him a final kiss on the cheek.

Argo grunted, then rolled over to go back to sleep. She allowed herself one final check to make sure she had everything, then picked up her carry bag and suitcase, and headed for the door.

"Bye! Love ya!" she called back to Argo, ready see what Munich had to offer.

Alex arrived at the airport with ample time to spare, having meticulously planned her departure. As she walked towards the gate, Alex unconsciously scanned the faces in the bustling terminal, hoping to catch a glimpse of the consultants. However, the sea of travelers remained a blur of strangers, and she couldn't spot either of them. Catching herself, she dismissed the thought, annoyed, and continued her journey.

Upon reaching the gate, Alex's shoulders visibly relaxed, and she let out a slow, deep breath when her eyes landed on the familiar logo of the airline, assuring her that she was in the correct place. Vampires may not faze her, but the thought of missing a flight had the power to reduce her to a barely functional puddle of anxiety.

With a sense of reassurance, Alex handed her boarding pass to the gate agent and proceeded down the jet bridge to settle into her luxurious Polaris seat. By the time the final boarding call echoed through the cabin, Alex still hadn't seen either Rory or Lucas, but she did notice something peculiar. The temperature on the plane seemed to increase subtly. Glancing around, she tried to identify the source of the sudden warmth, but nothing stuck out. A strange intuition gnawed at the pit of her stomach, a sense that Lucas must have boarded the plane, too. Alex shook her head slightly, dispelling the odd feeling. *You're being ridiculous, woman. Get it together*, she told herself.

Finally, blissfully, the plane's engines roared to life, and it began its ascent. Taking a deep breath, Alex settled into her seat and pulled out her presentation materials. Despite the lingering warmth, she forced herself to refocus on her materials, determined to make the most of her time in the air. With the information spread out before her, Alex delved into her work, trying to put aside her disrupting thoughts about Lucas. She intended on arriving well prepared.

Her concentration was eventually broken when a flight attendant approached, offering her the evening meal. A savory chicken piccata sat enticingly on her tray, accompanied by buttery garlic mashed potatoes and crisp green beans. Never one to pass up food, she pushed aside her laptop with satisfaction and savored each bite of the delicious meal.

Satisfied, Alex felt ready to delve into her other work. The recent string of murders did not have the usual slash-and-dash vibe she was used to seeing from the monsters. It seemed more organized and purposeful, not to mention the strange shimmer at the recent crime scene.

Drawing the privacy screens securely in place around her cubby, she carefully pulled out the case files Izzie had left on her porch the night before. The details of the two confirmed killings were disturbing: both young women were found in different parts of the city, each with a grotesque symbol seared into their abdomen.

The first victim, an older Anthropology professor from Northwestern, had been discovered south of downtown. The second, an Art History major from the same institution, was found near Navy Pier.

"Shit!" Alex cursed under her breath, searching for the younger victim's name. "Don't be Brittany, don't be Brittany."

"Fuck!" Alex's voice cracked as she felt the sting of tears threatening to spill. The name of the second victim, Brittany Santos, glared up at her from the page. "I should have checked up on her. I should have tracked that fucker down."

She had believed the girl would be safe after she chased off the vampire. If anything, the creep had seemed intent on finding Alex, not targeting Brittany again. *You were wrong, and now that girl is dead.*

Fueled by a renewed sense of determination and guilt, she dove back into the files, her resolve hardening with each page she turned.

The similarities didn't end with their academic profiles. Both crime scenes contained remnants of a rare blue lily known for its mystical properties. *That shit on her lips. It wasn't just some fruity drink.*

Next, it looked like the cops had been able to find some footage worth pulling. Alex remembered a surveillance camera from the Children's Museum near the second crime scene that matched the angle of the grainy photos in front of her. An inexplicable power outage had wiped out most of the data, but it had briefly captured a nearly transparent flash of a silhouette wearing a long dark coat before blacking out. This, combined with multiple witness accounts of a strange echoing laughter on the night of each murder, painted a chilling picture.

Poring over her notes, she found references to an old cult, the "Claws of the Flame," and recalled an unsolved string of murders from a decade ago south of the border that bore striking similarities to these recent killings. A local legend there spoke of a vampire lord rising from hell when the skies turned dark, marking his coming reign with a series of ritualistic sacrifices. It was interesting, but probably not related. Vampires tended to stick to certain territories and guarded them fiercely.

It was unlikely some vamp from down south would come up to Chicago.

Even still, Alex was sure that these weren't random acts of violence. It was an instinct that she couldn't quite shake, and she had learned to trust her intuition. Her mind was a whirlwind of theories and possibilities, each clue a piece of a larger puzzle she was determined to solve.

The ding of the fasten seat belt sign pulled her out of her deep concentration, indicating the initial descent into Munich. Taking a deep breath to steady her racing thoughts, Alex quickly pulled out her laptop. With a few swift keystrokes, she began composing an email to Izzie.

Izzie,

I met the second victim. Chased off a vamp targeting her Tuesday. Thought it was just a newbie testing the waters. Clearly, I fucked up.

Regardless, I've got one of my feelings. There's a pattern at play here, and the monsters may be meaner than we think. Stay safe.

Will update you soon.

Alex.

She sent the email just as the announcement was made to turn off all electronic devices. Still, she couldn't help the unease that settled in her stomach. Should she catch the soonest return flight, to hell with the meeting?

No, she thought. *Izzie can handle it.* Besides, she knew her friend would be pissed if Alex missed an opportunity like this because she didn't trust Izzie to get the job done. Or at least, Alex knew that was how Izzie would see it.

The plane landed smoothly, and the rush of passengers eager to disembark filled the cabin. As she stepped out into the Munich airport, the cool fall European air greeted her on the somewhat exposed walkway.

Exiting the terminal, her gaze was immediately drawn to a tall bulky man in a sharp, dark suit holding a placard with her name. His stance was assertive, his expression unreadable.

"Miss Alex?" he inquired in a heavy German accent, meeting her eyes.

"Yes," she responded cautiously, scanning him for any signs of ulterior motives.

"I am Otto. I've been instructed to take you to the Munich Offices of the Blackstone Group. The family will meet you there," he gestured toward the exit.

She hesitated for just a second, then decided to trust her judgment and follow Otto. The urgency of the business meeting allowed her little time to dawdle. Outside, a sleek black SUV had pulled up to the airport curb, the gleaming sun reflecting off its polished surface. She just had to get through the next couple hours, then she'd be on the first return flight to Chicago.

CHAPTER 10

OTTO HOISTED ALEX'S suitcase into the trunk while she took a moment to gather her thoughts and straighten her blazer. She couldn't shake the feeling of anticipation crashing over her like a wave.

Pulling open the rear door, her breath caught when she saw Lucas. Sitting across from the nearest seat, the elegant profile of his face momentarily froze her in place. His deep brown eyes lifted and locked onto hers. For a split second, it was as if they were back in the elevator, alone, the world outside non-existent.

Alex blinked, rapidly shaking off the memory, seeing Rory up in the front seat. Pushing aside the rogue thoughts threatening to cloud her judgment, she slid into the seat opposite Lucas, a respectful distance between them.

"Alex, it's good to see you again," he remarked, his tone measured, but the faintest hint of warmth seeping through.

She cleared her throat, searching for her voice. "Lucas," she began, nodding in acknowledgment, "always a surprise to find you in unexpected places." She hoped the slight tease might ease the tension.

Before Lucas could respond, Rory's voice chimed in from the front seat. "We always ensure the best consultants are present for our major clients. Did Steve not tell you we were coming? I hope your flight was comfortable."

"It was fine, Rory, thank you. I reviewed some of the preliminary findings for the EU business case during the flight."

Lucas leaned forward slightly, his fingertips brushing a tablet. "That's good to hear. I've compiled some additional insights I think you'll find useful. We can go over them before the meeting."

Alex felt a flutter in her stomach, acutely aware of his proximity, but she masked her thoughts with practiced ease. "I'd appreciate that."

"I'll leave you two to get a head start. Remember, our primary goal is to finalize the next steps for both the US and EU by the end of this visit," Rory said.

The SUV hummed to life, gliding effortlessly into the stream of airport traffic. With Rory's words hanging in the air, Alex refocused, reminding herself of the professional stakes. But as she and Lucas began discussing the data and the upcoming meeting, a part of her remained attuned to the man before her, battling the unwelcome—and undeniably enticing—desires threatening to pull her under.

"So, what drew you to supply chain initially?" Lucas inquired while tapping through a few slides on his tablet. "Especially when you could have had a career on the soccer pitch."

Alex snorted. "As if. I'm not that good."

"Agree to disagree." Lucas smiled. "So, what was it about operations, then?"

"Actually, it began when I was a teenager. One of my foster parents managed a local factory, and I was fascinated by the process - how you turned raw materials into a finished final product." Her gaze turned distant, a shadow crossing her features. "He was an absolute terror, but he'd let me hang out at work in the afternoons, and his procurement lead never tired of answering my questions."

Lucas's brow furrowed momentarily in concern at her words. Before he could voice it, though, Alex deftly redirected the conversation. "And what about you? How did you find your way into consulting?"

Lucas absently ran his fingers through his disheveled hair. "Well, my, um, family ran an enterprise of sorts in Brazil, and I was always spellbound watching how they managed all the moving parts. But beyond that..." He paused as if considering his words. "I've always had this urge to ensure all the pieces fit seamlessly, that everything flows just right. There's something inherently satisfying about solving problems in a realm where solutions are tangible and precise. Where things make sense. Besides"—the corners of his eyes crinkled with mischief—"I get to meet interesting people like you."

"Right," Alex laughed, pursing her lips. "But I've never thought about it that way. It's a puzzle that requires intricate precision, but almost always has a clear answer. You're absolutely right."

Rory snorted from the front. "As if I don't have a hard enough time managing his ego."

Alex raised an eyebrow, finding the man across from her wearing the biggest shit-eating grin she'd ever seen.

"You love it, old man," Lucas quipped.

Rory just grumbled incoherently in response, and the rhythm of their conversation gradually slowed. Alex was about to ask him another question about Brazil or soccer when Lucas's phone buzzed, and he glanced down at the incoming message. The corners of his mouth quirked up in a quick smile and he commented, "Speaking of challenges, keeping a puppy entertained in a small apartment is no joke."

His phone buzzed again, and after quickly reading the new message, he barked out a laugh. "It's from my colleague, Dan," he explained, showing Alex the screen, which had a playful picture of a mischievous-looking dog holding a sock in its mouth. "I was watching his dog this weekend before the call came for this trip. Honestly, keeping that little guy from tearing apart my apartment was harder than anything we've tackled at Sweet Temptations."

Intrigued, Alex asked, "Do you dog-sit often?"

"Yeah, I love it. I grew up with dogs. They were always there, looking out for each other and for me." His eyes grew distant for a moment.

Alex felt a warmth spreading in her chest, realizing she was enjoying getting to know Lucas beyond both the professional façade and the strange fiery passion that lurked between them. Eager to reciprocate, she quickly reached for her phone to show him a picture of Argo, even if Argo wasn't technically a dog.

But her haste and nerves betrayed her, and the device tumbled from her grasp. Both Lucas and Alex lunged for it, their fingers brushing against each other. For a split second, the world around them blurred as their eyes locked, a tangible spark igniting between them. But as quickly as it arrived, the moment passed.

And just as suddenly, a rush of memories flooded Alex's mind, chilling her to the core. The last time she'd allowed herself to genuinely care about someone like this, to let herself be swept up in passion and affection, it had ended in near tragedy. It was like an ice-cold bucket had been poured over her, dousing the warmth and budding connection she felt with Lucas.

She recoiled, sliding as far away from Lucas as the confines of the car would allow. The physical distance was a desperate attempt to shield herself—and him—from the potential dangers of her past mistakes. That boy from her past had nearly lost his life when her darkness had flared in an unexpected rage, and the weight of that guilt was a burden she carried with her always. Flirtation, even a one-night stand here or there—those were safe. But genuine feelings? That was a line she couldn't afford to cross. The stakes were too high, and she wouldn't risk Lucas's safety for her own pleasure.

"Sorry about that," he said, brows slightly furrowed.

"No worries."

Moving back to safer territory, the two continued discussing business. Munich's stunning landscape—the backdrop of historic churches, the English Garden with its serene river, and the distant Bavarian Alps—sped by outside.

At last, the SUV pulled up to Blackstone Group's offices. The building was modern, with sleek, darkened glass panels reflecting the overcast sky. Its imposing facade emitted an aura of strict professionalism.

Rory thanked their driver, explaining, "Otto's been with the Family for years."

Alex, extending her hand for a shake, nodded. "It's been a pleasure, Otto."

The trio then made their way into the building.

<h1 style="text-align:center">CHAPTER 11</h1>

THE BLACKSTONE GROUP'S boardroom was located on the top floor, offering an impressive panorama of Munich's skyline, punctuated by ancient spires and modern skyscrapers. As Alex stepped in, she was greeted by a long, polished mahogany table surrounded by high-back leather chairs.

Klaus Vogel, the EU CEO, stood from his chair to greet her, extending a firm hand. He was a tall, broad-shouldered man in his early fifties, with salt-and-pepper hair and piercing blue eyes that seemed to dissect everything they gazed upon.

Beside him was Hanna Bauer, Alex's EU Supply Chain counterpart—a petite woman with a tight, efficient bun of auburn hair. She gave Alex a nod of acknowledgment, her expression neutral yet attentive.

Next were the two younger members of the Von Mistel-weig family, responsible for leading the conglomerate of family businesses. Adrian was an attractive man in his early thirties with wavy blonde hair and a chiseled jaw. Beside him sat Greta, a woman of similar age, who bore an uncanny resemblance to Adrian in everything but hair color. With her straight black hair, high cheekbones, and confident posture, she looked every bit the business heiress she was.

Though Mr. Von Mistelweig's absence was noted, at Klaus's insistence, Alex began her presentation. She expertly wove through her plans for Sweet Temptations, each slide highlighting her vision for the company's potential dominance in the market. Throughout the meeting, Lucas played a supporting role, occasionally emphasizing Alex's points.

During her discourse, Hanna raised a hand and asked, "What about potential disruptions in raw materials? Have those been considered in your projections?"

Alex's response was smooth and composed, her words flowing effortlessly. "Absolutely, we've conducted a thorough risk assessment and have multiple contingency plans in place."

The room remained silent, the German attendees observing her with stoic, unreadable expressions. Yet, when she concluded, Greta began a slow clap, her face breaking into a rare smile. "Ms. Bain," she began, "that was commendable. This is exactly the vigor and innovation we need to make Sweet Temptations the global leader."

The room filled with nods of approval. As they wrapped up, Rory interjected, "Working with Alex and her team has been seamless. I'm confident we'll realize this vision in record time."

After handshakes and words of appreciation, Alex began to pack her things, ready to head back to the airport.

"Why the rush, Ms. Bain?" Klaus asked, suddenly standing next to her.

She looked up, explaining her flight plans, only to be met with Klaus's revelation about the Oktoberfest event.

He chuckled, his demeanor fatherly and warm. "Ah, Ms. Bain, work is important, but so is celebrating, especially traditions. We have reserved a significant section at the *Schottenhamel Festzelt,* one of the best festival tents for tonight. You must join us."

Seeing the surprise on her face, he continued, "And don't worry about attire or accommodations. We've arranged for traditional Bavarian clothing—dirndl for the ladies and lederhosen for the gentlemen—to be laid out in the hotel rooms we've booked for you and your colleagues for tonight. It's all been tailored to fit, and you can bring them home as souvenirs from Munich."

Before Alex could process all this, Klaus added, with a hint of regret in his voice, "And about today's presentation. As I'm sure you noticed, Mr. Von Mistelweig unfortunately could not be present. He was hoping he could meet you in person at tonight's event. He has expressed a keen interest in discussing your proposal further."

The opportunity to meet the patriarch of the Von Mistelweig family in such an informal setting added yet another layer to the evening's unexpected turn of events. Alex managed a smile. "I didn't even realize it was Oktoberfest. Work has been all-consuming lately."

A smile spread across Klaus's face. "It's an invitation we reserve for our most valued employees. It's the first year we've decided to include colleagues from the US."

Feeling the weight of the invitation and the opportunity it presented, Alex hesitated, then asked, "Would I be able to get the first flight out tomorrow? I have a dog waiting for me back home."

Klaus nodded. "Of course. We understand priorities. See you tonight."

Outside the building, the sleek black SUV was once again waiting for them, Otto standing at the ready. As they slid into the vehicle, Rory seemed to be riding a wave of adrenaline.

"That was phenomenal, Alex!" he exclaimed, replaying the best parts of the presentation with animated gestures. "The way you handled their questions, the confidence in your delivery. I couldn't have asked for more."

Brushing off the compliments with a humble smile, Alex replied, "I just presented what your team put together. It was a collective effort."

Rory acknowledged her words with a nod but soon lost himself in his phone, no doubt catching up with the onslaught of messages and emails that had accumulated during the meeting.

"So, what do you think about this sudden Oktoberfest invite? And the costumes? I've always wanted to wear lederhosen," Lucas said, clearly trying to draw her into conversation.

She gave a noncommittal shrug. "I wasn't expecting it, but it should be... interesting."

Undeterred, Lucas continued, "I've heard the *Schottenhamel Festzelt* is the place to be. And come on, who wouldn't want to see Rory in lederhosen?"

Alex chuckled at the mental image, but she kept her response brief. "It'll be a sight."

He looked at her, as if trying to gauge her emotions. There was an evident effort on his part to connect, to lighten the mood, but Alex stayed distant. She felt torn—part of her wanted to revel in the camaraderie, to enjoy this unexpected twist in her business trip. Yet, the palpable chemistry with Lucas, instead of exciting her, had made her cautious, reticent. The ghost of past experience was holding her back.

The Munich streets passed by in a blur, but for Alex, lost in her thoughts, the journey felt much longer as her mind wandered into the past.

High school had not been easy for Alex. Being in foster care made her an outsider, a loner, always feeling like she was on the periphery. Then, in her senior year, life threw her an unexpected curveball. Richard—the golden boy of their high school—acknowledged her and made his way through the layers of sullen protection she had spent years wrapping around herself.

His sudden interest in her was as baffling as it was exhilarating. He'd woo her in small, thoughtful ways: leaving anonymous notes in her locker with words of encouragement, surprising her with a book she had once mentioned wanting to read in class, or simply sharing his earphones during study hall, introducing her to his favorite artists.

And with this unexpected attention came something Alex had never experienced—acceptance. People were kinder and more open as she walked down the hallways hand in hand with him.

After months of being "official," Richard led her to a secluded spot in the woods and what started with roaming hands, and sweet caresses exploring each other's bodies, quickly came to an abrupt stillness. When Alex finally looked down and caught a glimpse of Richard's face, it was gripped in fear, rather than passion. She never knew for sure what he had seen in her, but his eyes had gone wide, his body trembling beneath her.

She suspected that her eyes had gone black, leaking streaks of darkness across her face, and that her canines had lengthened into fangs. That's what tended to happen when her vampiric side reared its head during states of heightened emotion. Either way, Richard bucked her off and hurriedly pulled his clothes on in a near panic before running away.

The next day, the cold shoulder she received from Richard and his friends left her feeling more isolated than ever. Determined to confront the boy who had turned her world upside down, she waited by his car, needing answers. Instead, she got

Richard's disdainful laughter and cruel confession that dating her had been a joke, a callous bet to see if he could take her virginity. The betrayal, humiliation, and rage crashed over her, too vast to contain.

Before she knew it, she had struck him. The power behind her punch sent him hurtling across the parking lot. Alex remembered looking down at her hands in shock and confusion, not understanding from where such strength had come. But the damage was done. Richard's smashed ribs were the testament to her unchecked rage.

He never told anyone that she was the cause of his injuries, and not long after, he transferred schools. His rejection and flight had left her more alone than she had ever been, with only her feelings of shame and self-disgust to keep her company. She remembered believing that she must be a monster. Heck, she still believed it sometimes. During those final months of high school, Alex made a solemn vow to herself: she would never allow herself to love another boy—or man, as time would have it.

After years of reflection, she no longer believed Richard had been playing her. She believed he had truly loved her, at least until she had inadvertently revealed herself. But it didn't matter. She couldn't risk unleashing either the darkness that he had glimpsed in her during their moment of passion or the out-of-control violence and power that had broken his ribs after he broke her heart.

She couldn't let her past control her present, but she also couldn't forget the lessons it had taught her. Emotions were dangerous, especially for her. As much as she wanted to get closer to Lucas, she knew she had to guard her heart. It was for his safety—and hers.

Pulling up to the grand façade of the "Hotel *Bayerischer Hof*," a renowned luxury hotel in Munich, Alex was quick to unlatch her seatbelt and step out. The opulent entrance, with its polished marble steps and glistening chandeliers visible through the tall glass doors, seemed a world away from her jumbled thoughts.

"See you soon, Alex!" Lucas's voice rang out cheerfully from behind her.

Without turning around, she raised her hand in a brief wave, her stride not breaking. But even as she tried to remain oblivious to Lucas, she couldn't help but offer a brief look back. The last thing she saw before entering the hotel was how he paused for a moment, running his fingers through his hair, his dark brows drawing together, not in frustration or confusion, but concern. For her.

CHAPTER 12

CLOSING THE HOTEL door behind her, Alex sagged in relief at the privacy the sumptuous room presented. Lifting her chin and glancing around the plush, luxurious interior, she saw the traditional Bavarian dress Klaus had mentioned lying on the enormous bed. Carefully arranged for her, the dirndl was a lovely mix of whites, pinks, and muted florals.

She stood still, her expression contemplative. Then, drawing in a deep, steadying breath, she relaxed her shoulders and nodded subtly, signaling her readiness to embrace the experience. After all, when in Munich...

Once changed, Alex paused to examine her reflection in the full-length mirror. The attire consisted of a white blouse, a floral vest that highlighted her waist, and a flared skirt that reached just past her knees. A pink ribbon laced its way through the front, offering a delicate contrast. A bit apprehensive at first, she had to admit that the dress was flattering and seemed to blend well with her features. She briefly wondered what Lucas would look like in his traditional outfit, then quickly squashed the thought.

Taking another look at herself, she was surprised to find that the traditional attire suited her. She looked... happy. Perhaps this small detour was just what she needed to take her mind off the pressing matters back home and her seemingly runaway emotions.

However, as her hand absentmindedly went to her phone, the harsh reminder of the investigation and the still unresolved murders weighed on her. The lack of news from Izzie was troublesome. But maybe no news was good news. She would try to enjoy the evening.

With a deep breath, Alex pushed her concerns to the back of her mind and headed for the door. Oktoberfest awaited.

The grandeur of the hotel's lobby was bathed in a soft golden glow, with chandeliers hanging majestically from the high ceiling. As Alex descended the sweeping staircase, she immediately noticed Otto standing near the entrance. Next to him, Klaus was engaged in animated conversation with Rory, both men dressed in traditional Bavarian lederhosen.

Her footsteps were silent on the plush carpet, but as she approached, Klaus caught sight of her and broke into a wide smile. "Ah, Frau Alex! You look *wunderbar!*"

"Thank you, Klaus. You and Rory look quite dashing yourselves," Alex responded, her eyes scanning the surroundings. A pang of relief washed over her when she didn't spot Lucas among them.

Once settled in the comfortable seats of the SUV, the journey to the Oktoberfest grounds began. The city outside was alive with excitement, the air thick with anticipation for the evening's festivities.

As they drove, Klaus, apparently an enthusiastic historian, began recounting the history of Oktoberfest. "You know, Oktoberfest began as a wedding celebration. In 1810, Prince Ludwig of Bavaria married Princess Therese, and they invited the entire city of Munich to join the festivities. The fields where the event took place were named "Theresienwiese" in honor of the princess, and the festival still happens there."

Rory chimed in, "It's more than just beer and pretzels, then?"

Klaus laughed. "Oh, yes, it's a celebration of Bavarian culture. But there's an old superstition, too. It's said that during the festival, the spirits of ancient Bavarians roam the grounds, blessing those who honor their traditions and seeking to make mischief with those who don't." He winked at Alex. "But don't worry, in our traditional outfits, we are showing our respect. We should be safe from any spirits."

Alex raised an eyebrow, intrigued. She had always had a soft spot for myths and superstitions, finding them often intertwined with history.

As the conversation flowed, Rory added, "Lucas sends his apologies. He got caught up with some emergency work for another client. He'll catch up with us later at the festival."

Alex nodded, doing her best to keep her face neutral. The drive, so far, had been pleasant. The tension between her and Lucas was absent, making it easier to immerse herself in Klaus's tales and the excitement of the night ahead.

Inside Oktoberfest's grand *Schottenhamel Festzelt*, the jovial atmosphere was contagious. Live bands played traditional German folk songs, causing patrons to sway to the rhythm. In between, unmistakable chords from classic American tracks filled the air, urging everyone to sing along. The tables reserved for the Family and employees of Sweet Temptations were bustling with laughter, clinking glasses, and the aroma of hearty Bavarian fare.

As enormous mugs of frothy beer were being served, a

robust serving girl, her muscles toned from carrying heavy trays, balanced an enormous bottle of Veuve Clicquot Champagne on her shoulder. She came around every thirty minutes or so with a new bottle, pouring generous servings into everyone's steins. Apparently, after nine PM most drinkers switched to champagne.

Alex, absorbed in the wild environment, was savoring the delightful array of meats and cheeses paired with the bubbly drink. She spent most of the evening talking with Klaus and his charming wife, who met him there. Freya was quick to share funny yet embarrassing stories of the big boss while he looked on helplessly. Thankfully, Lucas, who had been around briefly earlier, had vanished into the thickening crowd, leaving her to enjoy herself without his presence nagging her mind.

As time went on, the effervescent champagne made her head feel light and a little fuzzy. Add the inevitable build-up after too many drinks, and Alex felt a nudge from nature sending her to the restrooms to freshen up. Seamlessly, she maneuvered through the crowd, her low heels softly clicking against the sturdy wooden floor. Taking advantage of the momentary reprieve, she quickly checked her phone for any updates from Izzie about the murders in Chicago, though the screen still remained silent.

"Well, that's good," she said quietly to herself as she exited the restroom, head still looking down at her phone. When she raised her gaze to avoid tripping over another patron, her eyes locked onto Lucas, almost as if driven by some force she couldn't understand. He was standing casually by the rear exit, a silhouette of nonchalance, also looking down at his phone, as if scrolling through messages.

Whether it was the drink, or her general good mood, she didn't know. But the sight of him ignited an almost palpable wave of desire within her, drowning out any remains of her restraint. A tingling sensation rose from her core, surging forward like a rope of fire, magnetically drawing her closer. She stepped towards him, and Lucas pocketed his phone to look up. His eyes found her immediately, as if that had been their only purpose in life.

She'd blame it on the mischievous spirits Klaus had been talking about earlier, but now that she was standing face-to-face with him, she knew the inevitable was once again about to happen. Words did not seem to exist, only the sound of their rapidly beating hearts. Alex felt a shiver of anticipation as his eyes wandered over her, her skin prickling under his piercing gaze. She, in turn, drank in his appearance, the sharp angles of his face accentuated by the dim light, his traditional Bavarian attire giving him an air of rugged charm.

The muted sounds of Oktoberfest's revelry were a distant backdrop as Lucas turned without a word and ventured out of the hall and into a small grove of trees nearby. His back was still to her as he paused, seeming to gather himself.

She hesitated, just a moment, then Alex quietly made her way over, the soft crunch of autumn leaves underfoot. The slight chill in the air sharpened her senses, and she could detect the subtlest of fragrances from the trees around her, mixed with the ever-familiar scent of Lucas. Woodfire and bourbon.

"I needed to get away from the crowds," he admitted, turning to face her, his voice barely above a whisper.

Alex stepped closer, her voice matching his softness. "Is it overwhelming for you, too?"

For a moment, neither spoke, and the world seemed to hold its breath. Lucas slowly reached out to tuck a stray strand of hair behind her ear. "I didn't think you'd follow."

"Neither did I," Alex confessed. "But here we are."

His fingers brushed her cheek, sending shivers down her

spine. Alex's heart raced. The last time she felt like this, it had ended in heartbreak and confusion.

Lucas's eyes searched hers as if trying to decipher the secrets held within. "Alex," he began, but she silenced him with a gentle touch to his lips.

"Just... not now," she whispered. She knew she would bolt if she thought too much about what was about to happen. For now, she would simply let the moment take her, the rest of the universe forgotten amidst the rustling leaves and silver moonlight. She told herself she could keep this thing between her and Lucas physical and not put him at risk, because she was beyond resisting.

With the decision made, it was like a breaking dam, a rush of water tearing through the self-control that had held her back for so long.

Their hands explored, eagerly mapping each other's bodies. Every touch was fire, every sensation magnified, as if they were making up for lost time. The heat of Lucas's palms had her trembling with pure, unbridled need.

Suddenly, Lucas took hold of her, pressing her back against the rough bark of a tree. Her breath hitched, feeling the solid trunk behind her and the firm press of his body on top of her. She was utterly trapped.

Leaning against her, his forehead resting against hers, he looked into her eyes, seeking affirmation. And Alex responded the only way she knew how. Grasping a handful of his hair, she pulled him tighter to her, sealing their lips together.

The world blurred in a heady fog of longing as Alex fumbled with the stubborn belt at Lucas's waist. Frustration flared, and with a low growl, she sank her teeth into his lip hard enough to draw blood. The sharp tang hit her tongue, fueling the fire already consuming her. Lucas didn't recoil—he met her intensity, yanking her head back to bare her throat to his own biting claim. She hissed, ripping away the belt at last, tearing down the zipper, and freeing him from the ridiculous confines of the lederhosen.

Lucas didn't waste time. His hands slid beneath her skirts, tracing a slow, deliberate path upward. Heat coiled between them as he pushed higher, fingertips skimming silk—a barrier he had no intention of respecting. With a sharp tear, the fabric gave way, the sound cutting through the charged air like a promise.

The night melted away—the wind, the cold, the distant murmur of the forest—all of it swallowed by the fire crackling between them. Nothing existed but this, the raw pull dragging them closer. Every touch sent sparks racing across her skin, every brush of flesh against flesh stoking the heat higher, until sensation itself felt like an unbearable ache.

Lucas lifted her, muscles flexing beneath his shirt as her legs wrapped around him, feet hovering above the earth. Each thrust sent her back against the rough bark, the bite of it barely registering. It was reckless, unrestrained—the kind of hunger that burned away reason, leaving nothing but the primal need to lose herself in him completely.

And then, maybe it was the taste of Lucas's blood still fresh in her mouth, but just as suddenly, the world threatened to splinter apart. That familiar shadow, the encroaching darkness she'd known all too well, began to creep into the edges of her vision. Panic, sharp and unyielding, took root. The weight of her past and the looming shadow of her fears threatened to pull her under. She felt herself pulling away, desperate to escape the growing abyss.

But Lucas was there. His grip tightened, and his face buried into the crook of her neck with deep, passionate kisses. His touch, his strength or power, the feel of him inside her, anchored her to the present, a lifeline in the stormy sea of emotions. And just as quickly as the darkness had come, it receded, overpowered by their need to finish what they had started here in the secluded cove. The world lightened once more, their shared passion acting as a beacon, guiding Alex back from the edge and leading her to an entirely different threshold.

As if drawn by some unspoken command, Lucas's pace quickened, each movement feeding the fire already burning between them. They climbed higher, every thrust pushing them closer to the breaking point, until the tension snapped all at once. A cry tore from her lips, swallowed as his hand found her mouth—just as hers silenced his—muffling the unrestrained pleasure that shattered through them both.

As the intensity faded, reality pressed in. The distant hum of Oktoberfest revelry, once nothing more than background noise, now felt too close—too real. The laughter, the clinking of steins, the lively music all pressed in around her, a stark reminder of where they were.

Her breath still uneven, Alex hurried to adjust her clothing, smoothing down her dress with hands that weren't quite steady. The weight of their surroundings crashed down in layers—the sheer recklessness of this place, the impossibility of their timing, the unavoidable truth that they were still at a work event.

A wave of anxiety prickled at the edges of her pleasure-drunk mind, cooling the heat that had burned so fiercely just moments before.

Lucas, looking equally disheveled yet with an earnest gleam in his eyes, reached out and brushed a wayward strand of hair from Alex's face. "That was... unexpected."

Taking a deep breath, Alex finally mustered the courage to look into his eyes. They shimmered with satisfaction, yet she couldn't meet them for long. Her face turned a bright shade of red. "I can't believe we just... here, of all places."

Lucas reached out to touch her arm. "Alex," he began.

She flinched away. "Look, Lucas, it was... amazing. But..." She paused, grappling with her words. "Oh my god, what the fuck were we thinking?" Internally, she felt the weight of her hunger, still lurking, still pressing against the door.

"I don't understand. One moment we're—" Lucas frowned, his voice trailing off.

"Yes." Alex's eyes darted away. "I just think we should... I mean, I need to get back. Just to... clear my head."

"All right." His face flashed with a hint of surprise and disappointment. "But, Alex, it's not like that was a usual occurrence for me, either. I don't typically go about ripping off underwear," he said, reaching for her torn panties that had been carelessly flung to the ground, "from every beautiful woman I meet." He paused. "That was special. You're special."

"It was for me too, Lucas," she whispered, "I just... I need some space right now."

Confusion seemed to war with hope on his face. Offering her a half-smile, he ran his hands through his hair and then gestured towards the festival tent. "Okay, then. After you."

CHAPTER 13

ALEX'S HEART BEAT in sync with the rhythm of the foot-stomping music as she re-joined her table, attempting to blend in by standing on the benches like the others. Yet, even as she tried to lose herself in the fun around her, thoughts of her encounter with Lucas played on a loop in her mind, rendering her distant and introspective.

Interrupting her reflections, Klaus smoothly navigated through the sea of revelers to stand beside her. Leaning in so his words could cut through the raucous din, he hissed, "Where did you disappear to? Mr. Von Mistelweig arrived over ten minutes ago."

"I went to use the restroom and got a call. Had to take it outside, you know, with all the noise. Apologies!" She hoped her vague reasoning would suffice.

Klaus's expression was a cocktail of frustration, but he seemed to buy the excuse without challenge. With a subtle tilt of his head, he directed her attention to the corner of the table. An older gentleman was seated there, engaged in an animated discussion with a member of the Family, who seemed utterly captivated by his every word. Another nearby Family member observed the conversation with a nervous energy. Alex couldn't tell if he wanted to talk to the man or run in the opposite direction.

The patriarch of the Von Mistelweig family was distinguished. Age had weathered his face, accentuating the lines of experience, yet his posture was that of a younger man—upright, alert, and exuding a quiet strength. His traditional lederhosen was complemented by a distinctive silver broach holding his suspenders in place. It bore the detailed engraving of what appeared to be a mistletoe sprig. But it was the figures at the base of the sprig that intrigued Alex. One lay on the ground, pierced by something, while another stood above, wielding what might have been an ax. *Probably some age-old Germanic tale,* she mused inwardly.

Noticing her keen observation, the patriarch's eyes met hers. Gesturing her over, he beckoned her to sit next to him.

"Mr. Von Mistelweig," she started, her voice carrying a slight quiver. "Thank you for allowing me to present my findings. And for including me in this incredible tradition."

He nodded, his gaze not wavering from hers. "Of course."

Alex inhaled deeply, then confidently laid out her proposal's key points with clear, concise words, drawing strength from her expertise in the mundane.

Once she finished, Mr. Von Mistelweig was silent for a moment, pulling a small pipe from his pocket and chewing thoughtfully on its mouthpiece. "Very good."

Then, he tapped the ornate silver buckle on his suspenders. "Do you know what this signifies?"

Alex blinked, taken aback by the abrupt change in topic. "No... I don't."

"This represents our family's lineage. Our purpose, our

drive, and our eternal vow to shield the world from dangers most can't even fathom."

Alex was shaken, nervous now. She wondered what he was going on about and why he would be telling her. She was there for supply chain strategy, not creepy old men and monsters.

"Is it... a chocolate sprig?" she quipped, pointing to the intricate design on his buckle.

He chuckled a rich, deep sound. "You're sharp. But let me ask you this: Do you know why we hired you?"

She straightened up. "I assumed because I excel at managing supply chains."

"Indeed," he acknowledged. "But you are young and without experience in our specific sector. Ever wonder about that?"

She crossed her arms. "Why, then?"

"It's true," he began, "the skills you display in your day job are formidable. But it's what you do after dark that truly caught the Family's interest."

Alex's heart skipped a beat. How could he possibly know? Her pulse quickened, and she struggled to mask the shock from her face.

"A young female hunter from Chicago entered our purview about five years ago after the Preston Incident," he continued, observing her reaction closely.

The mention of the Preston Incident made Alex wince internally. That horrifying sequence of events, culminating in the final showdown with the monstrous vampire, was something she had hoped to leave behind.

She attempted a breezy tone. "Preston Incident? Doesn't ring any bells."

Undeterred, Mr. Von Mistelweig continued, "We noticed her potential. And so, we kept tabs, ready to assist if needed."

"Assist?"

"Yes." He leaned in slightly, his voice a murmur. "Because, like you, we hunt the monsters that the world denies."

She fought the urge to speak. It was ludicrous, all of it. Yet, there was an inexplicable connection to his words.

"We've been doing it for over a millennium," he declared proudly.

Alex arched an eyebrow. "You seem quite convinced of your story."

His deep laughter echoed across the room. "Stubbornness— a common trait among hunters, I've noticed."

Alex shifted uncomfortably.

"I assume you're aware that different vampires have varied vulnerabilities—save for sunlight, which is universally lethal. Some detest garlic, some can't bear silver, others need an invitation to enter."

She had indeed pieced together some of this knowledge over the years, but to hear it laid out so plainly was jarring. And yet, she couldn't resist a cheeky retort. "If all else fails, there's always decapitation."

The old man choked on his beer, spewing a little as he laughed heartily, a hand reaching out to pat her back. "Absolutely! A headless vampire is a problem-free vampire."

"All right, for argument's sake, let's say I believe you. If you've been watching me, why bring me here now?"

His gaze turned serious again, and in that look, Alex sensed the gravity of what was about to come.

"Because the Hidden Villages have become active again," he uttered solemnly, every syllable heavy with meaning.

Alex opened and closed her mouth, dumbfounded. "Hidden Villages?" She felt almost bad for the man. He had woven such a convincing narrative only to ruin it with this absurdity.

The room grew colder as his eyes bore into hers. "You

might be proficient in handling the newer breeds of vampires in your city, but it's evident you are unfamiliar with the ancient lore."

She could feel the other members of the Family withdrawing, sensing the brewing storm. "Hidden Villages? You want me to believe that old vampires have organized little towns?" She couldn't help but smirk a little.

He sighed heavily, pausing to take a long draw from his pipe. "Very well," he murmured, "let's begin from the beginning."

Mr. Von Mistelweig leaned forward, daring her to look away. "The Hidden Villages," he began, "are an ancient construct. Think of them as courts, each one uniquely different yet bound by the same bloodline."

Alex tried hard to mask her disbelief, reminding herself of where she was and the potential dangers of this situation.

"These older vampires, the ones that trace their lineage back to the Elders, they don't operate like the younger ones you might have encountered. They're organized, methodical, and vicious. Plus, each Village has its own set of characteristics. That's why a one-size-fits-all approach to hunting doesn't work."

He paused, giving Alex a moment to digest the information. "Most of these Villages are found in ancient cities, where they can operate from the shadows, away from the glare of modernity. Here in Europe, they can easily maintain their power, concealed from the prying eyes of humans. But they don't often get too involved in human affairs, preferring to stay, well, hidden."

"I suppose, then, North America has been left largely untouched?"

He took a sip from his drink before answering. "Initially, the Elders saw no appeal in the New World. Crossing the ocean was risky, and the perceived scarcity of human settlements meant fewer opportunities to feed. And then, as the new continent developed, its rapid advancement in technology became a deterrent for these ancient creatures. It was too... exposed, and privacy dwindled with every passing year."

His gaze became distant. "However, I am aware of one Hidden Village that braved the journey with the conquistadors to South America, adapting to the new world."

Alex felt a chill. "So, they're expanding their territories now?"

He nodded gravely. "Indeed. As the world evolves, so do they. We have reason to believe that Chicago, for instance, has recently caught their attention."

The tale was outrageous, yet captivating. Alex, despite herself, found her uncertainty eroding. "How do you know all this?"

Mr. Von Mistelweig leaned back. "The tale begins in 200 AD. Germany was not the nation you recognize today. It was fractured, tribal, and under the thrall of the Village Hidden in Stone. Those were dark times." He painted a grim picture of a world where the vampires did not lurk in the shadows but ruled openly. Human settlements were desolate, people lived in constant terror, and the nights were filled with screams.

"After generations of fear, our ancestors chanced upon a peculiar vulnerability the vampires had: Mistletoe. It wasn't just a festive plant. For us, it became a weapon, like the more well-known garlic." He paused, lost momentarily in the retelling of a tale that had been told over hundreds of years. "With this newfound knowledge, they orchestrated a large-scale daytime assault against the ruling vampire lord, whose name we never say. The battle was fierce and bloody, but in the end, the lord's son, Baldur, along with many others, were slain."

Alex listened, captivated.

"Devastated, the lord fled north with the remaining vampires of his bloodline, seeking refuge in Norway. There, they established what came to be known as the Village Hidden in Ice," he continued. "And interestingly, their influence in the region led to the birth of certain Norse legends. Ever heard of the tragic tale of Ragnarök or Baldur's death?"

He sighed deeply. "From that point on, the Von Mistelweig lineage has been devoted to combating these creatures. Over the centuries, we've built businesses like Sweet Temptations to amass the resources required for our operations. But, sadly," he said, casting a disdainful glance at some younger family members who looked away guiltily, "many of our kin have lost sight of the original mission."

There was a short silence, filled with the echoes of the past. Alex, contemplating everything she'd just heard, ventured, "So, you're sort of like Batman, but for vampires?"

The hint of a smile played on Mr. Von Mistelweig's lips. "Perhaps a more historic, less caped version, but yes, in essence."

"Thank you for sharing all of this with me," she began, trying to choose her words carefully. "While I can't say I fully understand or believe everything you've told me, I promise to consider your words." She paused, forcing a professional smile. "In the meantime, you can rely on me to keep delivering exceptional supply chain results for Sweet Temptations. I'll ensure your operations have the funds they need, even if it's for... less visible strategies."

Mr. Von Mistelweig chuckled warmly, the laughter lines deepening around his eyes. "I had a feeling you'd say something like that," he admitted, drawing out a card from his pocket and handing it to her. "Here. My direct line. Call if you have questions or find yourself in a situation with one of the Hidden Villages."

Alex accepted the card out of politeness, making a mental note to stash it away later. As she turned to leave, the weight of the day finally catching up with her, she felt a sudden grip on her hand. Looking down, she found Mr. Von Mistelweig's fingers wrapped around hers. He scanned the room intently, his gaze finally settling on Lucas, who was engrossed in a lively discussion with a younger member of the Family.

Mr. Von Mistelweig's voice dropped to a whisper, his eyes never leaving Lucas. "Be wary of him," he cautioned, his tone grave. "There's something... off about him. He's not one of them; I made sure to test all the consultants. But he carries their scent, like a lingering shadow."

Taken aback, Alex pulled her hand away, her eyes darting to Lucas and then back to the old man. "I really don't know what you're talking about."

Mr. Von Mistelweig simply sighed, a knowing look in his eyes. "Ah, youth. Sometimes ignorance can be bliss, but other times, it can be a curse." Offering her a nod, he added, "Thank you for your time, Ms. Bain. Stay safe." With that, he retreated into the crowd, leaving a perplexed Alex in his wake.

CHAPTER 14

A S MR. VON MISTELWEIG vanished into the swell of guests, Alex sat tiredly on the edge of the raised bench. The echo of his warnings, intertwined with ancient tales of hidden vampire villages, reverberated in her thoughts. Was this just the eccentricity of a billionaire, or was there truth in his stories? The logical part of her leaned towards the former; his tales of Norse gods and vampire courts seemed straight out of an Anne Rice novel.

She let out a soft chuckle, reassuring herself that he was just another wealthy man with too much time on his hands. Despite her nocturnal activities with Izzie, they had always been discreet, never leaving any evidence of their interference. The CPD looked the other way, leaving them out of any reports because they knew, in their heart of hearts, that the city was safer with her in the shadows. Would they admit it? No, never, but their deliberate omissions signaled an approval of sorts.

Feeling the weight of the day press on her shoulders, she scanned the room, her eyes instinctively searching for Lucas.

As their gazes met, a warm smile spread across his face. But Mr. Von Mistelweig's fleeting warning caused her to hesitate, her own smile waning for a split second. Lucas noticed, his eyes clouding with confusion and concern. Again. Fuck, she was probably giving him whiplash at this point. Shaking off the unsettling feeling, she mustered a halfhearted smile and a little wave before hurrying away in the opposite direction.

With the decision to leave solidified, she weaved through the crowd, grateful to see Otto stationed outside with the SUV. The evening streets of Munich, bustling with Oktoberfest celebrations, would have made it challenging to hail a cab.

Once she got back to the hotel, she carefully removed the complicated dirndl and got ready for an hour or two of much-needed sleep before she had to leave for the plane. Before she lay down, though, she checked her phone. "Fuck!" Izzie had called her five times in the last two hours. She cursed. How had she missed that? She immediately called Izzie back, knowing she would pick up wherever she was.

"Alex, where the hell have you been? Why haven't you answered? You said you'd be back tonight!" Izzie's voice crackled from the other end of the phone, frantic and full of worry and urgency.

"I got caught up at Oktoberfest with the Family," Alex explained, massaging her temples. "Met the patriarch, had a weird conversation. But what's going on? Why are you so worked up?"

Izzie's voice dropped to a somber tone. "Another murder, Alex. This time it was just a kid. A young girl."

The news struck Alex like a slap. Each death was a tragedy, but there was a particularly vile sense of injustice when a child was involved. Monsters taking kids was a brand of evil that seemed to defy the very order of the universe.

"Shit. Okay, details, Izzie. I'll be back by around ten AM your time tomorrow."

Izzie sighed deeply before beginning. "They found her body west of the city, in one of those small suburbs. Laid out like the others—branded stomach, drained of blood."

Silence stretched between them, oppressive and thick. Guilt churned in Alex's stomach; she'd been away, lost in the mundane world and a stupid crush. If only she'd been there, she might have made a difference.

"Alex, listen to me," Izzie said. "You being here wouldn't have changed a damn thing. That area wasn't even on our radar, and we definitely weren't expecting someone to target a child."

"You can't be certain, Izzie. Maybe I would've noticed something you overlooked. Tracked down that vampire from Tuesday. What about the shimmer? Was it there?"

"No shimmer this time," Izzie replied. "I brought Mary along. If the shimmer were there, she would've sensed it."

Mary's involvement brought some comfort to Alex. The local hedge witch might not be overwhelmingly powerful, but her ability to peer into the magical realm was unmatched.

"When I'm back, we're catching this bastard. I swear it."

"I know, hun. I'll send you everything we have by the time you board. Stay safe until then."

After hanging up, Alex took a moment to process everything. Lost in thought, she was jolted back to the present when she glanced at the clock. It was nearly time to leave for the airport. She cursed under her breath; how had she let time slip away so easily?

Descending to the hotel lobby, Otto awaited her, ever the reliable driver. However, Lucas and Rory were conspicuously absent. Reflecting on the previous night's festivities, she guessed they must have opted for a later flight.

Otto drove smoothly through Munich's streets, bringing her to the airport entrance. As he stepped out to help with her luggage, Alex noticed something odd in his demeanor. His gaze lingered on her, contemplative and searching.

"Thank you, Otto," she began, attempting to dispel the awkward atmosphere. "It's been great having you as our tour guide."

Without warning, he grunted and murmured almost inaudibly, "She doesn't look that tough." With that, he climbed back into the SUV and left, leaving Alex standing there, slightly baffled.

"Well, that wasn't weird at all," she muttered to herself, shaking her head. Putting the strange interaction behind her, she focused on navigating the airport. Security checks, boarding pass verification, and the whirl of pre-flight rituals occupied her attention.

Once settled in her airplane seat, Alex tapped her fingers impatiently, anticipating the plane's ascent to cruising altitude. As the familiar chime sounded and the fasten seat belt sign blinked off, Alex wasted no time retrieving her laptop and launching into Izzie's awaited email.

Just like the two files she had reviewed on the trip out, the report before her meticulously detailed the third murder. Every detail, every forensic finding, so far—Alex painstakingly read and re-read it all.

Committing each piece of evidence to memory, she leaned back, took a deep breath, and let her mind wander. Drawing upon the meditation technique Jiraiya had taught her, she used it to mentally organize and decipher the sea of data. This method, initially designed to understand intricate swordplay in combat and used to help her control her emotions, was one of the main reasons she was still alive and sane. Yet, today, it was being used for a grimmer purpose—to understand the mind of a killer.

The faces of the victims floated across her mind's eye, and patterns slowly began emerging. All victims were female, though their ages varied, and they all had connections to Northwestern University. Additionally, they all had that weird double triangle brand. But something about the latest victim, the child, stood out. It appeared she might have been moved post-mortem.

Alex's fingers flew over the laptop keyboard again, pulling up Google Maps. She homed in on an area, and a playground caught her eye. "Ha!" she exclaimed, drawing a few quizzical glances from fellow passengers. Ignoring them, she quickly typed out an email.

Izzie,

I think I've connected the dots. We're going to get this bastard before he kills again. Meet me at my place after I touch down. We need to strategize.

Alex

With the wheels of her plan turning, the remainder of the flight was a whirlwind. Alex mentally checked off what she'd need: Talon and the Twins, protective leather attire, additional knives, metal wire, an LED flash bomb, and a first aid kit. She had no idea what this asshole was, so she would be prepared for every possibility. The monster had sealed its fate, though. Tomorrow night, it would die, whatever it was. Izzie would surely disapprove of Alex's plan, but there was no other way. This reign of terror had to end.

CHAPTER 15

AFTER THE LONG FLIGHT, Alex tiredly pushed herself through the front door. As always, Argo was right there to greet her, his face full of mischief and energy.

"Missed me much?" she teased, slipping off her coat.

"Boss, please. While you've been off on your adventures, I've been engaged in mortal combat with my archenemy."

"You mean the squirrel from the backyard?" she guessed.

He shuddered for effect. "That treacherous fiend! The tales of his exploits are harrowing. The last to face him died quite horribly."

"But not you, of course."

He puffed out his fluffy chest. "Of course not! I expelled him from your domain. You're welcome."

Shaking her head in amusement, Alex retorted, "And I'm sure between these heroic battles, there was plenty of time for leisurely naps?"

"Naturally, but I did have a minor panic attack thinking I'd run out of food when you didn't come home yesterday."

"Sounds traumatic." She laughed, throwing her purse onto the nearby counter.

"Oh, it was, boss, you have no idea. But enough about me. So, how was the trip?" he asked, sitting down and licking his paws while Alex took off her boots and hung her coat.

"Well, the presentation went well, although I had an unusual chat with the patriarch, Mr. Von Mistelweig. He spun this weird ass tale about vampires and Hidden Villages. Thinks he's some modern-day vampire Batman."

Argo's jovial demeanor changed subtly at the mention of the Hidden Villages.

"Ever heard of these Vampire Hidden Villages, Argo?"

The pup sauntered over with an exaggerated nonchalance, his tail wagging just a bit too deliberately. "If they're hidden, how would I know?"

Alex eyed him skeptically but decided to drop it.

"So, any alone time with Lucas?" Argo's eyebrows danced.

Flustered, Alex retorted, "Why would that matter to you?"

Argo made little smooching sounds, almost cartoonish, given his canine face. "Oh, come on! Spill the beans!"

"All right, all right! We shared a... rather heated moment outside Oktoberfest." The blush in her cheeks rose even further. "He's... there's just something about him."

Argo's eyes widened, his back molars showing. "Oh, a 'heated moment,'" he said, accentuating the words with a wink. Suddenly, he arched his back up and began gyrating his little furry backside, mimicking a cheeky little dance against a nearby table leg. The sight was so ridiculous that Alex wasn't sure if he was trying to make love to the table or just poo on it.

Through her burst of laughter, Alex realized that his antics had successfully erased her previous embarrassment, probably just as he had intended.

Argo stopped his dance and nudged her. "I can see it in your eyes. You really like him, don't you?"

"Well, yes, obviously. But I can't, Argo. I can't risk losing control again, not after what happened in high school."

Argo's demeanor softened. "It's been years since Richard Delion. You can control your emotions much better now. And, besides, he got what he deserved. If he hadn't run away, I would have eaten him."

"Argo, even if he had it coming, which I'm not disputing, it doesn't make what happened right." Alex sighed. "The rat bastard."

"But with your training with Jiraiya, you've come so far. And Izzie has helped you understand and manage your triggers," Argo offered reassuringly.

Alex shook her head. "I appreciate that, but with Lucas, it's different. He doesn't just push my buttons. He's the bloody detonator. I'm an exposed nerve around him, and it terrifies me."

"Now you're just making excuses. You know it's not the person or how you feel about them that's triggering; it's certain situations. So, you have to ask yourself if you trust Lucas enough not to put you in those triggering situations."

Deep in thought, Alex mulled over their moments together. He had always been a perfect gentleman, or at least as much as she wanted him to be. He had never pushed her boundaries and always responded calmly to all her hot and cold, even though he must think she was a total basket-case. Smiling slightly, she thought that, just maybe, this was somebody she could trust. At least a little bit.

Argo seemed to notice the subtle change in her stance. "That's my girl!"

She blushed. "We'll see. Now, help me get ready. Izzie will be here soon."

It was just past six when Izzie walked in, greeted by the rich aroma of fragrant herbs and spices that hinted at a perfectly roasted meal. Exhausted, she took a moment to deeply inhale the enticing aroma before kicking off her boots. "For a creature without thumbs or the proper height, you sure know how to pull off culinary magic," she hollered, addressing Argo in the kitchen.

The little corgi, undeterred by the short joke, waggled out of the kitchen with his signature corgi butt shimmy, eager for some affection. "Hey, now." She chuckled, bending down to give him a scratch behind the ears. "How's Alex holding up after the journey?"

"Mostly hot and bothered," Argo cheekily replied, offering a sly wink before bouncing back to his kitchen duties.

Izzie's eyes widened, and she toppled backward in surprise, landing squarely on her backside. Even after all this time, Argo's sporadic vocal moments never ceased to catch her off guard. Even though Alex knew that she had no idea how chatty he could be with just her.

Emerging from the bedroom in cozy sweatpants, Alex stifled a giggle at the sight of her friend on the floor. But before she could chime in, Izzie raised an eyebrow. "So, 'hot and bothered,' was it?"

Alex's face flushed a shade of crimson. "That little chatterbox. I swear, one of these days, I'm going to turn him into a pair of fuzzy slippers." She glared at the future slippers. "But before diving into that, let's get something to eat and go over my plan for tomorrow. That's far more pressing than whatever escapades I might have had."

"Escapades?" Izzie's eyebrows danced. "Now you've really got my attention. But agreed, business first."

Upon entering the kitchen, the sight that met them was astounding. Though Alex was long used to Argo's gourmet tendencies, Izzie had never managed to fully wrap her head around it. A sumptuous feast was laid out, fit for royalty. A golden roasted chicken took pride of place at the table's center, surrounded by bowls of creamy mashed potatoes and glistening green beans adorned with buttery almond slivers. To the side, freshly baked bread rolls infused with garlic and butter were set in a basket.

As the women marveled at the spread, Argo sat off to the side with a pleased expression, his butt wagging slowly as if waiting for their reaction.

"Argo, how on earth..." Izzie began, looking from the corgi to the spread and back.

Alex chuckled, bending down to ruffle Argo's fur. "You've outdone yourself this time, little chef."

Argo barked happily, clearly enjoying the praise, though his mischievous eyes seemed to say, "Well, what did you expect, boss?"

The two women exchanged amused and impressed glances before taking their seats. With plates already served, they dug in, and for a few moments, there was only the sound of silverware against porcelain, interspersed with the occasional appreciative hum or sigh.

Izzie took a leisurely sip of her wine, no doubt savoring the velvety taste of dark fruits and subtle oak notes. "You never skimp on the wine, do you?"

Alex grinned, tilting her glass in acknowledgment before taking a sip herself. "Never," she replied, before setting her glass down to begin detailing her findings. "Every victim had connections to Northwestern. Different age groups. Different generations. But each was murdered in a place they would feel at ease."

Izzie nodded. "The older woman on the steps of a university, the younger one by a bar on the Navy Pier. But the child? How are you so certain?"

"I plotted the locations on a map of Chicago, using the symbol found on their bodies to triangulate. The third point? A playground."

Izzie inhaled sharply, her analytical mind working through the provided data. "God... it makes sense."

"And if we follow the pattern," Alex continued, her voice filled with urgency, "we can predict the next murder, likely tomorrow."

Izzie's eyes sparkled, and a wide, predatory smile spread across her face, but it quickly faded as she realized what Alex was proposing. "Using yourself as bait is out of the question. It's too risky."

Alex met her gaze unwaveringly. "Izzie, I fit the profile. I'm in my thirties, a working professional. I went to Northwestern, and to boot, I don't live far from where the next killing should take place. If not me, then someone else is at risk. We have to do it!"

"But you could be killed! We don't even know what this thing is. Or why it's doing this. And we still don't know the importance of that damn flower. It's too dangerous," Izzie argued, waving her fork around in front of her.

"It's too dangerous to someone else if we don't do it. You know that. Some woman, probably a mother, will die tomorrow unless we stop it or redirect it."

"You realize how insane this is, right?"

"I know. But someone's life is on the line," Alex responded, her voice firm. "I can't just stand by."

Izzie reluctantly nodded, her cop instincts kicking in. "All right, if you're set on this, then it's on my terms. We pick a location with full visibility, good street lighting, and an early start. And we'll have Mary stationed as our lookout."

"Abso-fucking-lutely not! It's too risky for her," Alex said, shoving the last piece of chicken into her mouth.

"It's too dangerous for you, Alex! This is non-negotiable. We need to get a heads up on the attack and if there's more than one asshole in on it."

"Fine, but you stay with her. And make sure your guns are ready to go," Alex relented.

"Obviously," Izzie agreed.

Alex took one last swig of her wine, emptying the glass. "So... we're really doing this, huh?"

"We are," Izzie replied, the decision made. "Now pour me another glass of wine and tell me about these escapades in Munich."

Grinning, Alex began regaling her with tales of her trip, including the rather scandalous event among the trees. Her face flushed as she spoke about the unanticipated moment of intimacy, recalling the feeling of tree bark against her back.

"It was... sudden. I was having a great time dancing on the benches and drinking champagne. Next thing I know, we're out in the trees, and..." She paused, waving her hands in the air. "When I finally managed to get out of that dirndl, there was actual tree bark stuck to it!"

Izzie chuckled. "Sounds amazing! And here I was, thinking it was supposed to be some boring business trip."

A groan escaped Alex's throat. "It was so embarrassing. I've never done anything so reckless!"

"You mean besides this half-baked plan to use you as bait?" Izzie said, then raised her hands in apology. "Sorry, go on, go on."

Alex frowned but couldn't keep a straight face, breaking into another wide grin. "It was amazing! I haven't felt like that in... I don't even know how long."

As she leaned forward, Izzie's face softened. "I'm really happy for you, Alex. It's about time you found someone who isn't a complete jerk or a one-night stand. Though I must admit, I'm a bit jealous."

Alex's smile faltered slightly. "Do you... think it's okay, though? You know, with everything?"

Izzie reached out, squeezing Alex's hand reassuringly. "Life's unpredictable. It might work out, or it might not. But it's all about taking that chance. And hey, even if it doesn't pan out, at least you put yourself out there. It's better than being permanently alone."

Before Alex could respond, a low, growling voice rumbled, "Hey! Woman. She's not alone."

Both women turned to see Argo, eyes gleaming with protective determination. Alex smiled, bending down to ruffle his fur, while Izzie once again raised her hands in a pantomimed apology. "I know, buddy. Thank you. But this is... different."

Argo's eyes met Alex's. "I just wanted to remind you, boss. You're never truly alone."

Izzie cleared her throat, shifting the topic back to the matter at hand. "Besides, you're not some naive teenager anymore. You face off with creatures that most people don't even believe exist. If anyone can handle a romance, it's you."

Alex laughed, relief flooding her. "Thanks, Izzie. I needed that."

The night grew darker, and as the final glasses were drained, Izzie stood up. "All right, I need to get some sleep. Tomorrow's going to be one hell of a day."

Alex nodded, walking her friend to the door. "Stay safe."

With Izzie gone, Alex descended into her basement, prepping her mind and body for the battles to come. Her thoughts occasionally wandered back to the stories she shared with Izzie, but she knew she had to focus. The next day at Sweet Temptations was going to be a long one knowing she'd be hunting a child-killer that night.

CHAPTER 16

ALEX WAS BURIED in emails. The sheer volume of correspondence generated from just one day out of the office never ceased to astonish her. It was as if her colleagues had an uncanny ability to synchronize their crises to coincide with her absence. One supplier's delay in corn syrup delivery threatened to halt operations, while another's flour delivery came infested with roaches, inciting a fit from the plant manager.

At the same time, her mind raced with the gruesome details of the latest murder victim. The mere thought of another body ignited sparks of fury in her heart. But for now, she had to center herself, clear the email backlog, and maintain the guise of a regular workday, at least until she could regroup with Izzie later. They were going to catch the motherfucker tonight, she promised herself.

A knock at her office door snapped her back to the present. Through the glass, she saw Lucas. Her cheeks flushed, thinking about what happened in Munich, but those were memories she needed to bury, for the moment at least. Giving a professional nod, she beckoned him inside. Lucas entered, dressed casually in a well-fitted charcoal Henley shirt that highlighted his toned arms. Paired with dark jeans and a pair of brown leather loafers, he looked every bit the modern professional but with a touch of laid-back charm.

Shutting the door behind him, he closed the privacy curtains on the large office windows. The gesture was primarily for confidentiality on this project, as per Legal's advice, but it also added an unintended intimacy to the room. He glanced at Alex, who sat poised in her high-back leather chair. She wore a silk blouse in muted teal that draped elegantly over her form, while a soft gray pencil skirt hugged her curves in all the right places. Alex could see Lucas's reaction to her presence. He seemed unable to tear his eyes away.

Clearing his throat, Lucas began, "I had a whole agenda planned, hoping to recap the Family's position and discuss our next steps for Chicago." He nervously ran a hand through his tousled brown hair, an all too familiar gesture that she was coming to love. "But here you are."

And then, as if a switch were flipped, he uttered, "Ah, fuck it," and any semblance of professionalism melted away.

Lucas closed the distance in a few swift strides, dropping to his knees before her. Alex's breath caught in her throught, her pulse hammering as his hands settled on her knees, warm and steady.

Their eyes met—held—and everything else faded.

Slowly, his gaze drifted downward, fingers tracing the edge of her skirt before pushing it higher, the fabric sliding up her thighs.

He looked up again, voice rough. "Should I stop?"

Alex's eyes widened, and she leaned back in her chair. "No."

He nodded and carefully reached up below the skirt's

surface, taking hold of the sides of her silk bikini underwear. He slid them down past her knees with utmost care and placed them gently on the floor beside him. He then reached back up with one hand and grabbed the soft mound between her thighs, squeezing gently, drawing a small, surprised moan from Alex.

His mouth twitched, but soon, a fiery intensity returned to his eyes. With both hands, he shoved her knees apart, then dove face-first into the depths of her skirt.

Alex clasped her mouth with her hands, trying to stifle the cry of pleasure before it could escape. As he continued his tender touches, she released one hand, reaching out to him, fingers entangling in his hair, trying to pull him closer.

He licked a slow, teasing path from top to bottom before withdrawing—only to return with deliberate, rhythmic strokes, each flick of his tongue sending a fresh wave of bliss through her. He was a starving man, and she was his feast.

As he continued, his wet strokes getting faster and harder with every passing second, Alex felt the darkness stirring once more, in tune with the growing pressure where Lucas was tending. Instead of changing her, though, it radiated through her body like tendrils of fiery warmth, escalating in fervor until the need for release became overwhelming. Her pelvic muscles contracted in one last burst of pleasure, and she shook wildly in the chair while Lucas held on, refusing to release his hold on either her thighs or what lay between them.

It felt like an eternity, but eventually, she descended from the peak, sinking into her chair with a deep, contented exhale. Looking down, she saw Lucas grinning back at her, as if he'd just gotten away with something terribly wicked. She couldn't even remember when exactly he had released her.

A bubble of near-hysterical laughter escaped her lips as she sat limp in the chair, knees knocking lightly together.

As he stood before her, though, she first noticed how

excited he had become while tasting her. The front of his pants strained against the seemingly unfair confinement of the fabric. When she looked up at his face, his mouth still wet and shiny from his efforts, she could have sworn she saw small flames dancing in the backs of his eyes. And just like that, it was as if her earlier release had never happened. She wanted this man even more than she had ever wanted anything in her life.

"My calendar is booked for the next fifty minutes. Nobody should disturb us." Her voice was a barely constrained growl. "And I'll be damned if I don't take my time with you this time." She had never felt more powerful than she did in that moment, one with the monster inside her, but unchanged.

He reached down, stretching a finger out under her chin, and gently guided her out of the chair. As she rose to face him, he seamlessly wrapped his other arm around her waist, pulling her closer.

He nestled his cheek against hers. Show me."

Alex grabbed him through his pants and dragged him to the back corner of her office. "Get on the floor. Lay on your back."

Lucas stared at her with wide eyes and an open mouth, seemingly processing the surprise role reversal. The seconds felt longer than they were until a playful glint appeared in his eyes. The edges of his lips curled up into a wolfish grin, and in what seemed like the blink of an eye, he was sprawled out on the floor, looking up at her with an expression that seemed to challenge, "What next?"

Slipping out of her sleek black stilettos, she positioned herself over him, straddling his waist. Responding to his silent beckoning, she smoothly hitched her skirt higher up her thighs, settling herself atop him.

She rocked back and forth, enjoying his frustrated little moans at feeling her weight and movement while still being trapped in his pants.

"Not yet," she snarled, swatting away his reaching hands.

Before he could take control, she beat him to it—fingers deftly undoing his belt, yanking open his pants. His briefs did little to contain him, and the moment she freed him, his length sprang forward, thick and hard, demanding her attention.

Alex paused, letting her gaze linger, a sly grin gracing her features. She hadn't actually seen it in Munich. It had been too dark, and events too rushed. But now, in her own space, she took a moment to indulge in the sight.

"Enjoying the view?"

She met his eyes, her grin still intact. Then she smoothly lifted her shirt over her head and undid the lacy purple bra that was holding her breasts in place. She intended to craft a memory he'd never forget.

He was immediately transfixed by the sight of her breasts hovering freely above him. When he unconsciously reached for them, Alex grabbed his hands and redirected their grip to the sides of her thighs. The flash of disappointment that briefly crossed his features was quickly replaced with bliss when she lowered herself onto him, directing him with one hand, inch by inch, into her soft, wet core.

"Oh, my god, Alex," he moaned, gripping her thighs hard enough to bruise as she began flexing her muscles to move on top of him, up and down, in slow, sensuous waves.

She leaned back, balancing herself with one extended arm, creating new angles that made them both pant in pleasure as she continued to move her hips in a slow, sinuous rhythm.

Lucas's hands moved up from her hips, locking onto her waist and buttocks. He clung to her with the desperation of a man lost at sea. But as she moved faster and faster, and harder and harder, nothing could stop the giant wave of pleasure from crashing down on them both.

"Alex!" Lucas groaned as she melted against him.

She sunk into his body, their heartbeats still racing in tandem. "Fuck," she sighed, allowing a fleeting moment of closeness before reality crept back in.

With a careful shift, she rolled onto her back, breath still unsteady, the air between them charged with the lingering remnants of pleasure. Then, she felt the now-familiar brush of his fingers—light at first, searching—finding hers and intertwining gently.

Lucas spoke up first. "Well, that was not at all how I envisioned our meeting." He began tucking himself back into his pants, securing his belt and zipper before shifting to his side to admire her.

Alex stared at the ceiling. "You don't say," she responded, laughter falling into a coughing fit.

His fingers traced soft patterns on her stomach, a light caress that made her shiver. As she made to sit up, he tugged at her arm gently, causing her to settle back down facing him. Their gazes locked, wrapped up in the depth of each other's eyes.

The discomfort of the carpet soon became evident, though, reminding them of their surroundings. Sitting up in unison, he handed her the shirt she had shed earlier, their fingers brushing briefly.

"So...um...should we..." Lucas faltered, his usual confidence gone.

Clad once again in her corporate armor, Alex sighed deeply before meeting his eyes. "That can absolutely not ever happen again."

His face fell, hurt evident in his gaze. "Oh... I'm sorry if I presumed or misread anything."

"Oh my gosh, you silly man, let me finish." She smiled. "I meant, we can't do that here, in the office. It was beyond crazy. But outside of this building? I might be persuaded."

As the weight of the moment settled between them, the soft ticks of a clock drifted into her consciousness.

Alex's gaze drifted to the elegant timekeeper on the wall, its slender hands indicating that their hour was rapidly drawing to a close. "Lucas," she began, still catching her breath, "it looks like our time is almost up. We'll have to discuss the project details later."

"How about catching up over an early dinner tonight?"

Alex's heart fluttered, but then she remembered her plans to catch a monster that night. "I can't tonight," she replied, noticing the disappointment in his eyes. "But how about lunch tomorrow?"

"Lunch sounds perfect," he agreed, his signature gorgeous smile returning in full force. "The restaurant across from the office at noon?"

"It's a date." She fumbled, realizing what she said. "Um, no, not a date. I mean a working lunch. Or something."

Lucas just smiled, laughter playing on his features, and turned toward the door.

As he exited her office, the atmosphere felt emptier, the space suddenly too big. Alex sat and leaned back in her chair, staring momentarily at the door he had just closed behind him. But duty beckoned. She had a mountain of emails awaiting her attention and needed to stay focused for the night ahead. With a sigh, she clicked her mouse and began her descent into the digital backlog, counting the hours until she could get the heck out of there.

CHAPTER 17

THE CONSTANT TICK of the old-fashioned wall clock in her office was the only soundtrack accompanying the dying minutes of Alex's workday. Each tock was a taunt, each tick a tease, until the hands of the clock aligned like stars—five o'clock, freedom's herald.

Her heels beat a tattoo on the polished floor, a staccato rhythm underscoring her escape. The cacophony of keyboards and gossip, the insistent blink of new email notifications—they all evaporated in the wake of her departure. Lucas, with his mischievous grin, the Munich shenanigans, even the possible seduction of tomorrow's lunch date—mere dust in her mental rearview mirror.

Finally heading home, Alex watched as Chicago's skyline unfolded before her, bathed in the hues of a reluctant sunset. With each heartbeat echoing like a drumbeat, a single thought reverberated within her—stop him.

She reached her house in record time, flinging open the door as fast as she could. Skidding on the floorboards, she burst in with all the subtlety of a hurricane. Argo, the ever-faithful fur missile, launched himself into her path, his excitement vibrating through the air. "Hey, boss," he yipped, but his greeting was brushed aside.

With a single-mindedness that bordered on feral, she streaked past his wagging booty and through the dimly lit kitchen, doubling as their strategic headquarters for this operation. Izzie, ever the general, hovered over a large map of the city scattered with the macabre breadcrumbs of a killer. She spared no glance for Alex; words were extraneous in the shadow of a hunt.

Without missing a beat, Alex moved to her bedroom. There, displayed on her bed like a warrior's arsenal, was her hunting kit for tonight's excursion. The sight struck her. The care with which her necessities had been laid out was a silent salute to her crusade. Her eyes caught Argo's, the liquid chocolate depths shimmering with something like pride, and something like fear.

"Sorry, buddy," she whispered as she enfolded the diminutive canine in her arms. "Thank you."

Argo's soft yip made her smile, his muzzle pushing closer as if to infuse her with courage.

Standing back up, she wrinkled her nose, seeing the boring trousers and bright pink shirt that he'd laid out on the back chair.

"You've got to rock the whole 'suburban mundane' camouflage tonight." Argo's voice threaded through her annoyance. "Which you shouldn't really have a problem with, given your age."

"My age? I'm in the prime of my thirties, thank you very much," Alex retorted, the corners of her mouth quirking up.

"Exactly, just young enough, barely," Argo countered. "And we'll still need to mask the scent of your weapons in case the killer has a heightened sense of smell. You know, like most of the monsters do. Cherry Blossom bath spray should do the trick."

Her face contorted at the scent's invocation, but the strategy was sound. She had to become the perfect bait—unassuming, vulnerable, the predator's ideal choice.

"All right, let's do this."

She slipped into her combat ensemble—leather pants tough as Kevlar and a similar shirt, whisper-thin yet laced with steel threads. Each weapon found its secret sheath: knives at her ankles and wrists, a pair of short swords at her lower back, and Talon perched along her spine—a dragon's tooth ready to bite. Gray slacks and the nondescript pink sweater cloaked her warrior's garb, her mundane camouflage.

She scrutinized her reflection in the full-length mirror, eyes sharp as the blades she concealed. With deft fingers, she tugged and adjusted, ensuring nothing hinted at the storm beneath the calm. Her hair, now a tactical accessory, was drawn back in a low ponytail, an innocuous curtain veiling the grip of Talon protruding above the sweater's collar.

With a nod, she pivoted on her heel, ready to rejoin Izzie. Together, they would do whatever it took to end this killer.

The kitchen was silent save for the soft shuffle of Alex's feet and the gentle hum of the refrigerator. She moved through the space, the air thick with the scent of freshly made turkey sandwiches—another offering from Argo laid out on the counter beside the sink. She picked up two without question, the heft of them satisfying in her palms. Then she made her way to the table where Izzie was hunched over a sprawling map, handing her one of the sandwiches.

"Thanks, Argo," Izzie and Alex mumbled appreciatively in tandem, their words slightly muffled by generous bites. The culinary reprieve was short-lived for Alex, though, as she saw the foreboding red circle Izzie had marked.

"That's where we're going to catch him?"

"Yeah, if you're right in your theory," Izzie responded as she chewed thoughtfully on her own sandwich.

A brief pause ensued as she took a swig of water. "But I do think you're right," Izzie conceded, meeting Alex's gaze. "So, we have to get this right. We get the bastard, and you don't get killed in the process."

"Of course."

Izzie lifted her head, her eyes scrutinizing Alex's ensemble. "You have both Talon and the Twins?"

Alex responded with a single nod. "And the knives?" Izzie pressed on.

"Of course," Alex assured, her hand instinctively gripping her wrist where the hidden blades lay snugly against her skin.

Izzie's brow furrowed. "I still don't get why you won't carry a gun too. It makes me nervous as hell. You're practically naked out there."

A sigh escaped Alex, a familiar exchange about to unfold. There was never a risk-free hunt, but this was riskier than their usual plans, and she knew revisiting this argument would soothe Izzie's jangled nerves. "We've been over this. I'm always too close to make good use of a gun, especially with how fast our targets usually move. I'm much faster drawing and striking with Talon close up than I would be with a gun, and besides, you're my gun." Alex grinned. "I trust you to have my back."

The exhale that left Izzie seemed to carry a weight with it. "Yeah, yeah, I know, and no pressure there, you twat," she muttered, the tension in her shoulders easing slightly. "Just had to say it one more time."

"I know," Alex replied softly.

Izzie's finger tapped on the map. "This is where we'll go," she announced, tracing the lines of Northbrook's streets to the familiar outline of the Sportsman's Country Club.

Pulling up the location on her phone, Alex's memory was nudged by the view of the clubhouse—a place of polished gatherings, echoing laughter, and the clink of glasses. She had been there once for a business golf tournament. Tonight would be vastly different than her last visit.

"What do they have going on tonight? It's not like we're members," she inquired, arching an eyebrow.

Izzie's smile was impish. Argo would have approved. "Oktoberfest beer tasting event. Open to the public for a charity thing—Toys for Tots, I think."

Color flooded Alex's cheeks at the mention of Oktoberfest, and a playful snort escaped her at the whimsy of the universe. "Well, I can certainly appreciate the coincidence. There's absolutely no way you picked this place just to tease me. This must have been the only suitable location."

"Of course! I would never!" Izzie replied with an exaggerated flutter of her lashes.

Their laughter mingled, a momentary lapse in the evening's gravity. Reaching across the table, Alex clasped Izzie's hand, a silent vow passing between them.

"All right then. Let's go get the bastard."

As they headed for the door, Argo sat by the exit. His posture was rigid, rather than sprawled out in his customary repose beneath the dining table. His dark eyes locked onto Alex with an uncharacteristic intensity.

"Hey, boss. Be careful, okay?" His voice was solemn. This was not his usual playful banter.

Then, even more surprising, Alex felt a nudge against her legs, a gesture so oddly reminiscent of a comforting feline that it brought a half-smile to her lips.

"Buddy, I'll be fine. And I'll probably be hungry when I get back," she replied with a reassuring wink, hoping to lift his spirits.

Instead of a quippy retort or a sardonic remark about his undervalued status in their operations, Argo simply nodded before he turned and retreated to the solitude of her bedroom.

"Huh, that was weird," she mumbled.

"Come on, let's go," Izzie's voice came from outside the door.

"Yeah, yeah, coming," Alex called back, then snatched the keys to her old Jeep from their designated hook by the door.

With a final glance back at the silent house, she steeled herself and stepped out into the crisp embrace of the early evening, Izzie's shadow already cast long against the driveway.

CHAPTER 18

WHEN THEY PULLED into the well-lit parking lot of the Sportsman's Country Club, the air was alive with excitement. The cheerful melody of traditional German folk music mingled with the chatter of guests as they streamed through the grand doors, eager to partake in the evening's revelries.

Alex glanced over at Izzie, whose focused gaze returned the unspoken communication with a nod. Without a sound, Izzie slipped out of the passenger door and disappeared into the shadows. Her role was clear: find a concealed vantage point from where she could oversee the area they'd designated for the trap. She knew Mary would already be there, hiding somewhere in silence, waiting for Izzie to take position.

Inside the Jeep, Alex allowed herself five minutes—a brief interlude to steady her breath and summon the facade she needed for the night. Then, with a composed exhale, she stepped out of the vehicle. Her smile was wide and genuine as she joined the throng of partygoers entering the clubhouse.

Blending in seamlessly, she weaved through the crowd. For

a good half hour, Alex became just another guest, engaging in idle chatter and ensuring her presence was noted without drawing undue attention.

She paused at the charity box, the bright display a beacon. With a practiced hand, she slipped in her donation, her movements part of the ebb and flow of the event.

The glasses of beer came and went, her apparent consumption increasing by the minute. Yet, unbeknownst to the onlookers, each beer barely touched her lips before its contents found a new home among the foliage of the display plants.

During this charade, she caught the attention of a handsome young man. His approach was smooth, and his offer to buy her another drink was delivered with a charming smile.

"Oh, no, thank you." She giggled with feigned tipsiness, brushing away the proposition. "I—I think I need some air, actually."

"Mind if I join you?" he inquired.

Her mind raced with suspicion, yet nothing about his demeanor suggested he was the predator they sought—just an utterly mundane young man caught up in the spirit of the event.

"No, that's okay," she managed to say, pulling her phone from her pocket. "I have a call I need to take." With a clumsy flourish, she pretended to answer an incoming call and staggered toward the exit.

Once outside, Alex put on a show of losing the call, cursing softly under her breath as she theatrically swiped at her phone screen. The silliness of the act didn't escape her, but she continued her uneven path, moving away from the comforting halo of the parking lot lights. Her destination was the darkness enveloping the driving range—the perfect place for them to lay their trap.

Even as she continued the drunken stumbling about, Alex's

senses were taut, stretched by anticipation as she lingered in the darkness of the driving range. She didn't have to wait long before she heard a quiet rustle and hiss from a nearby bush, Mary's signal that something was coming.

Her reactions were honed from countless encounters. As soon as the hiss reached her ears, her hands reached behind, fingers wrapping around the familiar hilts of the Twins. Pivoting on instinct, her blades cut through the air catching her attacker mid-lunge. It was a figure of medium build, now staggering backward, hands clasped over a chest from which dark liquid sprayed in a bloody arc. Even with Mary's warning, she had barely been fast enough.

In sync with the initial attack and out of nowhere, a voice, both familiar and fraught with urgency, cut through the chaos. "Alex! No!" The shout was a split-second precursor to a dazzling burst of light—a fireball tearing through the air with deadly intent.

The assailant, already reeling from Alex's unexpected resistance, was caught utterly unprepared. There was no time for evasion, no time for anything but the briefest flicker of surprise. The flames met flesh, and the figure was immediately swallowed by the conflagration, its screams piercing the night but for a fleeting moment.

Then, with a whoosh that seemed to suck the oxygen from the air, the burning man or vampire disintegrated. Ash and cinders fell like a grim rain, coating Alex in a fine dusting of residue. She blinked rapidly, wiping the gritty remnants from her eyes, trying to process how the hell a fireball had gotten there.

The acrid tang of charred remnants lingered in the air as Alex wiped the grime from her eyes. When her vision finally cleared, the tableau before her was so surreal it seemed ripped from the pages of a gothic novel.

There, standing at the far end of the driving range, was Lucas. He looked as if he had stepped out of the shadows themselves—dark slacks and a black shirt molded to his form, accentuating his lithe muscular build. Like the wings of some avian predator, a long black leather trench coat fluttered around him.

His raven hair, untamed and wild, danced with the night wind, each strand reflecting the distant lights of the parking lot. If that wasn't enough, fury etched his features into a silent scream of rage that held the world at bay. His eyes, those windows to the soul, were tempests of fury as he stared down at the remains of what presumably had been a vampire.

She had to blink again to make sure her eyes were working, because in his hands were orbs of brilliant molten fire. Large, pulsating spheres of white flame that should have devoured flesh and bone, yet they did not. Sitting in his hands, they burned with an intensity that defied nature, casting a hellish glow upon his visage.

The fireballs, seemingly an extension of his very being, flickered with a rhythm that matched the cadence of Alex's own heart. It was a wrath not to be underestimated. The night held its breath, the silence broken only by the distant echo of the German folk music, now an eerie soundtrack to the drama unfolding before her. In this moment, Lucas was not merely a man; he was the embodiment of the storm, the fire, the untamed force of nature that could either destroy or purify.

The clamor of the night receded into a tense hush. "Lucas?" Alex's voice wavered, the swords in her grip now feeling inadequate. She watched as Izzie broke through the underbrush, firearm ready, eyes locked on the man before them.

"Alex! What the fuck is going on?" Izzie's voice was sharp, her gun unwavering as she took in the sight of the man she only knew from Alex's breathless stories. "Please tell me that's not the guy from the office."

Lucas's face, etched in anger and concentration, melted into a look of relief as he saw Alex alive, then flickered to confusion, his gaze dropping to the swords by her sides. Then, as if shaking off the unexpected sight as inconsequential, he growled, "Get out of here. There will be more of them. They still need you to complete the ritual."

"Um, what?" Alex stammered, her mind racing. "Wait a second. What the fuck is going on?"

Simultaneously, Izzie's command sliced through the air like a warning shot, gun trained on Lucas. "Get down on the ground, hands behind your back! And douse those mother-fucking fireballs!"

With a frustrated sigh that seemed to carry the weight of the world, Lucas clenched his fists, and the flames dissipated into whiffs of smoke. "Look, I don't have time to explain. Alex, you were targeted at the party. I didn't recognize you, or I would have pulled you out sooner. But somebody marked you with the Azure Lily, and if they don't finish the ritual—killing you—they'll have to start all over."

"Fuck," she whispered, the image of the unsuspecting young man from the party haunting her thoughts.

"What? Who?" Izzie prodded, her attention snapping to Alex.

"Never mind, Izzie." Alex waved her off, her mind churning. She turned back to Lucas. "Look, clearly we need to talk," she said, nodding towards his now extinguished hands, "but Izzie and I, we've got this. We're the hunters here. We've been dealing with creeps like that for years. You should leave."

He ran a hand through his hair, a gesture so mundane and familiar that, for a moment, Alex allowed herself a smile amidst the madness. But then his voice was urgent, insistent. "You don't understand. This isn't a random rogue vampire attack. Just trust me and get out of here."

Izzie's laugh was brittle, like ice cracking on a frozen lake. "Yeah, not happening. How do we know you're not in on it?"

Before Lucas could respond, the night erupted into chaos as three more vampires descended from the swirling fog, their forms silhouetted against the ghostly backlight of the country club. Their eyes were hungry, and their intentions were clear. They landed with supernatural grace, fangs glinting in the stray beams of light that managed to pierce the sudden gloom surrounding them.

Their approach was a blur of speed and malice, the handsome man from the party leading the charge with a sneer.

"I must say, I didn't expect a challenge," he taunted, eyeing Alex with cruel amusement as he pulled out two knives. "You seemed so... compliant earlier."

Alex's grip on her twin swords tightened, her heart pounding with adrenaline. Izzie's gun roared in the night, but the vampires were swift, dodging with inhuman speed.

Alex matched their pace, her blades cutting through the night, trailing arcs of silver moonlight. The first, a stabbing thrust aimed at the vampire's heart, was parried aside by a knife too fast to see, though the vampire dropped his weapon in the exchange. The soft clang of metal on a nearby pole was music to Alex's ears. Smiling fiercely, she smoothly whirled into her second attack.

The vampire, cloaked in shadows, twisted with an almost beautiful grace, its body contorting in ways that defied the natural laws of human anatomy. It ducked under Alex's second blade, the sharp edge whistling mere inches from its face, taking only a small nick in the neck. With a mocking grin, it surged forward again, its hand snapping out, not to kill, but to disarm. The impact was precise, targeting the vulnerable wrists, and Alex felt the jarring force of the vampire's strike ripple through her bones. Her left sword clattered into the darkness, lost among the trees in the tumult.

Barely masking a grunt of frustration, Alex's instincts screamed, her training taking over. Her hand shot down to her ankle, swift as a striking viper, and from the sheath strapped there, she drew a silver-edged knife. With a flick of her wrist, the blade spun through the air, embedding itself in the vampire's shoulder. The attacker hissed, not from pain but annoyance, as the blessed metal sizzled against its flesh.

Instead of recoiling, it surged forward, a taloned hand lashing out and catching Alex off guard. The edge of a clawed finger raked across her thigh, leaving a line of fire in its wake that blossomed into wet warmth as blood began to seep through the tear in her pants. Gritting her teeth against the pain, Alex took a staggered step back, her mind already racing through her next move.

As the other two closed in on her companions, Lucas, with a sharp gesture, seemed to warp the very fabric of time around them. Movement slowed, but not enough—the vampires were adapting, resisting the magical lull. Fire erupted from Lucas's hands next, but the night was suddenly against them, dampness seeping into the air and muting the flames.

The handsome creep crackled, one hand on his neck, holding back the small stream of blood from Alex's attack. "Fool! As if we couldn't deal with you, slave," he yelled in Lucas's direction.

Then, he lunged with razor-sharp claws extended. Before she could stop him, Lucas stepped in front of Alex, flames meeting fangs, but human flesh yielded before the fire could cleanse. His grimace was a silent scream as he absorbed the blow meant for her.

"Get back!" Alex snarled, her eyes bleeding pitch black as the dhampir surged within her. She shoved Lucas aside, sending him flying over twenty feet out onto the driving range, her own body now a conduit of dark rage. She drew Talon with a hiss, the blade reflecting her newfound savagery. The vampire barely had time to register the change before Alex was on him. Talon arced through the air, slicing clearly through the neck, dispatching the cocky vampire in a spray of blood and a gout of unholy flame.

Izzie, despite a fresh gash along her arm, managed to injure the remaining two attackers while they were distracted by their leader's immolation. The roar of her gun covered their grunts of surprise as her bullets tore through undead flesh. It was the opening Alex needed.

Unleashing a primal snarl, Alex's humanity seemed to peel away. She flung the now superfluous short sword to the ground at her side and lunged with a recklessness that belied calculated risk. The predator within her sensed the kill and would not be delayed. She held Talon extended out before her, more claw than weapon.

The first vampire met her charge, its own inhuman prowess matching her fury. Fangs bared in a grotesque leer, it aimed to tear at the flesh it believed so fragile. But Alex was a whirlwind of wrath and steel. With Talon gripped in both hands, she parried a swipe from the vampire's clawed hand, taking it off at the wrist to its shock and horror.

The vampire stumbled back, cradling its injured arm, roaring in disbelief. It then launched itself back at her in a blur of speed and streaming blood. She ducked under the remaining grasping claw, and Talon arced through the air with a precision honed over years of combat. The blade, seemingly imbued with some ancient power, hummed with an eerie glow and found its mark, cleaving through the vampire's chest with an ease that mocked the concept of resistance.

As the sword punctured the undead heart, the vampire's

eyes widened in a split second of realization that it had under-estimated its prey. Before it could react, she dislodged her blade, whirled it once more in the air, and sliced the head clean off. More blood sprayed, and the creature's body crumbled, turning to ash as its essence was unmade with the loss of its head.

Wiping the ash once more from her eyes, her breath came in ragged gasps, the overwhelming power that had surged through her veins now retreating like a tide pulling away from the shore. The darkness that had clouded Alex's eyes faded, revealing the stark fear that she had been holding at bay. The inhuman strength that had bolstered her, that had allowed her to fight as more than merely a woman against these creatures of nightmare, was ebbing. And with it, her certainty crumbled.

Staggering, her knees buckled, and she collapsed, the manic rush of battle draining from her in an instant. Talon now hung from her fingertips, its tip kissing the ground as her arm drooped lifelessly. Agony lanced through Alex's leg; the adrenaline that had masked the pain flowed away. She clutched at the deep gash, her fingers pressing against the torn fabric of her clothing, attempting to staunch the bleeding. She was spent, the last vestiges of her monstrous inheritance leaving her hollow.

And now, as the silence of the aftermath wrapped around her, a different kind of darkness seeped in—the cold grip of guilt and fear. There was one more out there, still.

She thought of Lucas, of Izzie—the latter she had silently vowed to protect, a promise made in the quiet recesses of her heart. And now, with the approach of the last vampire, its shadow looming over them like an executioner's axe, she feared she had failed.

Tears carved paths through the grime and ash on her face as she tried to gather the shattered pieces of her resolve. She had fought and won against two vampires far faster, stronger, and cunning than anything she had faced before. But none of it mattered. If she couldn't rise, if she couldn't muster the strength to stand once more, both she and her friends would die.

The guilt was a crushing weight, and for a breath, it threatened to smother the fire that had always burned within her. She closed her eyes, willing the tears to stop, but they came unbidden—she had failed.

Lucas, though battered, was not yet broken. He rose, his hands once more becoming crucibles of seething arcane power. Whatever had smothered the flames before was no longer in effect. A surge of fiery vengeance emanated from his palms, directed at the remaining adversary. The night air shimmered with the heat of his fury as the inferno consumed the last vampire, its existence snuffed out in a final, desperate shriek. With the threat extinguished, Lucas's hands fell to his sides, the glow fading, leaving only the echo of his power in the air.

CHAPTER 19

IN THE AFTERMATH, her breaths came in labored gasps, her body a map of cuts and contusions. Her eyes, finally having shed the Hellish black, returned to their human hue. Looking around her, scanning for more enemies, she noticed Lucas wavering unsteadily on his feet, gaze staring unfocused out into the distance.

She rushed to him before he could stumble and fall, sliding an arm under his shoulder to steady him. Izzie, gun still in hand but now lowered, swept her gaze across the shadows that lingered beyond the light. They had survived, but the night's ordeal had exacted its toll, and Alex found herself grappling with more questions than before.

"Alex, you good?" Izzie's voice cut through the silence, her eyes probing Alex for any lingering darkness.

Alex managed a weary nod, her voice a hoarse whisper. "Yeah, back to normal." Then, her strength flagging, she and Lucas sank slowly to sit on the soft, short grass of the driving range. A laugh bubbled up from her, tinged with hysteria and relief at being alive. "I could really go for some rare steak right now. I hope Argo's got the sense to prep the kitchen."

"Sounds perfect. Mind if I crash that meal?" Izzie chuckled, holstering her weapon with practiced ease. Presumably, Mary had made herself scarce after the arrival of the first vampire.

"You'll have to negotiate with Argo. He's touchy about his kitchen privileges," Alex replied, her giggle fading to a contented sigh.

"True, true. I'll probably have to beg," Izzie agreed, rolling her eyes playfully.

"What, who's Argo? And why's he cooking for you?" Lucas's voice, though weak, carried a hint of jealousy, an emotion absurdly out of place given the gravity of their situation.

Alex and Izzie exchanged a glance, and then, as if on cue, both burst into unrestrained laughter.

Lucas looked at them, bewildered, his frown deepening. "What? What's so funny?"

"Oh, Lucas, no, no," Alex gasped between laughs, "Argo's my corgi. It's... it's an inside joke."

"A corgi, making you dinner?" Lucas echoed. "That's an odd joke, but given tonight, I suppose odd is relative."

As their laughter died down, the reality of their situation seemed to settle over them. They were out of immediate danger, but the implications of the night's events hung in the air.

"Any chance we can just pretend this never happened?" Lucas asked with a weak attempt at levity, now sitting upright without needing Alex's support. The sudden loss of his warmth and the press of his body left Alex feeling inexplicably colder, as though a vital source of heat had been snuffed out.

"Hell no, fire boy," Izzie shot back, her hands resting defiantly on her hips. "You owe us some answers."

He sighed a sound that was more surrender than exasperation. His eyes flickered to Alex, a tiny spark of longing smoldering in their depths. "Can we at least find somewhere safe? Somewhere private where we can grab a drink? This isn't the kind of conversation you have sober or with multiple people."

"There's no chance of that," Izzie cut in sharply. "You are a new, and very clearly dangerous, supernatural presence in my city. And you've definitely affected Alex in some way. There's no way I'm letting you out of my sight with her, especially not now." Her words were protective, her stance that of a guardian. Izzie would know that after such a display of her dhampiric nature, Alex would need time to recover, to regain her full strength.

Still, she was out of line. "Izzie, no, it's not like that," she said, climbing painfully to her feet. "He hasn't done anything to me." The ooze from the wound on her thigh was already slowing.

"Alex, no, you do not talk now," Izzie insisted, voice in full cop mode. She saw Lucas as a potential perp, and there was nothing Alex could do to talk her down until her questions were answered. Alex raised her hands in resignation and took off looking for her dropped short swords.

"What? Why not—No, never mind." Lucas caught himself. "Fine. You don't know me, and I'm in your territory. You pick the place. But please." His voice held a wry edge. "Can we at least ensure it serves something stronger than water?"

"Oh, don't think that charm will work on me," Izzie retorted with a scoff, though the corners of her mouth twitched in a reluctant smile. "But sure. There's a diner up the road. It's usually empty around this time, and they've got a full bar."

With that settled, the trio began collecting their belongings scattered across the battlefield. Alex felt the weight of her weapons in her hands, the solid and familiar grips offering a strange comfort. She stole glances at Lucas, whose attention was meticulously averted. Each evasion was a needle to her already frayed senses. Was he maintaining this distance for Izzie's sake, or was it something else?

Despite the weariness that pulled at their corners, Alex's eyes were alert as she fumbled with the straps and clasps of her gear, ensuring everything was secure. She could not shake the sense of unease that clung to her like a second skin.

Before they could exit the killing field, a low cackle of laughter drifted through the night.

Alex's eyes, no longer soft with the relief of survival, sharpened as she scanned their surroundings. "What now?" She groaned. Her heart, which had just started to slow its frenetic pace, now pounded with renewed urgency. Maybe it was just a partier from the clubhouse that had wandered too far. Izzie had her gun drawn again, and Lucas pulled what looked like a long knife out of the sleeve of his long trench coat. "A knife-wand?" Alex wondered blearily as she crouched in a ready stance, gripping her recently recovered Twins again.

"My, oh my, oh my," the voice teased from the shrouding fog, "to think I was worried the night's entertainment was ruined with the ritual's disruption."

From the shadow of a gnarled tree, a diminutive figure descended, hands clapping together to emit a crisp, eerie echo through the night. "Impressive work, really. I had my doubts whether the local guardian would figure it out, much less fell the Claw Quad we dispatched. But here you stand, victorious, an avenging angel," it said, directing a small, mocking bow towards Alex.

Her eyes locked onto the source of the emerging voice. It was a child, or so it seemed, no older than ten. Yet the way it moved, the cruel glint in its stony gaze, spoke of something far more ancient and sinister. She cursed as he stepped forward; his childlike clapping was juxtaposed horrifically against the dread he sowed.

As he stepped into the light, his hands found his hips, almost as if posing. He looked distinguished with his high and proud cheekbones framing his face and the subtle sharpness that defined his jaw. His attire straddled the realms of childish and mature, deceiving to those around him. The costume design allowed him to walk unnoticed among children and adults alike, masking the monster beneath with the guise of youthful nonchalance.

However, his skin betrayed any semblance of virtue. It bore the cold, matte finish of sculpted stone rather than the warm suppleness of a child's flesh. And his fingernails extended into cruel talons, while small, pointed fangs jutted out over his lower lip.

His eyes, though, held the most terrifying glamour of all. They were abyssal pools of pure black. It was like peering into the lowest chasms of hell itself. They spoke of ancient malice and dark secrets, of knowledge and hungers no mortal was meant to know. It was a mockery of innocence.

Alex's grip on the Twins tightened while Izzie visibly unraveled beside her. A quick glance to her side showed Lucas shaking, presumably in fear.

Izzie moved, her boots scraping softly against the dew-covered grass, bringing her shoulder to shoulder with Alex.

Alex watched as her friend's hands shook as she raised her firearm, aiming unsteadily at the small creature that seemed to defy all logic. Then, the gun slipped from Izzie's grasp, clattering to the ground with a jarring metallic clang.

"Mijo!" Izzie cried out, hands grasping frantically for a

child Alex knew was no longer there, the pain and longing in her voice cutting through the air.

Alex's hand reached out with a will of its own, her fingers closing around Izzie's with a desperate assurance she hoped was comforting.

Alex was one of the few who knew that Izzie had once been a mother, had once cradled life in her arms, a life that bore a chilling resemblance to the vampiric specter before them. Her son, vibrant and full of life, had been torn from the world by the crazed bloodlust of a creature Izzie had been hunting before she met Alex—a beast that had not only stolen her child and husband but had shattered her world as well.

The child-like vampire tugged at the buttons on his shirt, a sinister smirk playing on his lips. "I suppose I must remind you of your lost little one," he said. "I wonder if it hurt when the clanless tore through his tiny chest."

Without warning, a moan escaped Izzie's throat, a sound of such raw anguish that it seemed to echo off the trees. She tried to lunge forward, every muscle tensed to attack, but Alex's arms wrapped around her waist, holding her back with every ounce left of her depleted strength. Izzie thrashed, spitting venomous threats at the corrupted child that stood before them.

This creature was no ordinary vampire. It was not even like the overpowered 'Claw' they had just destroyed—this was something else, something far more insidious. It had delved into Izzie's mind and had plucked from it her most traumatic memories with a precision that left her reeling. They needed to escape, and they needed to do it now. But the cold, scornful laughter that followed them seemed to say it wouldn't be that easy.

As Alex thought frantically, trying to find a way to get them all out alive, Lucas's voice rang through the heavy night air. "No!"

In response, the diminutive fiend turned its attention toward Lucas, a twisted smile warping its child-like features. "Oh! And there he is! Little brother. The Master's lost, blood-thirsty little pet," it cooed, its voice a chilling sing-song that clawed at the edges of sanity.

Lucas's body seized, every muscle drawn tight with a conflict of emotions that seeped out like an ominous mist. Standing there, he vibrated with tension, an embodiment of internal turmoil that was almost visible to the naked eye. Beside him, Alex could almost see a golden thread connecting them, shaking in time with the man's clenching fists. And with it, a flood of his emotions washed over her—rage and fear, humiliation and an overwhelming sense of guilt and shame— so potent it was as if she bore the weight of his sins herself.

The creature continued with its twisted soliloquy, feeding on the chaos it sowed. "You know, he's been beside himself with worry since you left, wondering how you would fend for yourself out here in the cruel, mean old world."

A sidelong, cunning glance was cast towards Alex, its dark eyes gleaming. "We kept looking for the trail of bodies we were certain you'd leave behind—you never were one to keep your toys for long, after all. But we found none. The poor Master assumed you had been bested by some impetuous hunter."

With a theatrical pause, it leaned closer, its voice dropping to a conspiratorial whisper. "But here you are! Healthy and strong, if a bit rusty on the magical front." It tsked with a stern expression of disappointment.

Then, in a sudden shift to exhilaration, it exclaimed, "And you've bonded a true living and breathing dhampir!" Its voice pitched to a frenzied, gleeful shriek. It clapped its hands with an insanity-driven vigor. "Of all the scenarios we could have predicted, this was not one of them, especially after Margarete. But oh, it is by far the best!"

"Mattias, what the fuck are you talking about? Dhampir are just legends. If you're going to kill me, just do it. I'm done with the game. Just let them go. Don't think I've forgotten that you owe me a favor after Panama," Lucas snarled as he positioned himself between Alex and the sinister child.

An innocent yet vile laugh bubbled up from Mattias as he spun in a grotesque pirouette, hands lifting to the heavens in faux worship. "Oh, my dear naive little pet, are you truly so ignorant? Your beautiful hunter here is half-vampire. Astonishing, isn't it, that such legends walk among us?"

"No! That's a lie," Lucas snapped back, too stubborn, too desperate to glance at Alex for any form of validation.

"Oh, you poor sweet fool. How do you think she survived my Claw? And it's not like they were new. That was Daniel's Quad."

"No," Lucas whispered.

"And I suppose it was just 'mama bear strength' or something of the sort that sent you hurtling across the field? Did you even dare to look at her face when it happened? Into her eyes?"

"No! Shut up, you little freak!" The words clawed out of his throat, a desperate attempt to silence the truth that clawed its way out from the shadows of the unsaid and unseen.

Mattias's countenance momentarily darkened, a storm cloud passing over his childish features at Lucas's insult. "Then prove you're not the coward you've always been. Turn and face her."

Lucas was crumbling, a statue eroded by the relentless tides of doubt and despair. "Lucas?" Alex's voice was a lifeline thrown into the churning sea of his turmoil.

But Lucas was a fortress, his gaze locked to the ground. The golden thread that connected them slowly lost its brilliance, becoming murkier by the second.

"Just... just tell me he's lying," he pleaded, voice barely a whisper, laced with a desperation that tore at her heart.

Mattias stood aside, a spectator to the tragedy he'd authored, soaking in the aura of Lucas's unraveling like a connoisseur of fine wine.

Alex, still holding onto Izzie, who had more or less passed out from the psychic assault, was caught in the throes of her own battle.

"Lucas, please," she implored, the truth a bitter pill on her tongue.

He spun around then, the movement swift, his palms beginning to glow again. "Just tell me!"

"I can't lie to you, Lucas," she breathed out, her voice shaking.

The night's terrors culminated in that singular, suffocating moment—a tumultuous clash of truths unveiled, of loyalty ruptured, and of trust irreparably fragmented. It was as if every shadow now gathered, casting a heavy pall over the once shiny bond that had, only hours before, brought them both so much pleasure.

The warlock's hands, once aglow with a faint light, now blazed with incandescent fury, conjuring orbs of seething fire ready to be hurled. His arms drew back, muscles tensing to unleash his fiery vengeance upon Alex. With wide eyes full of shock, she moved, bracing to shield Izzie from the imminent blaze.

Yet, before the flames could be cast, the diminutive figure of Mattias was a blur, acting to protect Alex. A single double-handed shove repelled Lucas, dousing his fire mid-flight as he crumpled to the ground with the extinguished embers of his anger.

"Oh, Lucas. Lucas, Lucas, Lucas," Mattias drawled, a predator indulging in the savory taste of its prey's despair.

With grit and strain, Lucas attempted to regain his footing, only to collapse again and again.

"Freedom, my dear lost pet, is a delusion," Mattias continued, his tone dripping with toxic triumph. "You cannot strike her down without consigning yourself to oblivion. Perhaps martyrdom was your aim? Regardless, you will return to the Master, and you will bring the dhampir in tow. Together, you will be the Living Flame, the ultimate weapon of ancient prophecy. And none shall stand before the Village Hidden in Flame—no vampire, no mortal. We will finally have the reckoning that the Master has labored for these last many centuries."

Each fanatical word from Mattias struck Lucas like a blow, the final nails in the coffin of his resolve. He crumpled, not just in body but in spirit, sinking to the earth—a man shattered, his head bowed under the yoke of an inescapable fate.

Mattias cast a lingering, contemptuous gaze upon the fallen form of the warlock, his eyes then drifting towards Alex. Finally, his sinister stare settled on Izzie, whose limp figure lay cradled under Alex's protection. There was a momentary pause—a flicker of contemplation in the depth of those terrible eyes.

Alex's hands tightened instinctively around the hilts of the Twins, the weapons raised defensively before her. Her heart thundered against her ribcage, a crescendo of fear, bewilderment, and the sharp sting of betrayal, yet her stance was unyielding. Lucas's attempt to obliterate her had seared a wound deep within her, but it would not deter her. She would stand her ground against this beast. She would protect Izzie, no matter what.

A slow, chilling smile crept across Mattias's lips, not of warmth but of cold amusement, as if Alex's defiant posture was nothing more than a child's game to him. With an indifferent shrug, dismissing the scene as though it were beneath him, he turned back over to Lucas, voice delivering a command, "You will answer the summons when it comes." Then, he vanished, and Alex was left standing, shaking uncontrollably, as the cold air filled the space where evil had just stood.

She stayed as she was, still holding her blades in guard for she didn't know how long. Eventually, the muted rustle of Izzie's gradual awakening graced her ears, accompanied by the scraping sounds of Lucas crawling his way back to a stand. But to her dismay, he didn't move towards their makeshift stronghold. Instead, he staggered away, his figure shrinking towards the distant glow of the parking lot's lights.

"Oh no, you don't!" she bellowed. "You can't just barge in here, drop a bomb about being a magic-wielding pawn of homicidal vampires, and then just slink away!"

Lucas's departing back offered her no acknowledgment, his pace unfaltering. Once Izzie had managed a shaky ascent, Alex sheathed the Twins with a swift, fluid motion and chased after him. Her hand shot out, grasping for Lucas's arm to halt his retreat, only to have him spin around, his eyes ablaze with bitter rage. "Do not touch me, leech!" he seethed. "Do not touch me ever again!"

She reeled back, her heart stinging as though it had been lashed by the word. "What? Why would you say that?" she stammered. "You can't mean that."

"I mean every word, leech. I want nothing to do with you. Mystical bonding be damned. I'd rather die than let you near me again."

Stunned, Alex's mind whirled. The man before her was a stranger, his demeanor alien to the Lucas she had slowly gotten to know over the last week and whom she had started to care for more deeply than she'd ever admit. He wasn't the same

Lucas she had shared every inch of her body with, whose touch had sparked something within her she dared not name.

That budding connection felt as if it were being torn apart in her very grasp. With each word, Lucas's hate pulsed through their unseen bond with an invasive chill, a crawling dread that slithered beneath her skin. It was as if a dark stain had crept into the warm, shared space that the supposed bond created and turned it into a desolate expanse. Like a heavy weight on her chest, it made breathing hard, while spreading a continual ache through her bones. It was a sorrow she couldn't explain and couldn't escape, heavy and unyielding.

CHAPTER 20

LUCAS, HIS SILHOUETTE etched against the night, tried to retreat once more into the parking lot. But before he could get too far, the world erupted in thunder—a staccato of gunshots—and the dirt near his boots burst into a frenzy of dust and debris. He cursed, body jerking in a frantic attempt to escape, but there was no evading the determined wrath of Sergeant Isabella Bliss.

Recovered from the psychic onslaught she had endured, Izzie advanced, the authority of her service weapon extended before her, hands unshakably firm. Despite the undercurrent of pain that must have still tormented her, her voice was a serrated edge. "All right! Now, where were we, asshole?"

"It's not me you should be pointing that at, woman. It's that thing next to you," Lucas sneered.

With each poisonous word, Alex winced at the corresponding jolt of pain through the frayed golden threads of the bond.

Undeterred, Izzie closed in. "Now you listen here. That woman," she said, gesturing toward Alex with a tilt of her gun, "is the most honest-to-God good and brave person I've ever met. She's a goddamned hero, as far as I'm concerned. And I will not have the likes of you, who, apparently, is just as likely to leave bodies behind as those vampires, judging her."

"Then, you know what she is?" Lucas's voice was steeped in incredulity, eyes wide.

"You bet your dumb motherfucking ass I know," Izzie shot back, each word a bullet of its own. "I know she was born with a part of her that's hard to control and could drive her to behave monstrously if she gave it even an inch. And I know she has never once given in to it. Instead, she's put herself in harm's way, protecting this ungrateful city from the true monsters like yourself and your friends. Every night for the last twelve years. She has harnessed her power, which may have come from someplace dark, and turned it into a force for good. What have you done?"

Lucas's eyes narrowed, his expression a battleground of denial and dawning horror. The judgment he had so carelessly flung at Alex recoiled upon him.

"My friend Alex walks in the light," Izzie declared, her voice unwavering, a lance of clarity. "Where the fuck do you walk?"

The barrage of Izzie's words struck with the force of physical blows. He staggered, his posture crumbling until he found himself on his knees, his hands cradling his head as if to hold together the fragments of his shattered façade.

And then, the sobbing began—deep, wrenching sounds that tore through the night, so raw and full of anguish that it reverberated through Alex with the resonance of a cathedral bell. She could feel through their bond that the torrent of hate he had directed at her was a mirror reflecting the loathing he felt for himself. The realization was a blade twisted in her heart.

Tears etched pathways down Lucas's cheeks, mingling with

the dust and grime of battle, his whole body trembling. Alex, her heart aching and confused, fell to her knees beside him, driven by an instinct that went beyond anger, beyond betrayal. She crawled over, her movements hesitant but determined, and gently, she cradled his head in her lap.

Words failed her. The storm of emotions that should have rained down in a torrent of reprimands and accusations dissipated, leaving a silent empathy in its wake. Her fingers brushed through his hair, a soothing rhythm amidst the chaos. As she looked down at his broken form, she found herself wondering, pondering the path that had led him to this moment of complete unraveling.

She considered the weight of secrets and pain he must have carried, the anguish that she might have unwittingly unearthed from his carefully constructed sanctuary of denial and pretense.

The prophecy uttered by the childlike monster, the dehumanizing labels of "slave" and "pet" used by the vampires to brand Lucas, the mysterious ritual, and the elusive identity of the so-called Master—these were all enigmatic pieces of a larger puzzle that loomed, unresolved and imposing, in her thoughts.

"You've got to be kidding me," Izzie grunted, disbelief evident even as she holstered her weapon. "Just like that, eh?"

"What am I supposed to do?" Alex asked, her hand gesturing helplessly towards Lucas. "Look at him." In those three words lay an ocean of complexity—of compassion, confusion, and a plea for understanding. She didn't need to berate him; his own soul was doing that with a ferocity no words of hers could match.

As Lucas lay there, his fitful twitches a testament to the war within, Alex remained a sentinel of comfort in the bleakness.

Unable to feel the warlock's emotions, Izzie threw her hands up in exasperation and stalked off toward the parking lot.

Minutes later, she reappeared, toting a small black duffle—their medical kit. While Alex continued to cradle the shattered man, Izzie set to work treating the slash on Alex's thigh. She started with gauze to clean away the debris, followed by antiseptic, and finally, a bandage secured with more gauze to staunch the bleeding and protect the wound.

Alex mouthed her thanks, then gestured pointedly to the gash, marring Izzie's own arm. With a grumble, Izzie replicated the treatment on herself.

As she worked, she remarked, "I'm surprised the gunfire didn't have the cops swarming this place."

"Yeah, that's odd. Maybe the music from the clubhouse covered it up?" Alex suggested.

"No," Izzie began, only to be cut off.

Lifting his head, his eyes red-rimmed and his face a mask of tears and dirt, Lucas's voice seemed to traverse a great distance. "I left an area spell in place to muffle the sound as soon as I saw your gun."

Izzie responded with a noncommittal grunt. "Well, that's at least useful, Fireboy."

Lucas merely snorted in response, and silence settled over the trio.

Alex studied him, trying to weigh if he was back to himself or was going to turn on her again, or just run away. She didn't know what would be worse.

He tentatively reached out a hand towards hers, and Alex held her breath. His fingers halted, suspended in the tension of the moment, and she saw it—the hesitation, the flicker of conflict. Her eyebrows knitted in hurt at the additional rejection. Then, as if making an irrevocable decision, he continued his reach until his fingers entwined with hers. It wasn't lightning, but there was a small spark at their touch, and a tiny flame emerged. As Alex watched in wonder, it danced merrily between their tangled digits.

Relief sighed through Alex, tempered by a siege of doubts. She didn't trust that he wouldn't hurt her again, that he wouldn't still hate her or think of her as a monster, that he wouldn't run as soon as Izzie turned her back, or that she could ever feel the same way about him after having experienced that hate from him.

The delicate touch of their hands could reignite the blaze of their connection, but that was a bridge to cross at another time if she even wanted to take the risk. For now, the mere flicker was enough.

"Do you see it?" she asked him, her voice a whisper of awe.

His gaze, clouded with confusion, met hers. "See what?"

She sighed in disappointment. He couldn't perceive the bond visually as she did. Not wanting to appear needy or vulnerable, she said, "Oh, it's nothing, never mind," retracting her hand.

"All right, what's the game plan?" Izzie's said before Lucas could say anything else. "Our friendly neighborhood madman is probably not done with us. He could've finished us without breaking a sweat back there. I'm still not sure he didn't, to be honest."

Gathering her strength, Alex pressed herself to her feet, feeling the raw energy of survival instinct pushing her forward. She reached down to help Lucas stand, their movements synced in a moment of silent accord. Back to business.

"We've been thoroughly fucked tonight, and it's clear we're safer together than apart. I say we stick close, at least until first light. My place is the best bet for us to regroup and plan our next steps," Alex suggested, her tone leaving no room for argument.

"Makes sense. Let's do it," Izzie agreed, the medical kit slung over her shoulder like a badge of honor.

Alex turned to Lucas, her eyes searching his for some sign of the man she knew. "Lucas?" she asked tentatively. "There's still a lot of things we need answered. You should come too."

"It won't make any difference," he grumbled.

"And that's one more thing you are going to need to explain," Alex pressed, not letting him off the hook just because he looked pathetic. "You owe me."

He gritted his teeth, a muscle working in his jaw. In the supernatural world, debts were chains that could bind tighter than steel. "Fine."

Izzie, ever the one to cement plans into action, nodded. "So, it's settled then," she declared, "let's go."

CHAPTER 21

PULLING INTO HER driveway, the relentless strain that had gripped Alex's body throughout the silent drive began to ease. She was home, a word that felt like a protective charm after the harrowing events of the night. The hum of the engine died as she cut the ignition, her weary gaze sliding over to Izzie, who was already halfway out.

Alex's attention shifted back to Lucas. He had bowed his head, the fight seemingly drained out of him. She wondered fleetingly if he had succumbed to exhaustion.

"We're here," she announced, her voice a gentle prod.

Lucas sighed—a deep, soul-searching sound—and his shoulders lifted with the weight of the world before sagging again. His head came up, and there it was—that flicker in his eyes, a faint echo of the Lucas she had once known, a man she might have, in other circumstances, imagined something with.

"I can't say this is how I envisioned my first visit to your place," he murmured, a trace of the old humor in his voice.

A reluctant smile tugged at the edges of Alex's mouth, the

unexpected levity a gift in an otherwise objectively horrible night.

"Fuck," he exhaled, his fingers raking through his hair in that achingly familiar way. "I'd do anything to see that smile, even now... even knowing—"

The spell shattered. Her smile died as quickly as it had come. With a swift turn, Alex exited the Jeep, the slam of the door punctuating her feelings perfectly. His words had slashed through her, a reminder of the darkness she carried within her —the darkness she fought against every night.

She stalked to the back, popped the trunk, and began mechanically collecting her equipment, each movement touched with simmering anger.

"Coming in, or what?" Her voice was clipped, each word a sharp shard directed at Lucas. He still sat motionless, head leaning against the window, a ghost of regret in his posture.

"Yeah, fine," came his subdued reply. "If that's really what you want. I'm sorry, I didn't—"

"Stop." Her interruption was swift, final. "You meant it. And right now, it doesn't matter what I want. What matters is that you have the information we need to protect this city and survive the shit storm you've dragged down on us."

The trunk slammed with a thud. She strode toward her front door, trying to outrun the sting of Lucas's words.

She barely registered the sound of the Jeep's door opening and closing behind her. He was following, but it hardly mattered.

Finally, as Alex's hand pressed against the cool wood of her front door, pushing it open, a sense of peace began seeping into her veins. Feeling her shoulder relax, the house somehow managed to ease the adrenaline and hurt that had fueled her moments earlier. The familiar creak of the hinges and the soft brush of her feet across the threshold acted as a ceremonial end to the night's anarchy.

The aroma of comfort—food cooked with love—enveloped her, and tears pricked her eyes, unexpected in their intensity. Here, in this space, were the two people who accepted her fully, her dual nature notwithstanding. And that was all that should matter.

What do you care about some fool warlock, stupid enough to get himself mixed up with vampires? She was home, and for now, that would be her protection.

Argo immediately erupted into the entryway, his short, stubby legs motoring toward her, nails and feet slipping comically on the slick wood floor. His whole body wriggled with ecstatic energy impossible to contain, and he flung himself, full body, at her thighs.

"Boss! You're home!" The furry love missile was already airborne. She crouched down to catch him, and his little paws landed against her chest with the force of a friendly battering ram. "Oh, thank Lucifer, you're alive!"

"Lucifer, eh?" she teased while he lavished her face with eager kisses, each one a tiny affirmation of life and loyalty.

She allowed herself to be showered in his affection, feeling the dirt and soot from the night blending with the soft fur that now clung to her clothes.

"Fine, thank the stars, whatever. I'm just happy you're back, boss." Argo's words were barely out when the kisses abruptly stopped, and a deep, growling reverberation began to fill the space. It was a sound no ordinary corgi could make. It resonated, ominous and threatening like the forewarning of an ancient beast awakened.

Alex stepped back in surprise at the noise. Even still, she was not prepared for what happened next.

Where a happy, tail-wagging corgi had stood, a creature of

nightmare and myth emerged. Alex stumbled backward, her heart hammering against her ribcage as the creature's towering form eclipsed the doorway.

Its eyes were infernos of wrath, set deep within a skull that bore horns twisted like ancient brambles, each point scratching the ceiling above it. Its red, scaly body was a rippling expanse of muscle and malevolence, with jagged spines running down its back, culminating in a tail armed with a barb sharp enough to pierce the very veil between worlds. Atop its monstrous shoulders, wings unfurled, vast leathery expanses that could shroud the light of the moon, lined with spines and hooks that promised a deadly embrace. The air around it seemed to warp and weft with the heat of its breath.

"Begone warlock! You are not welcome here. And if you insist on your pursuit, I will gladly tear you limb from limb," called the creature that had once been Argo, focused on the man walking up the sidewalk to the house.

"Argo! No!" Alex yelled as Izzie came sprinting into the foyer, gun drawn.

"Um, Alex?" Lucas called from the sidewalk. "Should I start running?" Then he grumbled, "Honestly, I'm too tired to care at this point," wobbling unsteadily on his feet.

"Argo! Stop," Alex cried once more. She lifted herself to her feet, took a deep breath, and reached to grab the demon's arm, dragging him to face her.

The demon turned its gaze upon her, and for a moment, the air was electric with the potential for violence. But her resolve never wavered. Her eyes never blinked. Gradually, the fiery pits that were Argo's eyes dimmed, recognition dawning within.

"Boss?" he rumbled, a hint of his corgi self bleeding through the terrifying façade.

"Argo, he's with me. Please stand down."

The demon gave Lucas one last searching glare, a silent vow of retribution should he prove a threat. Then, with a surge of mystical energy, a cyclone of flames swallowed his demonic form. The three humans flinched back as the heat washed over them in a scorching wave.

When the flames dissipated, the hulking demon was gone. In its place, Argo sat panting. His corgi form was almost comical in its innocence compared to the beast that had stood there moments before.

"Sorry, boss," Argo apologized, his energy spent. "He reeks of destruction magic and hate. I assumed he was after you. It's not uncommon for the Hidden Villages to employ warlocks."

Alex knelt by Argo, her fingers brushing his fur tenderly. "It's okay, buddy. Given everything that happened tonight, the response wasn't far from warranted," she said, casting a stern glance toward Lucas.

Leaning closer, she lowered her voice for only Argo to hear. "Still, you owe me an explanation. 'Hidden Villages typically employ warlocks,' you say?"

Argo's gaze fell to the floor, a whimper of apology as he slunk off towards the kitchen, his small form disappearing in the direction Izzie had gone.

Lucas shuffled to the doorstep, hesitating just outside. "Oh yes, eaten by a crazed demon for trying to rescue you. Totally an appropriate response."

Standing, Alex brushed the fur from her battle-worn jeans and met his gaze squarely.

"Should I even be surprised that you have a demon pet?" He continued, staring right back at her, not backing down.

Her arms folded as she considered the weary man before her.

"Well, you demanded I come. Are you going to invite me

in?" He challenged, mirroring her body language, the invitation hanging between them like a test of wills.

Alex paused, weighing the gravity of Lucas's question. In her world, an invitation across the threshold was far more than a matter of courtesy; it was a covenant of trust, one not given lightly. Homes were bastions, imbued with the essence of their inhabitants. The daily rituals and love invested in these spaces wove a protective aura, an invisible barrier at the threshold. This barrier could diminish an uninvited being's intent to harm, stripping them of most arcane power if they crossed unbidden. An uninvited entry could be lethal for creatures dependent on such power to live, such as vampires.

For a warlock like Lucas, entering without an invitation would render him nearly helpless, especially to a creature like Alex. Without her express consent, her threshold could nullify his magical defenses, making him as harmless as a mortal. He would be unable to stop her if Alex, or, heaven forbid, Argo, decided to make a meal out of him.

The silent standoff between them stretched on, a tangible tension in the air. Lucas's shoulders eventually slumped, and with a heavy sigh, he steeled himself, his breath catching as he stepped over the threshold. As he crossed, there was a quiet pop of pressure like the equalizing of an airplane cabin thousands of feet above the ground. He shivered slightly, rubbing his arms as he acclimated to the prickling sensation of vulnerability that came with being uninvited.

Alex exhaled, a subtle easing of the lines around her eyes. Lucas crossing her threshold without her invitation was an act of trust, a tentative olive branch that might just allow them to come together to face their current supernatural crisis. She quashed the flicker of hope that it could mean something more personal, that maybe he could see her as more than just a half-vampire.

"Okay," she managed. "Thank you."

They moved in unison toward the kitchen, Lucas shadowing her. Izzie had already commandeered the dining table, a large goblet of wine cradled in her hand. Two loaded plates sat before her, spilling over with more food than they could imagine.

Alex's eyes lit up at the sight. "Oh, hell, yes, Argo!" A Philly cheesesteak sat on each plate. The bread, golden and slightly crispy, was stuffed to bursting with thinly sliced ribeye that glistened under the kitchen lights. The steak was enrobed in a blanket of melted provolone that draped over the sides of the sandwich, hinting at the caramelized onions and peppers nestled within.

With a gleeful shimmy and an enthusiastic clap, Alex sank into her chair and seized the sandwich. She took a ravenous bite, savoring the meld of savory meat and tangy cheese, the juices dribbling down her chin in an unapologetic display of joy. She moaned contentedly, her eyes fluttering closed as she relished the flavors.

Upon opening her eyes, she caught Lucas's expression of bemused astonishment. "Please don't tell me the demon corgi actually cooks."

His sentence was cut short by a low growl emanating from beneath the table.

"Rude," Alex interjected, her voice sharp but her eyes dancing with mirth as she wiped her mouth and reached for her wine. "You can't just go around calling people demons. In fact, a 'thank you' wouldn't kill you."

Lucas retreated a step, his hands lifting in a gesture of peace. "Uh, my bad, Argo. Thank you. You, uh, obviously cooked this delicious food."

Satisfied, the dog ceased his grumbling and resettled into the comfort of his bed, his eyes closing as if to dismiss the slight.

"It looks like Argo left out extra ingredients and plates by the oven. Help yourself," Alex said to Lucas, gesturing at the oven. "Glasses are in the cabinet to the right. Beer is in the fridge. And... we probably need another bottle of wine if you'd like that."

"Probably need one anyway!" Izzie said, waving her empty glass in the air, the last droplets of wine catching the light as they flung free.

"I only made extra in case Mary came," Argo mumbled, a touch of sulking in his tone. It was clear the idea of being seen as considerate towards Lucas didn't sit well with him.

From her position, Alex could see Lucas standing a bit removed from the action, his eyes wide with a mixture of wonder and disbelief. She noticed his gaze linger on them, watching as she, Izzie, and Argo seamlessly fell into their familiar routine. When Izzie praised Alex for swiftly taking down their first target, their playful fist bump seemed to captivate him even more.

She overheard him mutter, a note of envy mixed with confusion in his voice, "They're like some sort of... fucked up little family. Right out of a movie." It was clear to Alex that this tight-knit bond they shared was something entirely new to Lucas.

"Go on, fire boy!" Izzie hollered. "Get your food already."

From the corner of her eye, Alex watched as Lucas, unsure of his place in the lively kitchen atmosphere, obediently moved towards the oven. He carefully scooped up a generous helping of the sizzling steak. Alex noticed the meticulous way he assembled his sandwich on the toasted roll and his small smile when it crunched together.

But then, she saw him pause, a flicker of doubt crossing his face. Alex could almost hear his thoughts, wondering if Argo, in a final act of rebellion, had tampered with this last sandwich.

After a moment of hesitation, Lucas seemed to resign himself to trust, dismissing the paranoid thought with a shrug.

Alex watched as he took a cautious bite, his expression transforming into one of pleasant surprise. No tricks, no traps – just good food made with an unexpected dash of demon magic.

CHAPTER 22

FROM ACROSS THE TABLE, Alex watched as Lucas took another bite of the Philly cheesesteak. Smiling into her glass of wine, she saw his shoulders visibly relax and heard a small, contented sigh escape him, as if the rich flavors were dissolving all his stress. With a loud groan of satisfaction, he seemed to revel in the bliss of melted cheese.

It was like the food had some power to revive both his body and soul from the damage it had sustained through the night. When he raised his sandwich for another bite, though, he paused abruptly. His attention shifted, eyes narrowing slightly as he seemed to note the sudden hush that had fallen over the others, their chatter fading into silence.

"Wow, Alex. I think you might have competition for the warlock. Whether it's Argo or that sandwich, though, I can't be sure," Izzie smirked, pantomiming Lucas's groans of appreciation over her own sandwich.

Between Izzie's mock love at the cheesesteak, Lucas's grease-covered, embarrassed face, and Argo's fervent denials beneath her, she couldn't stop herself. In an uncontrolled laugh, Alex snorted wine out of her nose and all over the table. Quickly wiping away the droplets, she tried to muster a scowl. "Izzie, you're not as hilarious as you think."

"Too soon?" Izzie's grin only stretched wider.

The moment lingered briefly before Alex gave in, taking another, more cautious sip of her wine, her eyes playfully narrow as she peered over the rim of her glass. Not for the first time, she wondered if Argo put something special in the food. It always seemed to assuage her mood, no matter how difficult her day had been. And it seemed to be having the same effect on Izzie and Lucas.

"Come on, fire boy, join the party," Izzie said, gesturing to the vacant chair sandwiched between herself and Alex. "That cheesesteak won't run away."

Taking the hint, Lucas moved towards the table, a reluctant smile forming despite his embarrassment. As he set down his plate, Alex noticed a shift in his demeanor, a hint of longing in his eyes, and not just for the sandwich. It was clear to her that, despite his initial reservations, he found himself unexpectedly drawn to their group. And something in her eased at the thought of him joining their makeshift little family.

"All right, dig in." Izzie nodded to him, then focused once again on her own food.

Lingering over their meal, the silence was comfortable, punctuated only by the occasional soft clink of glass against wood as they sipped their wine. And when the last of the sandwiches were consigned to memory, Lucas regarded Alex and Izzie with an eyebrow cocked in intrigue. "You two are being suspiciously patient," he noted. "I thought the whole point of dragging me back here was to dig answers from me."

Izzie, dabbing her mouth with a napkin, met his gaze squarely. "Oh, it is. That hasn't changed. But that was a tough fight. We all needed the chance to recover before diving back in."

"Fair enough. Okay, what are your questions? I will do my best to answer them."

Alex caught Izzie's eye across the room, and in that brief moment, a silent understanding passed between them. Izzie gave a subtle nod, acknowledging Alex's need to take the lead in the situation. Alex inclined her head, silently thanking Izzie, as the weight of the moment settled upon her shoulders.

Whatever this thing with Lucas was, she needed to wrap her head around it and figure out how she felt about it. How he answered her questions would help determine that. With a deliberate pause, she formed a steeple with her fingers. "Okay, Lucas. Let's start simple. When did you land in Chicago?"

Lucas blinked, a flicker of surprise crossing his features—he'd no doubt braced for a barrage about secret villages and mystical bonds, not a timeline. "Six months ago. Why?"

She brushed aside his query with a flick of her hand. "And have you ever used your magic here?"

A frown creased his brow as he scratched his temple. "Just a light veil. The murder on the Navy Pier was too similar to Claw operations to ignore. I needed to see it. But nothing big. That would be like sending up a flare for those hunting me."

Izzie couldn't help but interject. "Just how many people are looking for you? It's not just the vamps?

He opened his mouth to respond, but the words tangled on his tongue. Alex cut through his hesitation. "Okay, so you were the shimmer on the pier. That answers that. But for larger magic, are you sure you didn't do anything? It's clear you have access to a great deal of power."

"That was you there, in the dark clothing?" he asked while Izzie snapped her fingers in recognition.

"Yes, now the other question," Alex pressed.

"Wait, hold a sec, Alex," Izzie interrupted, then looked at Lucas. "Why were you at the Clubhouse to begin with if it wasn't for Alex? You mentioned you didn't recognize her when she was targeted, so you were already there."

Lucas sighed. "After the murder on the Navy Pier, I suspected the Claw and kept my eye on the news. When I saw that a little girl was killed while we were in Munich, I thought their involvement was even more likely. But I needed to know for sure. If they were following the usual patterns, I knew they'd end up around the Clubhouse for the final murder tonight." He looked at Alex apologetically. "I was glad you turned me down for dinner. Tracking the vampires completely slipped my mind, um, during work."

Alex blushed, looking down. "Yeah, that makes sense, I guess." When she raised her gaze, she met his eyes. "I'm glad you were there."

"We'll see." Izzie snorted. "All right, back to Alex's question, though I'm not seeing the connection yet. So, no magic other than the veil?"

"No. Why?" he said, though she noted the dawning realization in his eyes as they traced the course of her thoughts.

"Fuck, the elevator. It's all my fault, isn't it?" His voice was barely a thread, frayed with guilt.

Izzie's brow furrowed. "I'm lost here. What are we talking about?"

But Alex was unyielding. "So, before you slowed time in the elevator, nothing, other than the small veil."

His nod was solemn.

"And these... Claw assholes the Hidden Village dispatches, does the little freak usually accompany them, too?"

His eyes widened in fear, almost looking around to see if the child vampire was there and had heard the remark. Izzie snorted a laugh. "Too soon, hun. Too soon."

Ignoring their responses, Alex waved her hand impatiently at Lucas to answer. "Now that you mention it. No. The Claw usually operate in a couple of cities at a given time. Mattias doesn't go unless something piques his interest. He's too important."

Izzie's patience frayed. "What in the hell is the Claw?"

Alex lifted a hand, halting the questions like a traffic warden. "Hold that thought, Izzie. I'm piecing it together."

With a huff, Izzie fell silent, giving Alex room to weave her thoughts into questions that might just unravel the knot of their current predicament.

"Okay, so the Claw probably already had Chicago in their sights, even before these ritual killings kicked off with Marsha Baterly," Alex reasoned, her mind racing to connect the dots. "So, your arrival here might be coincidental. But your magic? That could've signaled Mattias, whether he realized it was you or not."

Lucas nodded. "That makes sense. But what does that get us?"

"Just hang tight with me," Alex said, a calming hand motioning him to be patient. "The big question is, why target Chicago at all, right?"

Lucas rubbed his chin, contemplating. "Before I escaped, the Village Hidden in Flames had at least some degree of control or influence over most of South America."

The gravity of that statement was not lost on Izzie and Alex. They were used to handling the odd vampire—putting down lone predators and sometimes mediating for the rare peaceful ones who had settled down in the city, the 'vampire vegans,' so to speak. The notion of an entire organization, one with such extensive reach and influence, was staggering.

"But the Master is always looking to expand, hungry for more," Lucas went on. "And since there's no established

Hidden Village presence or other vampire faction claiming North America, I doubt he's seen much resistance."

The scope of what Lucas described made Alex's head reel. It wasn't just gang wars or political power plays—it was a chess game with supernatural kings and queens, and Chicago was just another square on the board. Reflecting on the ongoing situation south of the border, the implications for the US were ominous. The prevailing narrative had always pointed to political corruption as the root of persistent struggles in countries like Brazil and Mexico, impeding their progress to reach the prosperity seen further north. Yet, what Lucas was hinting at painted a far more sinister picture.

"Well, fuck," Izzie articulated what they were all thinking.

"All right." Alex tried to steady the quickening pulse of the conversation. "What's the Village Hidden in Flame planning to do now that we've thrown a wrench in their plans?"

"Well, if Mattias wasn't here, they likely wouldn't notice the disruption or absence of the Claw for a while. When they did notice, they would probably suspect the Claw went rogue and either ran or took each other out. That a local hunter could take out all of their operatives would be unthinkable. They'd be chasing their tails, looking inward for another couple of months."

"Then what?" Izzie pressed.

"They might get caught up in other territories or internal squabbles and forget about Chicago completely, or they could send another Quad in to check things out."

"So, if Mattias wasn't in the equation, we've bought ourselves a chunk of time, worst case. Best case, the vamps back off for good," Alex summarized with a hint of satisfaction.

"Yes, but it doesn't matter," Lucas countered flatly. "Mattias isn't going anywhere other than back to Brazil to update the Master."

"Right, let's table it for now. We need to dig into other things first," Alex said, sidestepping Lucas's bleak assertion.

Izzie was practically bouncing with eagerness to unravel the mystery.

"What in the hell is a 'Hidden Village' and who or what are 'The Claw'?" she blurted, slamming her hand on the table.

Alex raised a finger, signaling for a pause. "Hold that thought, Izzie. Let's go deeper first." Her gaze then settled on Lucas, who seemed to shrink a little under the scrutiny.

"So, Lucas," Alex began, her voice softening, "when did you first run into this Village Hidden in Flame? What's your story?"

Lucas pushed a hand through his hair, setting it back from his forehead as he sighed heavily. "It was when I was just a kid," he started, his voice trailing slightly as if the memories were painful to recollect. "Around four or five years old, I guess."

Both Izzie and Alex's expressions displayed a combination of shock and curiosity, but they held their silence, giving Lucas the floor. "I was born in a small town near Campu Grande in the central-western part of Brazil with my family. I barely remember it. And it's been difficult to separate the truth from the lies I was told later. But at some point, I must have shown signs of magical talent. Because shortly after, a Quad of Claw showed up."

"It's strange, you know," he started, a wistful note seeping into the edges of his tone, "how a room can seem like a palace and a prison at the same time." Alex watched him, saw the way his gaze seemed to focus on something far beyond the walls of the house. "That first night, I woke up in luxury, with the whole of São Paulo spread beneath me. I remember thinking it was a dream as I bounced on the bed, lost in the thrill of it. But dreams don't leave you alone and hungry, and I soon began to miss my mom and dad as the growls from my stomach grew."

His hands moved restlessly, tracing the grain of the wood on the table. "Mattias appeared then, like some pale ghost." A wry, sad smile touched Lucas's lips. "He was terrifying and fascinating to a kid who'd always longed for a brother."

He paused, and when he continued, there was a hardness in his words. "He fed me lies as easily as he breathed—told me my parents had traded me for a new roof, of all things." Lucas's eyes flickered to Alex. "I waited for them, you know? Waited for a sign they'd come back for me. But they never came."

Izzie's hand fluttered to her lips, and she let out a breath that sounded like it carried part of her soul with it.

"And the whole time"—Lucas's voice cracked, anger seeping through the veneer of control—"Mattias had erased my entire world, killing everyone in my little town. My family, my friends... gone, as if they were never there at all."

Alex's hand found his.

"Thinking my parents had abandoned me, I found a place with the vampires, and I dove into my new life, my new family, with a zeal I thought was righteous. Mattias came and played with me most days, discretely teaching me techniques to channel and control my magic, how to harness my anger, my pain." Lucas's hands clenched, knuckles white. "And the Master." He spat the title like it was poison. "He made me feel like I was something... special. But I was just another trophy, a rare trinket to be shown off."

His hands relaxed as he looked down at them, a faint glow of power simmering under his skin. "I was wanted, or so I told myself. Useful. And in a twisted way, loved. I was desperate to please, to make them proud. I was able to create an inferno that could engulf a building by twelve and threads of fire hot enough and thin enough to cut through marble by fifteen. The, um, time stuff didn't start until later..." Lucas trailed off, his voice hollow.

A hush blanketed the room, the kind that hangs in the air after a tempest, where the whispers of distant thunder linger and the tang of wet earth clings to the senses.

"Training with the Claw began on my thirteenth birthday," he continued, his gaze distant. "They're elite shadow operatives, the Master's personal guard and hit squad. They keep an eye on everything, snuffing out threats before they even have a chance to take root, both within our ranks and outside."

His hands clenched again, as if grasping the phantoms of a past he could never fully release. "Within *their* ranks," he corrected himself.

"They eliminate anyone who dares challenge the Master's reign. But their reach extends beyond mere assassinations. They're the vanguard, the harbingers of the Master's conquests. They infiltrate new territories before the Master claims them, laying the groundwork."

Alex and Izzie listened, their expressions a blend of horror and fascination as Lucas peeled back the veneer on a world they thought they knew. "They start with corruption, seeding it like a cancer—bribing officials, mapping the supernatural terrain, then tearing it down, piece by piece. They invest in industries meant to choke the sky, smothering the air we breathe with pollutants."

"They're the ones who penetrate, who corrupt and coerce. They're the rot that weakens the foundations long before the Master ever sets foot on new ground."

With each word, the reality of their situation became clearer and grimmer. "And their presence, when they move as a Quad... it can be potent enough to unsettle an entire city's balance, to warp the mood of its people, to twist the very weather itself."

Alex's brows furrowed in realization. "It has been unseasonably warm for October, and the city has been particularly on edge. I just assumed it was with the upcoming election. But it's been them, hasn't it? They got here way before the first murder, altering the very fabric of Chicago."

"Damn," Lucas breathed, slamming his free fist into the table. "I should've seen it—the signs were all there. I didn't notice anything until the second murder, too focused on hiding and pretending to be a consultant."

"You couldn't have known. You're not a local," Izzie said.

Lucas shook his head. "I still should have known."

Alex squeezed his hand and asked, "What happened when you started training with these Claw?"

He stared ahead, not saying anything, then seemed to deflate once more. "It didn't take long for them to start sending me on missions. In that first year, they sent me to destroy the property of those who had displeased the Master but hadn't earned worse. I remember watching the building burn and feeling proud of myself. I was an instrument of the Master's will, a destroyer for his cause." His words were clipped.

"The first time they asked me to act, to really act, was against a group of vampires who'd defied the Master. These vampires thought they could stand independent, live peaceably on their own, in harmony with humanity around them." Lucas's voice dropped. "And I... I brought down an entire building on them. They screamed as they burned."

Lucas's tale wasn't just a recount of events; it was an admission of the evils he'd committed, the bodies left in his wake.

"They were just vampires," Izzie offered.

"Yes, but I saw them as people. And besides, the next time they told me to act, there were human servants in the building, too. I still did it."

Silence fell, Izzie at a loss for words.

"With each mission completed, their approval felt like warmth, like belonging," he continued with a haunted look in his eyes.

"You were a child, Lucas, and they brainwashed you." Alex leaned forward.

"Doesn't make it okay, and certainly doesn't make me feel anything less than the monster I am. It only got worse after that. More burning and more killing. Mattias would meet me at the manor after every mission with a brotherly hug and words of praise. Even as I grew taller and older-looking than him, he was still my big brother. Or at least that's how I saw him."

"By the time I was sixteen, I was planning and leading missions. I was the Master's favorite enforcer. I was even given command of vampires on missions, something they loathed. But I saw myself as one of them, I suppose, and did more and more vile things to get them to accept me. Mattias's remark about leaving bodies and breaking my toys was not an exaggeration."

His gaze shifted to Izzie. "But I never harmed children. Never." She returned his look, her face a mask of mixed emotions.

"When I was seventeen, they gave me a companion. A vampire girl who looked about my age. The things she made me do to her." Lucas shuddered. "I thought I loved her, but she was just doing what she was ordered to do and ended up trying to kill me after growing tired of playing my girlfriend."

Alex's tone softened with recognition. "Margarete?"

"Yes, Margarete. By the time she was done with me, I was a broken body and soul. And when I finally turned the flames against her, part of me wished I hadn't. Maybe it would have been better if she had succeeded."

"No," came Alex's immediate, hushed rebuttal.

"It took a month to recover. Mattias cared for me then,

tending to my wounds with an almost tender diligence. Monster playing nurse to an even bigger monster."

"You're not a monster, Lucas. None of that was your true self," Alex's reply was a whisper.

Lucas offered a hollow shrug, the gesture failing to mask the torment behind his eyes. "Anyway, after I had healed, they laid a new mission at my feet—a mission so foul that I couldn't do it. Just hearing it... and feeling the corners of my mind start to entertain it, something in me snapped. I couldn't—wouldn't do it." His hands involuntarily traced the outline of an old wound on his forearm.

"When I refused, Mattias's facade crumbled." His voice was laden with anguish. "The brother I had looked up to revealed himself in his true form—a figure of sheer, unadulterated wrath." He paused, touching the scar again gently. "He attacked. I still have the scars. And as I lay wounded, he tormented me, dredging up the darkest recesses of my past. Then he looped them through my mind like a twisted highlight reel, feeding on my despair. It's a rare talent, even among the Flame vampires, and he's a master." Lucas shuddered, the memory all too vivid.

"Then, he broke me. He told me what had happened to my family. They hadn't abandoned me. They hadn't sold me. They had fought for me until their last breath." Tears were falling freely down Lucas's cheeks. "And he killed them. He killed them all. Even my little sister, who was only one year old."

"Once more, I snapped. My ability to slow time had only happened randomly with limited results until then. But, in that moment, I completely froze everything. Every vampire in the entire manor was immobilized." He recounted the scene with a distant look as if he could still see the frozen figures behind his eyes. "I didn't stop to consider the ramifications; I just ran. I ran until my lungs burned and my legs ached, using every trick and tactic the Claw had drilled into me to evade their pursuit and plot my survival."

"How did you manage to stay off their radar after that?"

Lucas's face clouded over, his eyes pleading for understanding. "I made a deal. That's all I can say about it."

Izzie opened her mouth, no doubt ready to interrogate, but Alex's subtle shake of her head stopped her. She knew all too well some pacts and promises bound one beyond the ordinary constraints of secrecy—oaths that held consequences if broken.

"What happened after that?" Alex nudged the conversation forward.

"I somehow ended up in the States, fumbling my way into the workforce. Turned out, I had a knack for convincing people I knew what I was doing." A grin played at the edges of his lips.

Izzie's laugh broke the tension in the room. "That figures. I've always said consultants are full of shit."

CHAPTER 23

"THANK YOU FOR SHARING, Lucas. I can understand why you have such strong feelings about vampires, or anything like them," Alex said.

Lucas's face fell. "Alex, I'm sorry—Izzie's right. You're nothing like them. My reaction was out of line."

"You're damn right, I was right." Izzie snorted, and Argo barked in agreement from under the table.

Alex raised her hands in a calming gesture. "No, guys, I appreciate the support, but he's not wrong either. I've got that in me. It doesn't matter what I do or how many people I save. It will always be there. It is what it is."

Izzie, poised to leap to her defense once more, was gently stopped.

"Love you too, Izzie, and I treasure that you can look beyond it. But there are more pressing issues we need to tackle than my longstanding battles with self-worth," Alex said.

Izzie crossed her arms and set her jaw. Alex knew this wasn't the end of it; the discussion would be revisited in private.

Shifting focus, Alex addressed Lucas again. "Now, tell me about this 'ultimate weapon' Mattias mentioned."

Beneath the table, Argo shifted his weight. He was a solid, reassuring presence against her legs.

"Well, to be honest, I'm not entirely sure," Lucas said, his hand running through his hair while Izzie frowned at him.

"No, I mean it," he pressed. "It's like a myth, this tale of the 'bond' and the 'Living Flame.' It's as much a part of vampire lore as any fairy tale is to humans."

Izzie's eyes flickered to Alex momentarily. "So, sort of like a dhampir?"

"Well, yes, now that you mention it," Lucas confirmed, a note of realization in his voice. "But there are historical accounts of dhampirs, at least. Sure, mostly from ages ago, but we know they existed. As for this prophecy, it always seemed like a story to me. I knew the Master valued me partly because my magic resonated with that legend, but I figured it was just his collector's obsession with unique abilities, not because he believed in the myth. It doesn't even explicitly state that the other half of the bond is a dhampir."

Alex leaned forward, eager for more. "What does the legend say exactly?"

Lucas took a moment, as if sifting through the archives of his memory for the precise wording. "I might not have it word-for-word, but it's along the lines of, 'When magic of pure destruction meets the vampire's true living blood, a bond of immense power will form, strong enough to stir the heavens. Together, they will kindle the Living Flame and set the earthly realms to tremble.'"

Izzie released a low whistle. "So, no pressure then, huh?"

Lucas matched her wry tone with a nod. "Right? It reads like something out of an ancient storybook—not to be taken literally. The real problem is that the Master and Mattias might believe in it. Whether or not it's true, if they think it is, that belief alone will be enough for them to come after us."

Alex's brow creased in thought as she mulled over the myth, her gaze intermittently flickering to the ethereal gold threads that connected her to Lucas—threads visible to her alone.

Argo's whimper drew her attention downward; the little corgi looked up at her, his eyes round with a concern that seemed far too knowing. "But why would he even think you had this bond?" He asked.

Lucas hesitated for a moment, his cheeks flushing with embarrassment. "Um, well, he was likely able to smell, um, that we had recently been, um, well, intimate."

Alex's eyes widened in mortification, and Izzie burst into laughter. "When on earth would you two have had time for that? Unless..." Izzie trailed off, her expression morphing into a scandalized look as she covered her mouth. "Oh my god. Did you two do it at the office? Animals!" She dissolved into laughter.

Alex sank into her chair, practically melting in embarrassment, while Argo couldn't help but chime in, his tone dripping with disdain. "Well, that answers that. The vamp was not the only one who could smell it. You reeked of lust and bodily juices."

"OMG, gross, Argo!" Alex exclaimed, her face flushing even redder.

"You're telling me!" he retorted, his impish grin evident. "You're not the one who had to smell it."

Amid the awkwardness and laughter, Alex realized they had gotten off track from their previous conversation, and she refocused her attention on Argo, her tone stern as she leaned forward. "So, Argo, what do you know about this legend? I haven't forgotten you left out the bit about the

Hidden Villages earlier, either. If there's more, I need to know now."

Izzie's mocking laughter ceased, and Argo hesitated, his usually playful demeanor subdued. "Boss? You sure?"

She nodded, and all three humans turned their attention to the fluffy little corgi. "In my world, before I came here, they wouldn't dismiss it as just a fairy tale," he admitted.

Izzie let out a derisive snort, but Lucas leaned forward. "And what world is that exactly, Argo?"

Alex watched the exchange, a faint smile curling her lips at the unlikely alliance forming before her eyes.

Argo paid no mind to their probing. "The Prophecy of the Living Flame is taken quite seriously where I'm from. For some, it's a beacon of hope, a chance to gain the power to overturn the established order, both High and Low. Others fear it could unravel Hell itself, while some believe it might pave the way for the Master—Lucifer's—dominion on Earth."

The weight of Argo's words hung heavy in the air, hinting at the vast and dangerous implications beyond the impending vampire threat to Chicago.

"But who or what the prophecy is about is left largely vague. Dhampir, warlock, faery prince, who knows."

Ever the pragmatist, Izzie spread her hands wide, drawing their attention. "Well, that's all very interesting. Thanks for the demonic insight, Argo. But let's get real—it doesn't change the situation we're in."

Still grappling with the surreal nature of their gathering, Lucas muttered, "Is no one else questioning why there's an actual demon in the house, culinary skills notwithstanding?"

Argo, seemingly offended, returned to under the table, his grumbles about being underappreciated barely audible.

Alex, however, was focused on the more pressing matters. She turned to Lucas. "Do you think Mattias has already reached out to the Master? How soon should we expect another visit from the Claw, or worse, the Master himself?"

Lucas pondered for a moment. "No, Mattias would want to report this in person. He doesn't like phones or most modern technology. And it's too close to dawn now for him to travel tonight. He avoids flying during daylight hours at all costs. Something about being too close to the sun. Either way, he's quite the traditionalist, preferring to lie dormant during the day."

A spark of realization flickered in Izzie's eyes as she snapped her fingers. "So, we still have a chance to intercept him before he can report back to the Master. He must be hiding out somewhere in the city until tomorrow night!"

But Lucas was quick to dismiss the idea, shaking his head. "No, it's impossible. Mattias is far too strong for us to take on. He's a master-level vampire who chooses to stay subservient to the Master of the Village Hidden in Flame, out of some weird loyalty, rather than pursue his own territory. Our best option is to get out of here, as far away as we can."

Izzie began to sputter in disbelief at the suggestion of retreat, while Argo, from his shelter beneath the table, murmured his agreement with Lucas's assessment.

Alex's mind raced as she weighed their bleak choices. None of them were good. They'd had their asses handed to them the first time facing Mattias, but they'd been worn out from their earlier scuffle with the Claw. They were also completely ignorant of his capabilities. Knowledge was power, and this time, they wouldn't be caught off guard. Well, she hoped. Yet, the risks were monumental; Mattias was unlike any monster she'd faced before. Moreover, his daytime hideout remained a mystery.

Determined to shift the dynamics of their predicament, Alex ended the escalating debate. "We need to change the game," she declared, capturing the attention of everyone in the room.

She rose from her chair and strode to the coat closet near the front door. Reaching in, her fingers dug into one of the coat's pockets, rummaging until they emerged with a sleek white business card. Nothing more than a phone number was printed on the card in bold, black font, accompanied by an EU area code.

"What's that?" Lucas asked.

"It's Mr. Von Mistelweig's personal contact," she explained, ignoring Izzie's quip about a 'vampire Batman.'

Lucas still looked perplexed, not quite seeing how a business magnate could shift the balance in their current predicament. On the other hand, Izzie seemed to be mulling over the possibilities.

With a gesture for patience, Alex took out her phone and began dialing the number. As the call connected, she set her phone to speaker mode, placing it on the kitchen counter so that Izzie and Lucas could listen in.

The phone barely rang twice before Mr. Von Mistelweig answered, his voice firm and imposing. "You obviously survived the Village Claw and stopped the ritual that was underway. My informants tell me the final murder was supposed to happen earlier this evening. Well done, Ms. Bain."

Lucas and Izzie exchanged glances, both eyebrows arching in surprise at the man's awareness of their situation.

"Good afternoon, Mr. Von Mistelweig," Alex replied, her tone professional yet direct. "You're well informed. It saves me the trouble of explaining."

His deep chuckle resonated through the speaker. "How can I assist you?"

"I need help locating an ancient vampire before he can fly back to Brazil and inform the Master of the Village Hidden in

Flame about the failed ritual." She deliberately left out any mention of Lucas or their bond.

There was a pause on the line, a few moments of silence that stretched taut with anticipation. "Ms. Bain, your intelligence is... intriguing for an independent hunter from Chicago."

"Can you help me or not?"

"The target's name?"

"Mattias," she responded, her tone steady.

"The abomination," he hissed, more a statement of fact than a question, revealing his own understanding of the gravity of their request.

Mr. Von Mistelweig's voice leveled. "Ms. Bain, if I may ask, how have you managed to stay alive amidst all this?"

"I'm not entirely sure myself," Alex replied. "But I've been warned that if we can't intercept Mattias before he gets back to Brazil, it will only escalate from here. The Master himself might intervene."

"Trust is a currency not easily spent," Mr. Von Mistelweig noted, aware that Alex was withholding information. "I can respect that."

After a moment's contemplation, he spoke again. "All right, I have someone who can assist you. Otto is currently in Denver, but he will be on the first flight to Chicago this morning."

"The driver?" Alex's eyes widened, mouth open in surprise.

"Yes, the same. He was assigned to observe you in Munich, but his skills go far beyond chauffeuring. Otto is among my most capable hunters."

"And you believe he can handle someone like Mattias?"

"Otto is proficient in explosives and precision strikes. His particular set of skills should prove to be a valuable asset alongside your own expertise in swordsmanship. You might succeed with help if you're able to find Mattias while he sleeps and surprise him. And even though that chance is still small, it's worth it, considering the cost of failure."

Alex glanced at Lucas, considering how Otto's skills might align with Lucas's fiery abilities as well.

"I'll take any help I can get," she said. "But we still need to locate Mattias before sundown tomorrow."

"Yes, facing a vampire of his age in the night would be... inadvisable," Mr. Von Mistelweig agreed. "Give me a few hours. I should have a location for you by the time Otto arrives. Meanwhile, I suggest you and your police officer friend get some rest."

The call ended, leaving Alex, Lucas, and Izzie with a brief respite but a growing sense of urgency. They had potentially gained a powerful ally, but the race against the sunset had only just begun.

CHAPTER 24

IZZIE'S RHYTHMIC TAPPING on the table betrayed her underlying unease. "Can we really trust this guy?"

Alex sighed. "We have to trust someone, Izzie, and right now, he seems like our best shot."

"Great, so we wait for this Otto guy to show up with the location and, apparently, an arsenal. Sounds totally above board."

Alex started to counter, but Izzie cut her off. "Yeah, yeah, I get it. It's what we've got. But I'm still going to snoop around, see if I can dig up anything on recent hideouts fit for a day-sleeping vampire."

"Izzie, you need rest," Alex insisted.

"I'll grab a few hours," replied Izzie, standing up and heading towards the guest bedroom. "But I'm not putting all our hopes on this mystery man from your day job."

Alex watched her. "Where are you going?"

"To get some sleep, like you said. What does it look like?"

"Izzie, there's no need to stick around. Besides, Lucas will need somewhere to crash," Alex pointed out.

Izzie stopped, turning to face her with a determined look. "Alex, hell will freeze over before I leave you alone here with him," she said, her voice unwavering. "No offense, Argo."

The little corgi just rolled his eyes and grumbled, "For the second time, she's not alone, you frustrating woman."

Alex nodded. "Exactly. Argo's here, and besides, look at Lucas." She gestured toward the man. "He's about to fall out of his seat. I'll be fine. Head back to your place. It's just down the road. Clean up, catch a few hours of sleep, then we'll meet up for a late breakfast. I've already told Steve I won't be coming into work tomorrow."

Izzie's gaze lingered on Alex, her eyes narrowing slightly.

"All right, you win," her friend conceded, though not without a hint of reluctance. "I'll be back by nine. Otto should be landing around then." She then turned her attention to Lucas, her voice an unyielding force. "If you do anything—and I mean anything—to cause Alex any more trouble, I won't hesitate to fill your face with bullets."

Her words were a clear, unambiguous warning, and Lucas visibly flinched, but he nodded sadly. With that, Izzie left, her footsteps echoing, a silent promise of a swift return.

"Alone at last, with only a corgi for company," he mumbled without looking up.

Alex observed him thoughtfully, contemplating whether to delve into more personal matters now that they were alone. But she decided against it, recognizing the need to heed her own advice about rest. She needed to get her shit in order. It was the only way they would survive the next twenty-four hours.

Lucas let out a weary sigh. "I could use a place to clean up before I crash. I'd rather not leave soot and ash everywhere."

With a light chuckle, Alex gestured for him to follow her. "Sure, come on."

Lucas groaned as he rose from the chair, glancing questioningly at the dirty dishes. Alex dismissed his unspoken offer with a wave of her hand. "Leave them. We'll deal with it in the morning."

She led him down the hallway, pausing to retrieve a few spare towels from the hall closet before entering the guest bedroom. The room was simple yet tastefully decorated in hues of blue and gold, creating a calming ambiance. She placed the towels on the bed and then pointed to the bathroom at the far end of the room.

Feeling Lucas's presence close behind her, Alex became acutely aware of their proximity. She glanced back as if pulled and saw the bond between them. It was slender, the gold threads, shimmering mutedly yet unmistakable. A wave of heat rushed to her cheeks as fleeting memories of their previous encounters flickered through her mind.

Turning back to face the room, her words came out slightly awkward. "All right, um, make yourself comfortable." Like Lucas's earlier sentiment, she couldn't help but think how different this situation was from any scenario she had imagined about bringing the man into her home.

As Alex turned to leave, Lucas stood close, almost startlingly so. She found herself pausing, her gaze meeting his. Still clad in the remnants of the night's battle, Lucas looked like a shadow of a man. His dark slacks and black shirt were smeared with ash and char. His trench coat hung off him wearily, no longer fluttering with the same predatory grace.

His hair, which had been wild and untamed, dancing with the night wind, now lay limp and disheveled, streaked with grime. The fury that had etched his features at the driving range, transforming him into a wrathful avatar of the storm, was replaced with an expression of exhaustion and vulnerability. Yet, the intensity of his eyes remained, fierce and deep, hinting at the tumultuous emotions that churned beneath his tired facade.

Now, in the aftermath of their ordeal, he seemed a broken blend of extremes. In him, she saw the raw power of the elemental force she had witnessed at the driving range, tempered by the vulnerability of a man who had just bared his soul. And beneath it all, she couldn't deny it, there was still a magnetic attraction that went beyond the physical, stirring something deeper within her. She sighed and backed away. Now was not the time.

"Let me know if you need anything else." As she moved around him and down the hall to her own bedroom, she could still feel his presence burning with potential behind her.

"Good night, Alex," she heard him whisper before she crossed into her room.

CHAPTER 25

IN THE SANCTUARY of her room, Alex took a moment to assess her own state. She was covered in the same grime and residue of the night's events as Lucas. The thought of her luxurious shower, with its promise of warmth and cleanliness, was immensely appealing.

"You okay, boss?" Argo's voice came from his usual spot on her bed.

"Yeah, buddy, I will be," she replied, managing a weary smile. "Just need to unwind a bit."

"You and me both. That shift was rough. I much prefer being like this, you know."

Her laughter broke the room's quiet tension. "I almost forgot about that, Argo! That was actually quite terrifying. The scales, the horns, the fire, oh my!"

Argo's grumble about the lack of appreciation for his efforts only made her laugh more, though she quickly softened. "I'm sorry, buddy. It was impressive, really. And I think Izzie may have even peed her pants a bit. But are you okay? Shifting like that can't be easy."

As he rolled over, presenting his belly for a rub, he sighed. "Just tired. Shifts that far from my true nature take a lot out of me."

Alex, careful not to soil the bed, leaned over and gently stroked his belly. "I'm sorry you felt the need to do it. I'll give you a heads-up next time. Promise."

His tongue lolled out the side of his mouth as his eyes practically rolled up into his head in pure puppy pleasure.

"Well, then," she said, standing up. "I need to shower. I feel like I've been rolled in ash."

Argo's parting shot was typical. "Next time, maybe skip bringing home warlocks, no matter how pitiful or pretty they look."

She laughed, heading to her closet to strip off the dirty clothes. "Got it, no more strays. You're the only one for me."

His bark was almost reproachful before he settled down, quickly succumbing to sleep.

As she readied for her shower, the sound of water from the guest bathroom reached her. Lucas was showering, too. A pang of disappointment and confusion hit her. Why did she wish he was with her, especially given how he felt about vampires? She couldn't change her nature any more than he could change his feelings, she thought as she stepped into the shower.

The warm embrace of water enveloped Alex, cascading from multiple directions. The dirt, the blood, and the lingering shroud of fear began to dissipate under the relentless streams. As she lathered soap into her skin and worked shampoo through her hair, there was a deliberate intent to purge, to cleanse not just the physical filth but also the emotional residue that clung to her.

She wanted to wash away every vestige, to emerge renewed, especially after the night's events had brought her so close to unleashing the darker aspects of her nature. The soap suds swirled down the drain, taking with them the superficial layers of the ordeal she had endured.

Leaning forward, her hand pressed firmly against the far wall. She allowed her body to relax, her head bowing under the steady downpour. The water muffled the world around her, offering a rare moment of solitude, a refuge where she could let her guard down. In that private, watery cocoon, the emotions she had kept at bay started to surface. Tears mingled with the shower's spray, a silent release of the pent-up stress, fear, and confusion.

"Why does it have to be so hard," she cried into the water. It was all overwhelming—the battle, the revelations about Lucas, the bond they shared that only she could see, and the looming threat that still hung over them.

She didn't know how long she had been in there, but at some point, she heard the soft creak of a door opening. She didn't want to look. She didn't want it to be another fantasy like the one she'd had in the basement. She knew it was stupid. She knew it didn't make any sense, but right now, she wanted Lucas to be behind that opening door.

As it clicked shut, proving the reality of the intruder, a jolt of apprehension surged through her. Her heart raced, torn between the fear of being alone and the vulnerability of facing Lucas in such an intimate setting.

Through the steam swirling around her, she heard a deep exhale from the other side of the glass. Summoning her courage, Alex slowly opened her eyes. The vapor blurred her vision, but she could still make out his shadowy form, his head bowed.

Compelled, she reached out, wiping a clear patch on the fogged-up glass of the shower. Through the window, she saw Lucas lift his head, their eyes locking in a silent exchange. In that gaze, she saw a reflection of her own deep-seated need, a raw and burning desire mirrored in his eyes.

"May I come in?" His question was laden with meaning, whether he knew it in that moment or not, extending beyond the physical space of her shower. Alex understood that her invitation would relinquish the protective threshold of her home, restoring his magical powers.

She hesitated for a heartbeat, considering the weight of her decision. Then, with a quiet resolve, she decided to trust him. "Come in."

As Lucas slowly opened the glass door, the magic seemed to rush back to him. He took a deep breath, stretching out his palms with a faint, mesmerizing glow. "Thank you," he whispered, stepping into the shower.

The towel wrapped around his waist fell away, forgotten, as the water splashed around him, merging with the droplets already caressing Alex's skin.

Whether it was the mystical binding, or a completely natural bond forged in a crucible of chemistry and danger, it burned like an ember within her. Lucas moved, the space between them diminishing with each deliberate step, and Alex could feel the heat radiating from him.

Her hands, unsure yet drawn by a power not their own, slowly reached out, mirroring his. Fingers tentatively brushed, exploring each other's bodies. His fingers tenderly traced the line of her jaw, down her neck, gliding over the curves of her breasts with a softness that spoke more than words could. It was a touch filled with care, perhaps even a hint of wonder, as if rediscovering something precious and fragile.

Alex leaned in, her eyes fluttering shut as her hands began their own journey. They traced the contours of Lucas's shoulders, down his back, and across his chest. The water flowed around them, wrapping them in a soothing rhythm.

Her fingers continued their dance over the firm lines of his body, soon discovering a tapestry of scars, a rough landscape of healed wounds crisscrossing his skin. *Fuck!* Her breath hitched. They engulfed his entire upper body.

Then, she found the brand etched into his chest. It was a unmistakable outline, mirroring the marking she and Izzie had discovered on the murdered women. This sigil, the emblem of the Village Hidden in Flame, was a permanent scar, a relentless reminder of Lucas's tormented past that would carry with him always.

"Oh, Lucas." Her voice held a well of sadness for the pain he had endured.

Lucas grasped her hand, pulling it away from his chest. "Don't."

She simply nodded as her fingers found their way to his wet hair. Her touch mimicked the way he often tended to his own locks, a gesture she had observed countless times now.

In response, Lucas leaned forward, his lips curving into a broad smile, a silent thank you. His eyes held her as he closed the gap between them, meeting her lips with his own.

Face to face, Lucas's lips were soft against Alex's, moving with a gentle insistence. As the water dripped down their faces, the kiss deepened, her own lips parting to welcome his searching tongue into her mouth.

Lucas's hands, previously tentative, cradled Alex's face as his thumbs traced her cheeks and jawline. Alex's hands, once lost in his hair, now slid down his neck, tracking the contours of his shoulders, feeling the play of muscles beneath his skin.

The taste of him, the soft sound of their mingled moans, and the feel of his hair under her fingertips was nearly enough to send her over the edge. It was as if the shower had become their small universe, where only the spray of water accompanied their quickened, intertwined breaths.

Then, like a man coming up for air, Lucas disengaged, stepping back awkwardly, before a vulpine grin sprung onto his lips. The air itself seemed to shift, charged with a sudden anticipation, and with a subtle gesture from the warlock, time stood still within their steamy haven. The droplets of water that had been cascading around them now hung suspended in air, each one a tiny, shimmering jewel caught in a frozen dance.

Alex, awestruck, tentatively reached out toward the droplets. Her fingers gently brushed against one, and it quivered at her touch yet remained floating, defying gravity.

Lucas watched her, his smile broadening. "You think this is cool? Wait until I show you what's next."

Alex looked at him and it was as if the water had washed away all the barriers they had built. Here, together, they were left utterly bare. And just like that, the dam of restraint they'd been mostly holding in place since Izzie left seemed to burst between them.

Time started again, and the water fell. Their hands roamed with a newfound urgency, each touch more insistent than the last, as if they were both desperate to lay claim to every inch of the other's body.

He leaned into her with his whole body, squeezing her against the cool tiles of the shower wall. She moaned under weight of him, needing more. More of his hands on her, more of his kisses, more of him. The firmness of him was undeniable, insistent against her belly. When she reached down to grab him, their lips clashed in another passionate embrace.

She pressed her forehead against his for long, slow exhale before her hand continued its exploration of the throbbing shaft between them. But it still wasn't enough. Amid the gentle cascade of water flowing over them, the contrast of his rough hands, the coarse texture of his scars, and the firmness of his desire drove her to the brink of frenzy.

With a feral growl simmering in her throat, Alex pushed Lucas away and maneuvered him onto the small bench at the back of the shower. Lucas reached out from his position on the bench, his hands finding the back of her buttocks and pulling her roughly atop him, as she wrapped her legs around his waist.

His gaze lingered on her neck. She could see him intently following the path of water rolling down her body, as if memorizing each curve and line.

She stilled, then, as her vampiric nature emerged, and her eyes began to darken at the edges. Alex watched him closely. Nervous, she braced for his reaction to the change.

But Lucas's expression remained unshaken, his gaze only deepening with an adoration. The darkening of her eyes, a visual display of her vampiric nature, did not make him look away.

Through the bond, she could see how he saw her.

He saw not just a woman or a vampire but a beacon of strength and resilience, someone who carried the weight of her dual nature not as a curse but as a unique strength. He cursed himself that he ever saw anything else in her.

She was a mirror in which he saw the possibility of overcoming his own inner demons, hope that even he could find a path to reconcile the disparate parts of his own existence.

She smiled, and any flicker of hesitation or nervousness that had momentarily dimmed her passion vanished.

Renewed, she extended one hand to grasp the cool, solid bar of the towel rack above the bench. Using it for leverage, she lifted herself into a poised hover slightly over the warlock. He, in turn, maintained a steady hold on her hips, his wet grip firm yet tender, never allowing even the slightest distance to disrupt the magnetic pull that hung between them.

As she hung in the air, chest expanding and contracting and breaths coming faster, Lucas's eyes widened in surprise and damn near childlike glee. It was as if he had just noticed her breasts rising and falling mere inches from his face.

Alex chuckled a deep throaty sound and closed her eyes as his hands roamed further up her back, pulling her closer until she felt the flick of his tongue. She hissed in pleasure, her nipples tightening under his touch. Then, with a slow, deliberate hunger, Lucas took nearly her entire breast into his mouth, the heat of it sending a shudder through her. He started gently, teasing, then sucked harder, his tongue and lips claiming every inch of the sensitive peak.

With her free hand, she reached down to grab his still throbbing member and slowly lower herself, guiding him to the soft entrance between her thighs. Maintaining her grip, she caressed herself with his silken tip in tight, stroking circles—in and out and around the edges.

"Alex," he panted, trying to pull her down further and end the teasing. But she repositioned her grip on the towel rack, holding herself in place.

When she didn't immediately give in, his eyes darkened, and a slow, knowing smirk curved his lips.

Then—heat.

His fingers against her back warmed, a soft, teasing glow at first, then steadily intensifying. But it wasn't painful. It seeped into her skin, unfurling in waves, each touch sending a cascade of shivering pleasure rippling outward, wrapping her in sensation until every nerve was attuned to him.

Heat bloomed where his fingers roamed, igniting her shoulders with liquid pleasure. Then, as his hands slid to the sides of her neck, a bliss surged upward, pooling at the base of her skull like a spark catching fire.

Overwhelmed, Alex arched back, a sigh slipping from her lips.

"Lucas," she gasped, breathless. "What are you doing?"

His smile was pure mischief, playful yet predatory, as he ignored her question and let his magic do the answering. His hands glided lower, each movement trailing an electric thrill over her skin.

"What did you expect?" he murmured, voice thick. "I'm a no-good, rotten-to-the-core warlock."

For a fleeting second, she felt like Little Red staring down a wolf in disguise—charming, deceptive, dangerous.

Then his fingers reached the tops of her thighs, a teasing brush before pleasure struck deep, curling through her like molten lightning. Her legs buckled, and with a helpless wriggle, she collapsed against him.

If she thought the feel of his touch down her arms or back was bliss, feeling him plunge deep inside her, filling every inch of her as she sat and writhed on top of him nearly blew apart what little was left of her sane, rational mind.

"Lucas," she started to moan before he trapped her mouth in another infinite, all-encompassing kiss. The pressure coiled deep, but it wasn't a slow, measured crescendo—it was urgent, insistent, a fire igniting from within and racing outward, setting every nerve alight with a tingling, all-consuming heat.

Lucas moved with her, and his hands sent wave after wave of euphoria through her lower back in time with her rocking motions atop him. Her heart rate increased, and her breath became quicker and more shallow.

Whether it was a minute or an hour, the fire wove through her, pulling the ecstasy along every nerve and sinew. It rolled in great waves, each one more potent and profound than the last, washing over her in a continuous, unending flow. It radiated from her core to the tips of her fingers and toes in an overpowering, all-encompassing exultation.

At the height of it, Alex felt complete surrender. Nothing

else mattered but the profound sense of fulfillment and connection. As the sweet relief engulfed her, she looked at Lucas and saw in him a miraculous new light. He was no longer the man marred by self-hatred and torment she had seen earlier that night. Instead, he appeared infused with a golden glow that emanated from the bond they shared. His smile was genuine and filled with happiness, touched with a roguish, endearing charm. His eyes sparkled, not with the pain of his past, but with the light of the present moment and hope for a future worth having.

Water dripped down the walls of the shower, and eventually, the waves of release gradually began to subside. It seemed impossible after such an encounter, but Alex felt herself returning to the present, as the extraordinary magic-induced ecstasy left her little by little with each successive exhale. Contented, she leaned against Lucas, wondering what he had seen in her at the moment of release.

Finally, Alex untangled her legs and stepped away from him to turn off the water and step out. Standing on the plush fuzzy bathmat, she wrapped a towel around herself, glancing at Lucas as he reached for a fluffy purple towel of his own.

"That was... um, out of this world. Have you ever felt anything like that before? With the magic and, um, everything else?"

Lucas paused for a moment. "Honestly, no. That was unlike anything I've ever felt. The magic... it's always been a part of me, but what happened between us, that was, um, unexpected." He smiled sheepishly. "It was more than just me doing something with my power—it was us, how my power interacted and intermingled with you. It made everything feel more intense, more real."

"Oh, well, all right." Alex blushed, feeling silly that she would feel embarrassed. Then she tried to change the topic, joking, "You know, at this rate, I'm starting to think we'll never make it to an actual bed."

Lucas chuckled and pointed towards Alex's luxurious bed, visible from where they stood. "Well, there happens to be a bed right there." Eyes wide, she dropped her damp towel and reached for his outstretched hand. Thankfully, Argo was nowhere in sight.

CHAPTER 26

AS THE FIRST RAYS of dawn began to seep through the bedroom windows, Alex lay awake, her eyes wide open. Despite the brief respite of sleep—a mere hour since she and Lucas had succumbed to exhaustion—she felt an unexpected surge of energy pulsating through her veins. The weight of the evening's physical and emotional trials had dissolved in the face of a burgeoning hope. They might just survive the day.

Her gaze drifted to Lucas, who lay beside her, bathed in the morning's tender glow. His features were softened in repose, exuding tranquility that belied the chaos in their lives. The golden threads of their mystical bond shimmered faintly, weaving an invisible tapestry between them. With a mixture of wonder and apprehension, Alex noticed that these ethereal strands seemed denser, more intricate than they had the night before.

Compelled by curiosity, Alex tentatively reached out. The moment her fingers brushed against the thread, a flood of emotions washed through her. Initially, there was a warmth, a sensation akin to love, painting a vivid picture in her mind of waking up to Lucas's serene face each morning. But then, the vision morphed rapidly, turning sinister. She saw Lucas, lifeless, sprawled on the ground with dirt clinging to his still form. Her own wrists streamed with blood, the pain so acute and overwhelming that it felt as though her heart was tearing itself apart beneath her ribs.

Gasping, Alex withdrew her hand sharply, severing the connection. Her chest heaved with labored breaths as she grappled with the shock of what she had just witnessed. Was it a glimpse of the future? A foreboding premonition? Her eyes flicked back to the bond, a tremor of fear mingling with the fading echoes of the vision. With a hesitant, almost reluctant motion, she pulled her hand to her chest, even as the memory of what she'd just seen faded from her mind.

Feeling a bit foolish yet shaken, Alex decided to redirect her focus. A quick workout would be the ideal distraction, a way to regain some sense of normalcy before Izzie arrived.

She eased out of the bed, taking care not to rouse the man, and slipped into loose shorts and a sports bra. Her hair was quickly gathered into a long, practical ponytail. As she stepped out of her bedroom, the rich scent of freshly brewed coffee filled the air.

"Oh, Argo, you are a godsend," she murmured.

Argo merely grunted in response, lifting his head from its resting place on the edge of his dog bed.

"Hey, buddy. Are you feeling okay?" Alex inquired, noting that his tone was grumpier than his usual morning demeanor.

"Well, I would have been, boss," Argo retorted, "if someone hadn't kept me awake all night with their moaning and... thumping."

Alex snorted coffee through her nose. She quickly grabbed

a paper towel, wiping away the droplets from the countertop and her chest. "You heard that, huh?"

Stretching luxuriously, Argo extended his front paws while pushing his hindquarters in the opposite direction, groaning contentedly. "Boss," he said. "I'd bet half the street heard you. And that's saying something, given that most of them have limited human hearing."

Her cheeks warmed with a blush. "Most have human hearing?" she queried, one eyebrow arched.

"It's nothing," Argo dismissed haughtily. "And besides, if others wanted you to know, they'd tell you. It's impolite to pry."

"Fair enough," Alex conceded, playing with a strand of her hair. "Well, um, sorry if we disturbed you. Things got a bit... intense."

Argo snorted and trotted over to her. "That's one way to put it."

He then flopped onto his back, paws waving in the air, inviting a belly rub. Alex chuckled and obliged, her fingers gently kneading his soft fur as she sipped her coffee. Argo's mouth opened in a wide grin, his tongue lolling out in bliss.

"You think it was wise?" he asked, his tone serious despite his playful posture. "Not to be that guy, but there's kinda a lot going on right now..."

She exhaled slowly, standing up. "You're right, but I don't know. I think it needed to happen. Facing Mattias with anything, um, icky or unresolved between us, wouldn't be good, especially since he can fuck with our heads."

Argo barked a laugh. "Well, there was no shortage of 'icky' between you last night."

"Argo!" she exclaimed.

He rolled back onto his paws, gazing up at her with thoughtful eyes. "You might be right, though. Resentment would be ammunition for him. But you've also opened yourself to a new kind of vulnerability, you know?"

Alex was about to question Argo's cryptic remark when an unnerving image flashed through her mind. Lucas lying lifeless before her, his body smeared with blood and dirt. A sharp breath escaped her lips as she dropped her empty coffee cup, the unsettling vision vanishing as quickly as it had appeared. Her heart raced, and her hand instinctively moved to her chest for support.

"Boss?" Argo's concerned voice floated up to her.

"I'm fine," she assured him, her composure swiftly returning as the haunting image faded from her memory. Glancing down, she sighed at the sight of the shattered mug. "Damn," she muttered.

"Don't worry about it. I'll clean up. You should get to your workout."

"Yeah, okay, thanks," she replied, already turning to leave before pausing. "What were you saying earlier?"

"Nothing important. Don't worry about it."

"Sure, thanks again for the coffee and cleaning up."

"I live to serve, boss," Argo said. "Now get going."

Nodding, Alex headed to the basement, a nagging sense of unease still sitting in her mind. She spent the next hour engaged in a rigorous calisthenics routine, trying to shake off the discomfort.

Returning to the kitchen, she found the floor spotless and Argo dozing comfortably under the table. A smile crossed her face at the familiar scene. Peeking into her room, she saw Lucas still deeply asleep. Careful not to disturb him, she tiptoed past and headed for the bathroom.

After a brisk shower, she allowed herself a brief moment of disappointment that Lucas hadn't awakened to join her.

She quickly dried off and dressed in simple black leggings

and a T-shirt, the underlayer to her tactical gear for later. Exiting her closet, she heard the distinct sound of a key turning the lock on her front door. Izzie was early.

A chorus of sharp, loud barks echoed through the house at the noise. Alex rolled her eyes, amused yet slightly exasperated. She often wondered if Argo barked out of genuine alarm at intruders or just enjoyed embracing his role as a vigilant corgi.

Either way, the mutt's vocal warning stirred Lucas from his slumber. She observed him as his eyes fluttered open, slowly taking in his surroundings: the soft morning light filtering through the curtains, the unfamiliar yet comforting setting of Alex's bedroom, and her standing before him, dressed in simple gear, her damp hair framing her face.

Lucas propped himself up on one elbow, offering a slightly disoriented smile. "Um, morning." He smiled and raked his fingers through his hair, seemingly mixed up in trying to look confident and being completely nervous.

Catching his tentative look, Alex decided to ease the awkwardness. She crawled onto the bed, closed the distance with a quick, sweet peck on his lips, then scrambled back before he could grab her and deepen the embrace.

She laughed as she landed on her butt outside the bed. "Izzie's here," she announced, her tone shifting to a more serious note. "It's time to switch gears. We've only got a couple of hours to figure out how we're going to kill the biggest, baddest monster we've ever faced."

His smile vanished, replaced by a somber expression. "Okay, we're really doing this then."

"There aren't any other options," she said. "I'll be in the kitchen. You can take a shower if you want and join us when you're ready." She gestured towards a neat pile of clothes on her dresser. "It looks like Argo cleaned your clothes, so, um, no need to come out naked."

His deep, resonant laughter reverberated through the room, igniting a warm flutter in Alex's stomach. "That corgi is a miracle worker. And here I was planning to just borrow your clothes."

Her laughter mingled with his, the absurdity of Lucas wearing her clothes casting a brief, welcome lightness over the gravity of the day ahead. "Now that," she said, still chuckling, "would have been truly terrifying. Forget Mattias."

"Alex! You here?" she heard Izzie call from the kitchen.

"Whelp. That's my cue," she said to Lucas, who gave her a little salute from the bed, then walked out of the bedroom, closing the door behind her.

"Hey, hun! There you are. I was starting to think you'd vanished." Izzie was standing behind the kitchen counter, balancing a large cup of coffee in one hand and a piece of buttered toast in the other. The island before her was a gastronomic masterpiece, courtesy of Argo. An array of freshly baked croissants, a platter of crisp bacon and savory sausages, a bowl of scrambled eggs fluffy as clouds, and an assortment of fruits, freshly cut and glistening with dewy freshness, adorned the surface. It was a spread that could rival any high-end brunch spot.

"Hey! Just finished showering after a workout," Alex replied, gesturing to her damp hair.

"Well, you look a thousand times better than last night. I guess you were right that we all just needed a good sleep and shower. I'm so ready to get that little asshole today," Izzie said with a confident bite into her toast.

"Haha, yeah. Sleep, exactly what we needed," Alex agreed, her smile masking the fact that her night had been anything but restful. "Argo, this is incredible," she complimented, diverting the conversation as she moved to get some food for herself, suddenly ravenous.

Her plate quickly piled high with the delicious offerings, drawing a dubious look from Izzie, before she crashed down into her usual spot at the dining table to dig in.

"Hun." Izzie eyed the small mountain of food. "That must have been some workout."

"By the way, where's the warlock?" she continued. "He didn't sneak off in the night, did he?"

Alex, mouth full of eggs, shook her head and gestured vaguely towards the bedrooms.

"Hmm, I half expected him to bail," Izzie mused. "Not sure if it's good or bad that he stayed, though. He seemed pretty rattled last night. Could be a wild card in battle, especially with his ties to the target."

Alex simply shrugged, continuing her meal, while Argo snorted softly from his spot under the table.

Izzie took a bite of her toast, probably gearing up for another round of banter when the door to Alex's bedroom swung open. Lucas emerged, looking rejuvenated in his freshly cleaned clothes, his hair damp and a tentative smile gracing his lips.

Izzie halted mid-chew, her mouth agape and eyebrows arching in surprise. She theatrically swung her toast in Lucas's direction, then comically turned her gaze to Alex, who deliberately focused on her meal, feigning ignorance.

"What are you doing coming out of that room, Fireboy?" Izzie questioned, her tone filled with mock incredulity and amusement. Lucas paused, glancing uncertainly toward Alex, who continued to eat unperturbed.

"And your hair is wet?" Izzie nearly shrieked. "You let him use your shower? You've never even let me near that luxurious monstrosity!"

Alex couldn't help but choke on her eggs, a burst of laughter escaping her at Izzie's scandalized reaction.

Lucas, clearly bewildered by the unfolding scene, turned to Alex. "Um, Alex?" he stammered.

"She's just messing with you, Lucas. It's fine," Alex reassured him with a calm smile. "And she only messes with people she doesn't hate, which is good. Go ahead and grab some breakfast."

"I knew what I was walking into. I'm not blind," Izzie interjected with a smirk, plucking a strawberry from the spread and popping it into her mouth. "But I am still shocked she let you into her sacred shower space. I've not even gotten to use those godly shower heads."

Lucas, his cheeks tinged with red, moved towards the table without a word. Izzie's eyes flicked between him and Alex, who was now trying to hide her own blush behind her coffee cup.

"Oh, my gawd! In the shower?! You animals! I'll say it again. You animals!" Izzie cackled, reveling in their discomfort, then sauntered over to Alex, giving her a playful fist bump of solidarity before sinking into her chair.

Alex mumbled something unintelligible, clearly embarrassed, while Argo grumbled from under the table, "You didn't have to listen to it all night."

Izzie's eyebrows shot up. "All night?" She then glanced at Lucas, a newfound respect in her eyes. "Not bad, fire boy."

Lucas, like Alex, could only muster half-coherent grumbles in response to Izzie's teasing remarks.

"Anyway." Alex steered the conversation back on track. "Izzie, did you manage to uncover anything useful?"

Izzie's expression darkened. "Not much. But there's been a worrying spike in suicides downtown these past few days. Given the target's proclivities, it might be connected to our current situation."

Lucas, pausing between bites of bacon, chimed in. "That

tracks. Mattias doesn't need much blood due to his size, but his victims often end up mentally shattered."

"Great," Izzie remarked dryly. "Anything else we should know about him?"

"Tactically, not much," Lucas replied. "He's usually protected by a Quad, so I've never seen him in direct combat. But since we neutralized the Claw here, he's likely relying on human servants now."

Alex pondered the situation, biting her lip. "So, our main threat is one vampire, elusive and mentally manipulative. Human servants, though, are a complication." She turned to Izzie, concern etched on her face.

"Right," Izzie agreed. "We can't just eliminate humans without due process. We'll need to incapacitate them non-lethally."

Lucas interjected, "That won't be easy. Those humans will be utterly devoted. They worship the vampires like gods."

Izzie glanced at her watch, then at Lucas. "And speaking of complications, Otto's due soon. What's our story for him? I'm still not thrilled about involving someone we barely know."

Alex nodded in agreement. "But we need the help."

"Ugh, fine," Izzie conceded.

"We can say Lucas was at the club looking for me, to ask me out. It's plausible and aligns with Mistelweig's suspicions about us."

Izzie couldn't help but snort. "And what about Lucas's ability to conjure fire? That's a game-changer against Mattias."

"I could say it's a family ability I usually ignore, but I acted on impulse to help Alex. However, Mattias might expose our connection during the battle."

"We'll deal with that when it happens," Alex said. "We can't afford to let the Family know too much about us. They're unnervingly well-informed."

Izzie grumbled. "We're keeping them in the dark then. And I assume we're not revealing your dhampir nature, Alex?"

"Absolutely not," Alex responded firmly, echoed by simultaneous barks of agreement from Lucas and Argo.

Alex chuckled. "Well, there's a unanimous decision. Argo, go check if Hell has frozen over."

"Haha, very funny," Argo retorted from under the table. "Nope, it's still as hot as ever." The group shared a laugh, but their amusement was short-lived as a knock at the door interrupted them.

Alex turned to her companions, a serious edge to her voice. "Looks like it's time to figure out how to kill an ancient evil." She nodded firmly and got up to open the door. "Let's do this."

CHAPTER 27

THE DOOR CREAKED open, revealing a man who, with his blond hair and broad, muscular build, could have been mistaken for a modern-day Viking. His black jeans and tactical jacket were utilitarian, yet they fit him like a second skin, complementing his imposing stature. Otto's steely blue eyes scanned the room, a hint of skepticism etched in his sharp features.

"Otto, come in," Alex invited, her voice steady yet warm. "You already know Lucas."

Otto nodded curtly at Lucas, his gaze lingering with a hint of curiosity before he addressed the group. "Heard you took down a Quad. Hard to believe."

Alex leaned back against the wall, arms crossed over her chest and a wry smile on her lips. "It was a close call. We got lucky, and Lucas here was the wildcard that gave us the edge." Her words were factual, devoid of any boastfulness, as she subtly underscored the unexpectedness of their victory.

Otto's eyes narrowed as he looked her over, clearly

weighing her words. He then turned to Lucas, suspicious. "Wildcard? And why were you there in the first place?"

Lucas replied, his voice holding a hint of embarrassment. "I was there to ask Alex out. We had a good time in Munich, and she mentioned Oktoberfest at the Clubhouse earlier that day. It seemed like a good idea at the time." He paused, then added, "And, for the other part, well, I guess it's easier to show than tell." He extended an arm, and in his palm, a small orb of fire flickered to life, glowing softly yet intensely.

Otto's eyes narrowed. "A warlock? Wielding fire? And you just 'happened' to be there when a Quad of Hidden Village vampires showed up?"

Lucas maintained a calm demeanor, sticking to the narrative they had crafted. "It's a family trait that we've spent generations avoiding. It's too dangerous to use." He shook his head, then glanced at Alex. "But when I saw Alex in trouble, I had to act. It was instinctual."

Otto huffed. "If you say so." He then turned his attention to the duffel bags he was carrying, dropping them with a heavy thud. Striding to the counter, he surveyed the array of breakfast items. "When did you find time to cook all this?"

Alex, Lucas, and Izzie exchanged a quick, knowing glance, stifling their giggles. Otto looked at them, puzzled. Alex waved it off nonchalantly. "I had it delivered."

Now focusing on his plate, Otto shared the information they were all waiting for. "We think we've located Mattias's daytime hideout. There's also a private jet booked for Brazil at nine tonight, so he should still be there."

Alex and Izzie exhaled in unison, a collective sigh of relief. The pieces of the puzzle were falling into place.

"Where is it, Otto? And what do we know about his daytime defenses?"

Otto's gaze shifted to Izzie, sizing her up for a moment. "The cop, right?"

"Obviously," Izzie retorted, her arms crossed defiantly.

Otto's lips curled into a slight smile. "Mattias is holed up in a middle-class neighborhood close to downtown. It's quiet, unassuming. The kind of place where a kid walking around at night wouldn't raise any eyebrows."

He leaned against the counter, his eyes scanning the group. "From what we've gathered, he's got one human bodyguard with him, posing as a parental figure. This bodyguard is likely his only immediate defense during the day."

Over the ensuing hour, the team huddled together, meticulously reviewing their individual skills and piecing together a strategy to infiltrate Mattias's suburban stronghold. Their main objective was clear: take out the vampire without involving or harming the neighborhood's residents. It was a strict set of parameters.

By the time they finalized their approach, the clock had crept past eleven in the morning, and they still had an hour's drive to get there. Hastily, Alex retreated to her room to prepare for the impending confrontation. She donned her most protective gear, meticulously arranging her various holsters and blades.

For today's hunt, she pulled on a lightweight, Kevlar-lined vest that offered protection against blades and bullets without sacrificing mobility. The vest was molded to her form, allowing her to move freely and stealthily. Over the vest, she wore a durable, black tactical jacket with hidden pockets and compartments, ideal for concealing various tools and weapons.

Her second layer of pants was made of a rugged, dark material with reinforced stitching at critical points. The pants were paired with sturdy, lightweight boots, their soles designed for silent movement. Holsters were strategically placed around her waist, back, and thighs, providing easy access to her arsenal of blades.

Before leaving, she secured the swords in their specialized carrying cases, ready for transport to the car.

Emerging from her room, Alex found Otto, Izzie, and Lucas standing in a solemn huddle, ready to depart. Otto's eyes scanned her, pausing at the swords at her side. "I assume you know how to use those?"

She rolled her eyes. "I guess we're about to find out, aren't we?"

Argo's head emerged from under the table as they moved toward the door, his whine cutting through the tense atmosphere. Alex knelt down, her hand gently caressing his face, her forehead pressed softly against his. "I'll be safe. Love you, buddy," she whispered, planting a kiss on his cheek. Argo's large puppy eyes followed her as she stood to leave with the others.

Otto chuckled softly. "Cute dog, though hardly what I'd call proper."

As Otto made his comment, Alex noticed Lucas glance nervously back at Argo. The corgi sat calmly, his attention on the group but showing no signs of transforming into a demonic entity. Alex chuckled to herself as Lucas cautiously stepped through the door. Then she heard the faint, barely audible threat from the dog: "You keep her safe, or I will eat you."

She paused, not sure what to make of that. Surprisingly, Lucas didn't physically react. As he carefully shut the door behind them, Alex could almost hear his silent response in her mind: *If she gets hurt, I'll roast myself so you don't have to worry about the flavor.*

CHAPTER 28

THE NONDESCRIPT SUV, piloted by Otto, slid quietly into a parking spot a block away from their objective. The low hum of the engine ceased, plunging the vehicle into silence.

"Okay, we should have more than enough time before the sun starts to set," Otto said, doing a final check on the various guns within reach and a small bag of explosives sitting in Izzie's lap. But before the rest of them could begin their final checks, Izzie's phone buzzed to life.

She looked down at the caller ID, and her brows scrunched up in confusion. "It's the LT. I'm off today. Not sure why he would be calling. Let me just take it real quick."

As Izzie's conversation unfolded, the rest of the team sat in weighted silence, their attention riveted on her changing expressions. The transformation was subtle yet telling—her brows furrowed in surprise, her lips tightened into a thin line, and her eyes hardened as the call progressed. Each mumbled response seemed to draw her deeper into a well of anger and frustration.

The moment the call ended with that definitive click, Izzie threw her phone against the nearest window in frustration. When she turned to face her team, her usual composure was replaced with a look of steely determination and rage.

"Mary's dead," she said. "She walked right in front of a Metra train down by Ravinia." Her hands clenched into fists as if grappling with the reality of the news. "Witnesses said she looked absolutely terrified, like she was running from something, or someone, right before she ran onto the tracks."

"Mattias," Alex hissed. A shadow seemed to pass over her eyes as the darkness stirred within her.

Lucas, seated close to Alex in the back seat, was the only one to notice the subtle shift in her demeanor. He reached out, his hand finding hers in a silent offer of support. "I'm so sorry," he murmured.

Izzie's voice quivered. "It's my fault," she said, the weight of guilt pressing heavily on each syllable. Her eyes, usually so steady, flickered with grief. "I was the one who insisted she be there as a lookout. He must have targeted her... a twisted trade for not getting to me."

Alex's focus shifted from her own simmering anger to Izzie's palpable distress. The guilt and pain in Izzie's voice acted as a catalyst, even more than Lucas's comforting touch, pulling Alex back from the edge of her dark emotions.

"Izzie, listen to me," Alex said. "You made the right decision. Mary's warning was crucial—it saved us. Without her, I wouldn't have stood a chance. None of us would have. And the Master would be en route to Chicago right now."

"Fuck. It doesn't matter. It's still my fault. Let's go kill the little fucker." She threw open the door, signaling the beginning of their assault.

Lucas, pulling his hand back from Alex, whispered an incantation, and a barely perceptible veil covered the SUV and its occupants, rendering them almost invisible to the casual observer.

The team stepped out into the quiet street, each member mentally preparing for the confrontation ahead. Otto took point, his eyes scanning the quiet street with the practiced ease of a seasoned operator. He moved with a silent grace that belied his muscular frame, each step deliberate and calculated.

Izzie followed a few paces behind, her movements equally fluid. Her hands were steady on her silenced weapon, her eyes darting to shadowed corners and potential hiding spots behind cars and trees, ready to neutralize any threat that might compromise their mission.

Lucas, sandwiched between Otto and Izzie, whispered another incantation under his breath. Time around them seemed to compress; their movements accelerated yet remained soundless, a clever manipulation that allowed them to cover ground swiftly without attracting attention. The earlier veil likely wouldn't deter a focused guard for long.

As they reached the door of the house, Otto paused, carefully inspecting the frame and lock. His fingers trailed over the surface, searching for any sign of hidden traps or alarms.

Lucas then stepped forward, his eyes narrowing in concentration. He extended his hand, fingers twitching slightly as he sensed the magic woven into the doorway. "There's a barrier spell here, and an alarm," he murmured, more to himself than to the others. With a few more whispered words and a deft gesture, the magical barriers unraveled, dissolving into the air like mist. Both men had obviously done this sort of thing before, a detail not lost on Otto as he narrowed his eyes at Lucas.

Before opening the door, Lucas's expression turned somber. "The threshold's been destroyed," he said quietly, a note of sadness in his voice. "It means he likely killed the family living here."

With a nod from Otto, they entered the house, slipping into the dimly lit interior. Once inside, it looked like any other family home in the neighborhood, with signs of life and normalcy that were now hauntingly out of place. Children's toys were scattered in the corners, a chilling reminder of the family that once lived here. In the dining room, spoiled leftovers sat on the table.

In the living room, just off the entryway, stood the human bodyguard. He was a tall, imposing figure, his eyes cold and calculating. He smirked at their entrance, like he had been waiting for them. "Welcome. It'll be my pleasure to kill anyone who dares disturb my master's sleep. He's resting so peacefully after feasting on that little witch last night."

Izzie's hand moved to her gun, a growl escaping her lips. But Otto was quick to gently press her hand down, his eyes conveying a silent message of caution. They needed to keep quiet; waking the vampire was not an option yet. Izzie nodded, understanding, and took a strategic position, her weapon at the ready but not raised.

Following the plan, Lucas attempted to use his time-slowing ability on the bodyguard. But the man seemed to shake off the magical influence with surprising ease, a hint of a sneer on his face. "Nice try, warlock," he taunted. Lucas muttered a curse under his breath, his hands beginning to glow with the beginnings of a fiery spell.

But before he could unleash his magic, Alex sprang into action. Her movements were a blur, fueled by anger at the man's flippant disregard for human life. She closed the distance between them in the blink of an eye, her hands moving in a precise, calculated manner. She ducked under his outstretched arm, twisting it behind his back and using his own momentum to unbalance him. Then, she applied a chokehold, expertly cutting off his air supply. The bodyguard struggled, his face turning red, but Alex's hold was unyielding. Within moments, he slumped in her grasp, unconscious but unharmed.

Otto quickly stepped in, dragging the incapacitated bodyguard to the kitchen. He found a sturdy chair and tied the man to it with a length of rope he had in his bag. He worked methodically, ensuring the knots were tight and the man was securely bound. Once satisfied, he used a piece of cloth to gag the bodyguard, guaranteeing he couldn't raise an alarm.

The team exchanged glances, their expressions filled with relief. They had neutralized the immediate threat without raising an alarm.

Otto grunted, looking over at Alex. "That was excellent."

She nodded in response. "We're lucky it was only the one."

"That was too easy. No offense, Alex," Lucas said, concerned.

"And what would you know about it?" Otto asked.

Lucas remained silent and turned to look for the basement door. His search led them to a concealed entrance to the basement, a narrow door that seamlessly blended into the wall. As Izzie stood guard, her eyes scanning for any sudden movement, Otto carefully inspected the door for electronic security measures. Finding none, he cautiously pushed the door open, revealing a steep staircase descending into darkness.

He flipped the switch by the door, but there was no response. The electricity had been cut off, leaving the stairs engulfed in shadows. Alex drew her twin swords, the first to descend. As the rest joined her, Lucas stepped forward, cupping his hands to summon a small orb of fire. The soft, flickering light illuminated the first room of the basement—a simple, barren space with bare walls and a cold concrete floor. Two doors, one closed and the other slightly ajar, led to further areas beyond.

"Where the fuck is he?" Izzie whispered, her voice a low hiss.

With a silent gesture towards the partially open door, Alex began to move forward, her steps silent and measured. Lucas followed close behind, his conjured flame casting eerie shadows against the walls. Otto pulled an automatic rifle from his bag. He clicked off the safety, holding it in a ready position, his eyes fixed on the darkness ahead.

As the team moved forward, the silence was suddenly shattered by a sound that sent shivers down Alex's spine—a chittering, like hundreds of tiny legs scratching against concrete. It grew louder, more frantic, as they neared the closest door, echoing ominously through the darkened space.

Izzie's voice sliced through the unnerving cacophony, her whisper sharp. "Alex, can you see anything?"

"No! It's pitch black. But..." Alex trailed off, her voice full of confusion. "The darkness, it's... moving." Her sentence was cut short as the first spider lurched from the room.

It was a grotesque creature, the size of a small dog but with the unmistakable anatomy of a spider. Its body was bulbous, covered in a glossy, black carapace that absorbed the faint light. Long, spindly legs, each tipped with sharp, hook-like appendages, moved in a disoriented dance. The spider's mandibles clicked menacingly, revealing needle-like fangs that were dripping with what was probably venom.

But it was the creature's eyes that were most disturbing. Large and multifaceted, they glimmered with an unnatural intelligence. As the spider steadied itself, its gaze fixed intently on Alex, there was a malicious understanding in its stare. Then, with a shrill, piercing trill that resonated through the basement, it signaled an attack.

The wave of darkness behind it suddenly erupted into a nightmarish frenzy as hundreds of similar spiders surged forward. They moved as one, a seething mass of legs and fangs, their collective presence transforming the room into a living, writhing nightmare.

The basement erupted into chaos as the throng of giant spiders surged toward the team, their legs clicking against the concrete in a rapid, rhythmic assault. Each spider was a nightmarish fusion of speed and tearing claws, their fangs glistening in the dim light cast by Lucas's fire.

Standing his ground, Lucas conjured a wall of flames, sweeping it toward the advancing creatures. The spiders hissed and recoiled, but their numbers were overwhelming. "Keep back!" he shouted as he manipulated the fire, moving the barrier to follow the pulsing horde.

Alex moved like a whirlwind, her twin swords slicing through the air with deadly precision. Each strike delivered death, severing spider limbs and carving a path ichor with each step. "On your left!" she called out to Otto, who was steadily firing his muffled assault rifle, the muzzle flash briefly illuminating the grotesque scene.

Otto's shots were good, each bullet finding its mark. He moved in tandem with Alex, covering her back as she engaged the spindly monsters up close. "How many are there?" He grunted, ejecting an empty magazine and slamming a new one into place.

"No fucking clue," Alex answered, looking over at Izzie.

Despite her fast and careful shooting, Alex saw Izzie cornered by several spiders that had managed to evade her gunfire. One leaped, its fangs bared, only to be knocked aside by a well-timed kick.

"Damn it!" Alex cursed, feeling the brush of death too close for comfort. In response, Lucas moved to cover Izzie's back with another wall of fire.

The team fought for their lives, a unified whole against the relentless tide of spiders. With every slash, shot, and burst of flame, they pushed the creatures back, but their numbers seemed endless.

"Shit, what are these things?" Izzie yelled, her voice laced with disbelief and adrenaline as she fired her silenced weapon. The bullets tore through the nearest spiders, but for each one that fell, more took its place.

The battle descended into desperation. The spiders, relentless and seemingly numberless, found ways to breach their defenses, turning the fight into a grueling struggle for survival.

Lucas continued incinerating swathes with his fire, but he couldn't cover every angle. A spider managed to dart through the flames, its pincers clamping down on his leg. He cried out, flinging the creature off with a burst of magic, but the pain was evident. "They're getting through!" he yelled.

Alex moved faster than ever before, yet even she couldn't fend off every attack. A spider fang grazed her arm, drawing blood. She grimaced, her attack unrelenting, but the venom was already slowing her down. "We can't keep this up forever!" she shouted, slicing through another spider.

Otto's methodical rifle firing was interrupted as he wrestled with a creature before finally crushing it against the wall. "We need an out!" he barked, checking his ammo and searching for where he had dropped his bag.

The spiders, as if sensing their growing fatigue, became even more frenzied.

Otto dove towards his bag, rummaging briefly before pulling out a small, nondescript device. With a swift motion, he flipped some switches and lobbed it into the darkened room. "Get down!"

Moving instantly, Otto wrapped his arm around Izzie's waist and yanked her towards the relative safety behind the stairs. Izzie, caught off guard but quick to understand, helped brace their impromptu cover.

Lucas, catching onto Otto's plan, sprinted towards Alex. Dodging the deadly arc of her blades, he grabbed her and pulled her forcefully towards the back of the room. As they fell to the ground, Lucas positioned himself between Alex and the mass of spiders, shielding her with his body.

Moments later, the device detonated. The explosion was deafening, a concussive force that reverberated through the basement. A bright, searing light momentarily blinded them, followed by a wave of intense heat that washed over the space, sending shockwaves that rattled the very foundations of the house.

The spiders, caught in the heart of the explosion, let out shrill, agonized screams that pierced the air. The sound was a grotesque symphony of torment, echoing off the walls.

From behind Lucas, debris and dust filled the air, creating a choking haze that obscured Alex's vision.

"Fuck!" she cursed. The sensation of heat was almost unbearable, singeing her skin and clothes.

She heard Izzie retching from across the room. The stench of burning chitin and venom—a pungent, acrid smell that made her eyes water and throat burn—had permeated the air.

The room where the spiders had been was now a charred, smoldering ruin. And the creatures that had just moments before overwhelmed them were now reduced to ash and cinders.

As they slowly emerged from their cover, ears ringing and senses reeling, the sound of coughing came from each one of them as thick smoke enveloped the group like a suffocating shroud.

"Otto! My love! Where have you been all my life?" Izzie said, her cough transforming into hysterical laughter.

"Women," Otto grunted, still trying to clear his lungs of the smoke. But when Alex looked over at him, she was surprised to see him blushing at Izzie's outburst.

With relief at her friends' safety washing over her, she felt Lucas reach out, his hand brushing against her arm. "You okay?"

Alex nodded, her eyes meeting his. "Yeah, thanks to you."

His brows knit as he tried to form an answer, but the moment was shattered by another trilling scream and heavy thud that resonated from the top of the basement stairs.

CHAPTER 29

"FUCK, WHAT NOW?" Izzie groaned, struggling to her feet alongside the others.

Alex's eyes shot to the staircase where the bodyguard, who should have been securely tied up, appeared.

Lucas growled at Otto, "I thought you handled him."

"I did, warlock. With steel-lined fiber. No human could break free from that."

Before anyone could respond, Izzie whispered, "He's no longer human."

The bodyguard was a grotesque amalgamation of human and spider. His flesh seemed to flow seamlessly into chitinous plates, and his two human arms were grotesquely juxtaposed with six spindly spider limbs. His face was a nightmare come to life, spider eyes gleaming with malevolence and huge pincers pushing out from his gaping mouth, snapping in rage. Venom dripped from his fangs as he screamed and reached his elongated legs down the stairs, preparing to launch himself at them.

The few spiders that had survived the explosion echoed their master's fury, their shrill yells filling the air.

"Stars in Heaven," Otto cursed, his face a mask of disbelief.

"Holy hell," Alex muttered, drawing Talon from her back.

Lucas stammered, his voice a mix of fear and disbelief, "It was just a legend. None of the Claw actually believed it. A werespider... it couldn't be real."

Otto spat, boiling over at the implied confession in Lucas's words, "Fuck you, warlock. I will kill you if we ever make it out of here."

"Not now, Otto!" Alex said through gritted teeth, stepping up to the bottom of the stairs and planting her feet. The big man nodded in frustration, and they all braced themselves, facing this new, unthinkable threat that defied both nature and belief.

The battle with the werespider escalated rapidly. Alex watched as each member of the team sprung into action. Otto moved, pulling out his handgun and positioning himself next to Izzie, ensuring they wouldn't catch each other in the crossfire. His eyes were focused, seemingly calculating the best moment to strike without endangering his allies.

Meanwhile, Lucas conjured an inferno along the hallway surrounding the stairs. The flames roared, creating a fiery wall that the beast would have to breach to reach them.

But it didn't stop the monster. With a shrill, agonized cry, the creature flung itself forward, its terrible form soaring over Alex.

Knowing her part, Alex was ready. She swung Talon in a graceful arc, slicing through the spider's underbelly. The chitin was tough, absorbing much of the blow, but she managed to inflict a deep gash. The creature roared more in frustration than pain as it landed and swiped a massive leg, sending Lucas crashing against the wall with a sickening thud.

Alex's eyes widened for a split second, but she immediately refocused on the threat behind her. She pivoted in a blur, her speed a match for the spider's own agility, and the two danced a deadly ballet, their movements too fast to follow.

But even as she engaged the spider, concern for her friends weighed heavy on her mind. She knew that all this noise was bound to wake the sleeping vampire. And then, without notice, her perspective shifted, and she was somehow in two places at once.

While tracking the frenetic battle, she saw Otto and Izzie looking for an opening to injure the spider, but Alex's movements were too fast. She saw Izzie's frustration grow with each passing second, her curses barely audible under her breath as she kept her weapon trained on the rapidly moving figures.

Alex almost faltered a step, ducking last minute under a sweeping spider leg. Risking a glance over her shoulder, she saw Lucas sitting up, rubbing his head, and looking back and forth between her fight with the werespider and Izzie.

Otto gently guided Izzie's gun downward with a firm hand, his gaze fixed behind Alex and the monster. He must have known that there was nothing they could do for Alex, but the second door, which had previously been shut, was now slightly ajar.

Izzie nodded, seeming to understand his intention, and they both shifted their stances, firearms trained on the partially opened door. Their bodies were tense, their expressions a blend of focus and wariness, ready to react to any danger that might emerge from the unexplored darkness.

Holy fuck. Am I seeing through Lucas's eyes? she asked herself silently, before the spider thing attacked again.

With shifter speed, the creature lunged forward with a massive spider leg. Alex parried with Talon, the clang of her blade against chitin ringing out. She pivoted on her heel, narrowly avoiding a swipe from another grotesque limb.

The werespider reared up, its numerous eyes focusing

intently on Alex. It thrust towards her, its mandibles snapping in an attempt to catch her. Alex dodged, feeling the rush of air as the fangs narrowly missed her head. She countered with a swift upward slash, her crimson blade leaving another shallow cut along the creature's underbelly.

The creature, growing increasingly frenzied, overextended in its next strike. Seizing the opportunity, Alex sidestepped and slid under its guard. With a swift, fluid motion, she brought Talon up, targeting the slimmest portion of its neck. The blade sang through the air, finding its mark with deadly precision.

In a split second, the creature's head was severed, tumbling away from its body. The monstrous body stumbled for a moment, then collapsed in a heap.

Alex panted, then fell into a half-hysterical laugh. "Ha! You can always count on decapitation."

Expecting some response from her companions, she turned to find them silent, their attention fixated on the back door, guns raised and ready. The fight might have ended, but the danger was far from over.

CHAPTER 30

WITH THE SPIDER-LIKE thing defeated, Otto cast an appraising, somewhat wary glance at Alex. "I don't know what that thing was, and I don't know how you moved like that or how you managed to kill it," he said. "But I do know that the warlock"—he gestured at Lucas, raising his gun at the man—"is mixed up with the vampires."

Lucas raised his hands in a non-threatening gesture as Izzie stepped in, her hand gently lowering Otto's gun. "Hun, we can sort this out later. Right now, we've still got to deal with Mattias and make it out alive."

Otto seemed to weigh her words, his suspicion lingering. "You're not some monster, too, are you?"

"No, hun. Plain old, 100% human."

"And you trust them?" Otto's eyes flicked between Alex and Lucas.

"I trust Alex with my life and my soul," Izzie stated with unwavering seriousness.

Otto grunted, a reluctant acceptance in his tone. "Good enough for now. But we're not done talking about this. You dragged me into this mess without the full picture. I don't trust you."

Alex's expression tightened. "I'm sorry."

"Good enough," Otto repeated, his anger subsiding slightly.

Their momentary truce was interrupted by the sound of soft, childlike whimpers from behind the door. It creaked open further, revealing Mattias's small form. He rubbed his eyes, mewling softly, clad in pajamas adorned with tiny spiders.

"Little brother," Mattias whined, "you woke me up."

"Fuck!" Otto exhaled, his anger flaring anew as he turned toward Lucas. Whatever he saw in Lucas's expression, though, seemed to calm him slightly, and he refocused on the true threat.

"But you brought a new friend! How fun!" Mattias perked up, his gaze shifting to Otto.

Without hesitation, Otto and Izzie opened fire, but Mattias transformed into an indiscernible blur, dodging the bullets with supernatural speed. The sound of thuds into the far wall was the only indication of their futile attempt.

"How rude!" Mattias exclaimed, lifting a small hand towards Otto and Izzie. They immediately doubled over in pain, clutching their heads.

Alex's muscles tensed, ready to leap to Izzie's aid, but Mattias's swift gesture halted her. "Naughty dhampir, no. You should stay right there," he chided, his voice sing-songy.

Reluctantly, Alex lowered her sword, her other hand raised in a gesture of surrender. The stakes were too high to risk a reckless move. She stood, a statue of frustrated defiance, as Mattias toyed with her friends like a cat with a cornered mouse.

"Now, what am I going to do to them?" He placed his hands on his hips, tilting his head in mock contemplation.

Meanwhile, Otto and Izzie slumped to the ground, their consciousness slipping away under his influence.

Alex shifted slightly, intending to check on Izzie, but Mattias's hand shot up again. "Simon says, stop!" he commanded. She froze in place, and he clapped his hands delightedly. "Well done, little dhampir!" His attention then returned to Otto and Izzie. "But it's very rude to touch somebody else's meal. These are things you will need to know when you join us in the Village Hidden in Flame."

"Fuck that! You little freak!" Alex spat.

In an instant, Mattias's eyes turned pitch black, his childish demeanor replaced by seething rage. He flew across the room, striking Alex with a force that sent her sprawling.

"No! Alex!" Lucas called, moving to her defense.

Mattias stood still, glancing at Alex, who was already pushing herself back to her feet. Then, he turned his chilling gaze to Lucas, who involuntarily recoiled.

"Now, what am I supposed to do with you both?" he mused. "I can't kill you. The Master would be displeased." He tapped his chin mockingly. "But this behavior"—he gestured around—"is unacceptable for the Master's presence."

Suddenly, his face brightened as if struck by inspiration. "I know! I shall train you! Make you perfect little pets. Yes, that's what we'll do."

His words hung in the air, a twisted promise of a fate worse than death. Alex and Lucas exchanged a look of fear. Then Alex saw Lucas's expression shift, his mouth hardening.

He stood tall as Mattias faced him. And with a swift incantation, he summoned a burst of fire, the flames leaping from his palms toward the child vampire. At the same time, he whispered another spell, attempting to slow the flow of time around Mattias.

For a moment, it seemed to work. The fire engulfed

Mattias's arm, the flames licking up his sleeve and eliciting a hiss of pain. But it didn't last. With an almost inhuman speed, the monster extinguished the flames, leaving a charred scar along his arm.

Seizing the moment, Lucas lunged forward to strike again, but Mattias countered too fast to see. He reached out, his small hand touching Lucas's forehead. Instantly, Lucas's body stiffened, his eyes going wide with an indescribable terror.

Mattias, holding his injured arm, turned to Alex, his voice calm but cruel. "He's reliving one of my memories now. The night I took his parents from him," he explained with a twisted glee. "For him, it's like years of experiencing the same horror, over and over, while we stand here."

Alex, petrified, looked at Lucas. He was frozen, his gaze fixed on a point in space, lost in a torment that only he could see. As they stood in the dim basement, the air heavy with the scent of burnt flesh and fear, the reality of their situation settled heavily on Alex.

Alex knew she had to act fast to save her friends. With Talon in hand, her eyes darkened, and she surged towards Mattias, moving quicker than ever before. Time itself seemed to stretch, elongating the moment, though she knew Lucas was in no state to cast any spells.

As she moved, Mattias, his face twisted in surprise, turned toward her in what seemed like slow motion. Aiming to sever his head from his body and end it, Alex brought her sword down with all her might.

At the last second, Mattias leaped back, releasing Lucas from his nightmare hold. He had narrowly avoided the fatal blow but did not escape entirely unscathed as Talon left a shallow cut across his chest.

"How dare you!" he shrieked, his voice a mix of pain and

rage. From the back of his pants, he pulled what appeared to be a coiled wire.

Alex lunged at him again, but Mattias shifted his stance, and the wire shot out with unimaginable speed. It slipped past her blade, slicing into her forearm, leaving a deep gash in the now visible bone. "Fuck!" she screamed, Talon clattering to the floor as her arm hung limply at her side.

"You think that hurt? You half-breed little freak!" Mattias taunted. "Let's continue what we started." Sinister webs of darkness stretched across his face as his attention went back to Lucas, who was groaning on the ground, slowly regaining his senses.

"Oh, little brother. Remember the night you left? What I told you?" Mattias purred, his voice twisted with glee as he watched blood drip from Alex's arm.

"Well, my little pet"—he giggled maniacally—"I lied!"

He danced over to Lucas, grabbing him by the chin and forcefully lifting him to his knees. "I didn't kill your sister. I kept her. She's been my special little toy all these years."

Lucas's voice was filled with anguish. "No!"

"Yes! I told her we rescued her from a mean old warlock who killed her parents. And who do you think we told her killed them? What mean old warlock could it have been?" Mattias laughed cruelly.

Lucas began to weep, his body shaking.

"You! You killed your parents and everyone in your town. But lucky for Sarah, heroic Mattias was there to save her," the creature crowed. "The gallant Mattias battled the fiend and saved her. He even gave her a new home and showed her everything she needed to know to grow up to be a strong and loyal supporter of the Master!"

Lucas collapsed, curling into a fetal position, utterly broken by the revelation. "And now she's the most effective assassin we've had since, well, you. Oh, my little animal, I've never seen anyone take such exquisite joy in causing pain. It's a thing of beauty! If I didn't know she was human, I'd swear she was already a vampire. Though of course, the Master will turn her anyway, before she gets too old. He's been looking for a new concubine," Mattias added with a malicious grin.

Looking down, Alex saw the golden threads of their bond practically vibrating with the intensity of his psychological agony. Connected to Lucas, she felt a tsunami of his emotions wash over her. She felt his pain, his fear, his overwhelming despair. It was as if she were living through his memories, feeling the depth of his loss. The realization hit her that Lucas might not withstand this mental onslaught much longer. His psyche was fracturing, and she felt every piece of it as if it were her own.

With each cry and whimper from Lucas and giggle from Mattias, the bond vibrated louder, like it was etched into her very soul. Responding to his agony with a primal, protective rage, her vampire heritage surfaced once more, more powerfully than it ever had before.

It felt like a fire had been lit within her, not just a flickering flame but a roaring blaze. Her body temperature rose, her skin feeling too tight, too hot, as if she were a vessel for a volcanic eruption. The wrath coursed through her veins like molten lava, demanding action and retribution.

Her fangs elongated, unsheathing as her eyes changed color, mirroring the darkness that had taken hold of her. The need to protect Lucas, to destroy the monster that tormented him, was all-consuming. It was a visceral, overpowering urge that left no room for doubt or hesitation.

She stepped forward, a predator ready to strike, driven by a bond that was as much a part of her as her own heart. In that moment, she was more than just a dhampir; she was a living inferno, ready to burn, and kill, and destroy anything that threatened her people.

As the blood continued to seep from the deep gash in her arm, Alex observed something extraordinary. Instead of dripping to the ground, it began to congeal, hanging suspended in the air before her. Intrigued, she turned her wrist, watching as the crimson liquid defied gravity, floating and swirling as if endowed with its own consciousness.

The blood moved in a mesmerizing dance, forming intricate patterns that ebbed and flowed. It shimmered in the dim light, a living tapestry of droplets joining and separating. It was as if her life force had taken on a spectral form, responding to her inner turmoil.

Mattias, preoccupied with tormenting Lucas, failed to notice this strange phenomenon. Acting on a deep, instinctual level, Alex flexed her hand into a fist. The blood reacted to her need, coalescing into a solid shape. She swiped her arm downward, flicking the blood below her, willing it to be something more.

Before her eyes, the blood transformed, flowing and twisting into the form of a sword. It was shorter in length than Talon but no less menacing. The edges of the blade undulated in waves, each movement creating jagged, serrated edges that vibrated with a life of their own. Spikes protruded along the blade's spine, giving it a savage, primal appearance. It was a living weapon, a manifestation of her rage.

Holding this newly formed sword, Alex felt a surge of power within her. Wasting no time, Alex lunged at Mattias once more. The child vampire, caught off guard by her sudden aggression, barely had time to look up before her blade made contact. She landed a swift slash across his small chest, the blood sword slicing through the air with lethal precision. Mattias leaped back, a snarl contorting his young face.

Lucas, momentarily freed from Mattias's mental torture, collapsed to the floor, gasping for breath. The victory, however, was short-lived as Mattias quickly regained his composure.

"You embrace your vampire nature well," Mattias taunted, his voice dripping with malice. "It suits you, little dhampir."

Panting from exertion, Alex shot back, "Better a monster than whatever twisted tiny thing you are."

Mattias's face stretched into another wide snarl. Still oblivious to the true nature of her weapon, he lashed out with his metal whip again before Alex could defend herself. Two quick strikes landed across Alex's face and shoulder, leaving searing lines of pain. She cursed, stumbling back. The loss of blood was beginning to take its toll, and her movements grew sluggish.

Overwhelmed by desperation and driven by instinct rather than any conscious plan, Alex acted. With a raw, almost primal resolve, she turned the hilt of her blood sword against her other arm. She didn't think; she just acted, drawing another deep slash across her skin. As the blood flowed freely, a sense of urgency overcame her. She wasn't sure what was happening to her or what she was doing, but deep down, something compelled her.

Mattias, misunderstanding her intent, sneered, "Trying to kill yourself, dhampir? I won't let you escape that easily."

Alex looked up at him, a fierce grin spreading across her face. In the reflection of Mattias's eyes, she saw a fire blazing in her own, a mirror of Lucas's magical gaze.

With a flick of her left arm, she formed a twin to her first living blade. The two swords pulsed with her life force, beating steady with each heartbeat, though she didn't know how long she could continue with so little blood left in her.

Facing the twin blood swords, Mattias's demeanor shifted

profoundly. The once confident, almost gleefully cruel expression on his childlike face began to falter. His eyes now flickered with the first signs of uncertainty. He took an involuntary step back, his gaze darting between the glowing blades in Alex's hands.

For the first time, a hint of genuine fear crept into Mattias's features. He swallowed hard, a subtle but telling sign that Alex's transformation and newfound ferocity had unnerved him.

Her life force draining away, she tapped into her rage, fear, and in a display of raw, unbridled power, the blood swords in Alex's hands suddenly ignited. The newly formed flames engulfed the blades in an intense, fiery glow.

Simultaneously, the blood droplets suspended in the air around her began to crystallize, frozen in time. They glittered like rubies caught in a spider's web, each droplet perfectly preserved in its own moment. It was as if the very essence of her anger and fear had combined with Lucas's magic to create this petrified firestorm.

Drawing upon the remnants of her strength, Alex lunged at Mattias with a desperate yell. The fire from the swords seemed to fuel her, just as they drained her, lending her movements a ferocity and speed that was downright otherworldly. Each step she took left a trail of flickering embers in the air.

As she closed on Mattias, the frozen blood droplets began to shudder and vibrate. And the air itself seemed to thrum with the power she wielded.

His eyes widened in frozen surprise when she brought both swords down on his neck in quick succession. The left blade cut through his defenses, burying deep, while the right completed the execution, severing his head cleanly from his shoulders.

Alex stumbled to keep her feet under her, looking over at

the now tiny still form of Mattias. It stayed where it was on the ground, and Alex held her breath. He couldn't possibly survive decapitation, she thought to herself.

Then, after a few breaths, the body started to crackle and burn, before disintegrating completely in a cloud of dust. Her deep exhale of relief was a hoarse cough, as she choked on his remains. She couldn't quite believe that it was actually over and that they had all survived. Attacking a master-level vampire who was awake was practically suicide in the most painful way possible, a reality they had all almost experienced.

As an almost unbearable fatigue set upon her, she barely noticed that the fire on her swords was turning against her. The blood continued to pull, and the flames grew hotter. She could actually feel the heat now. Even worse, the flames started to crawl up her arms with a voracious hunger. They licked at her skin, a fiery embrace that threatened to consume her entirely. Alex, drained of all strength, had nothing left to fight this new danger. She wouldn't have known how to stop it even if she did. She was done.

Her legs gave way, and she fell to her knees, her body no longer able to support her. In the distance, she heard Izzie's voice, fraught with panic. "Alex!" A blurry image of Izzie rushing toward her flickered at the edge of her vision.

But before Izzie could reach her, Otto grabbed her, his arms wrapping around her waist and pulling her back, away from the inferno that Alex had become. Alex heard Izzie's screams and sobs fading into the background, her friend's anguish a distant echo in her ears.

She knew her time was ending; she had literally burnt herself out. But it didn't matter. The others would survive.

Then, unexpectedly, she felt strong, cool arms encircle her chest. Her eyes, too heavy to keep open, fluttered shut, and the unbearable heat began to recede. Eventually, the blood swords in her hands liquefied, their fiery essence extinguishing as they splashed onto the floor in a sizzling puddle.

The last thing Alex was conscious of before succumbing to the darkness was Lucas's voice, laced with desperation and something deeper. "Alex, No! Don't leave me. I... I..." His words trailed off as she drifted into unconsciousness, his voice the final tether to the world she was leaving behind.

CHAPTER 31

ALEX'S RETURN TO CONSCIOUSNESS was gradual, her senses slowly reawakening. The first thing she noticed was the sterile, antiseptic smell that filled her nostrils, a scent unmistakably associated with hospitals. Her eyes cracked open, revealing a bland, white ceiling above her. The room was bathed in the harsh glow of fluorescent lights, creating a stark contrast with the dimness of the basement where she last remembered being.

In the background, the soft murmur of people talking and moving echoed through the walls—the familiar sounds of a busy hospital. Nurses and doctors conversed in hushed tones, their words blending into a soothing, indistinct hum that provided a backdrop to her thoughts.

She was lying in a bed, the sheets crisp and clean against her skin. An IV drip was hooked up to her arm, its clear tube snaking down from a bag of saline solution. Her hospital gown was standard-issue, pale blue, and slightly scratchy, offering only modest comfort and privacy. It felt foreign against her skin, a far cry from the battle gear she had been wearing.

She felt the gentle tug of bandages wrapped around her wrists, face, and shoulder and looked down, only to inwardly flinch at the reminder of the injuries she had sustained.

As Alex lay there, taking in her surroundings, she tried to piece together the events that had led her to this place, the memories slowly knitting themselves back together in her mind.

Her awareness grew, and she became conscious of a comforting weight snuggled against her side. She turned her head slightly, her movements still sluggish, and there was Argo, the little stinker, curled up on the bed beside her. She breathed a sigh of relief at his furry presence, taking whatever sense of comfort and normalcy she could get amidst the sterile hospital environment.

Argo's eyes were closed, his breathing steady and rhythmic, a sign of deep relaxation. His coat was soft and warm against her skin. The dog seemed at ease, as if his sole purpose at that moment was to be there for Alex, providing silent support.

The sight of him, so peaceful and content, brought a faint smile to Alex's lips. Despite the pain and disorientation, his presence was a balm to her frayed nerves. It was a small reminder of the life she had just fought so hard to keep.

The room, previously submerged in a tense silence, stirred to life with Izzie's hushed exclamation. "Oh my god, she's awake," she said. "She's finally awake!"

Before Alex could fully process the scene, she felt the firm, reassuring grip of Izzie's hand clasping hers. Izzie's eyes, usually so bright and confident, were red and puffy. Her makeup, typically flawless, was smudged, giving her a weary, disheveled appearance. Even her fresh clothes bore the rumpled look of being slept in.

"Izzie?" Alex's voice was hoarse, a rough whisper barely escaping her throat.

"Oh, hun!" Izzie swiped at her eyes. "We were so worried about you. It was touch there and go for a bit."

"What?" Alex asked, her brow furrowing in confusion. Her body usually healed quickly; hospital stays were foreign to her despite years on the front lines against the supernatural. "We?"

"You lost so much blood," Izzie explained, her voice laced with concern. "And you're going to have to tell me what happened. I was, um, not exactly conscious for most of it there at the end."

"Izz!" Alex sighed wearily.

"Fine, fine." Izzie waved her hands in a gesture of defeat. "But you lost almost as much blood as a person can lose and not die. You had burns all over your body, but um, those cleared up pretty fast, and your breathing... it was like your lungs were singed."

Izzie paused, her lips quivering. "Honey, I thought I might lose you." The tears broke free, streaming down her cheeks. "I can't go through that again, Alex. Don't you ever do that to me again."

Alex watched, eyes wide. "Oh, Izzie. I'm sorry," Alex murmured. She had always loved Izzie like a big sister or even like a mother that she never had, but she'd never thought Izzie felt so deeply about her. She didn't think the woman could after losing her own child.

"Boss, oh, thank Lucifer. You're up." Argo's voice echoed in her mind. He nuzzled into the crook of her hip, and Alex freed her other hand, gently stroking Argo's smooth fur.

Looking from Argo to Izzie, she saw an ocean of affection and concern in their eyes. "Oh, you guys. I love you."

Izzie, her face brightening with joy, stroked Alex's hair, while Alex continued to pet Argo, savoring the simple pleasure of their presence. It was moments like these, she realized, that truly signified victory.

"How on Earth did you get Argo in here? Seems a bit against the rules," Alex asked.

Argo let out a yip, feigning shock at the suggestion of rule-breaking.

"Well, hun," Izzie chuckled, "apparently, Argo already had all the necessary paperwork for a service dog. He showed up at my door, insisting on coming along, and just breezed right in. Another corgi miracle, I suppose."

"Argo, I didn't even know you could leave the house," Alex said.

Argo merely scowled at her, giving her a disdainful side-eye.

"Well, either way, thank you," Alex said, leaning forward to plant a soft kiss on his head. In response, his little furry back-side started wiggling, eliciting another smile from Alex.

As the laughter and warmth continued to fill the room, a sudden interruption came in the form of a soft yet distinctly deep cough from the corner. The sound, resonant in its basso quality, immediately captured everyone's attention.

Alex felt a surge of anticipation. For a brief, hopeful second, her heart raced at the thought of seeing a certain raven-haired warlock. However, as she turned towards the source of the cough, her expression shifted to a slight frown. It wasn't Lucas, but rather the looming figure of Otto making his way toward her bed, his expression composed and unreadable.

"Oh! Otto! Get over here. You're a part of this victory cele-bration too, even if you're always grumpy," Izzie teased, waving him closer.

Otto positioned himself at the end of the bed, crossing his arms in front of his chest. "You're alive. This is good."

Alex exchanged a glance with Izzie, and they both burst into laughter.

"This is funny?" Otto asked.

His deadpan expression only fueled their laughter. Despite the odds they had faced, they were together, alive, and that was something worth celebrating.

Izzie stepped closer to the end of the bed where Otto stood and hit him with a playful nudge of her hip against his leg. "Hey, big guy. We're just enjoying your skill at understatement," she said with a gentle tease, her hand reaching out to give his forearm a reassuring squeeze. "That was a close one. Closer than I've ever been."

Otto's rigid posture eased slightly at Izzie's touch, his arms uncrossing as he allowed a brief moment of ease. However, his expression soon turned serious again, his eyes narrowing with concern. "But how are we alive? The warlock was acting awfully twitchy once he woke up, and I haven't even seen him for the last day. I still have questions for him, some very pointed questions," he said, his fists flexing instinctively.

Alex, hearing this, turned to Izzie with wide, alarmed eyes. "Izzie, what happened after I passed out?"

"Oh hun, I'm not even sure if 'passed out' is the right word. I think you may have, um, died a little," Izzie said hesitantly.

"What?!" Alex squeaked.

"Yeah, um, I didn't come to until it was practically over. Before that..." Izzie shook her head as if trying to dispel the harrowing images. "It was bad. But I opened my eyes right there at the end when you took his head with the Twins, but they were on fire. Or at least it looked like the Twins," she added, her voice trailing off in confusion.

Alex didn't respond immediately to Izzie's implied question. Instead, she prompted, "Then what?"

Izzie continued, her voice growing softer, "Then you stumbled back, and the fire crawled up from the swords and over your arms until your entire body was engulfed. It was terrifying. I tried to get to you, to save you, but, but..."

The room fell into a heavy silence, the weight of Izzie's words hanging in the air.

Otto's gruff voice carried a rare hint of emotion. "I grabbed you and pulled you back. There was nothing you could do but throw your life away," he said, looking at Izzie.

Alex smiled faintly, touched by the concern in Otto's voice. It seemed Izzie's influence had extended to the stoic giant during their brief time together.

"Then what?" she asked, her voice still weak.

"Well, then Lucas pulled himself up from the ground and threw himself at you," Izzie recounted. "I don't know exactly what happened, but it was like he pulled the flames from you and into himself."

"What?" Alex's concern spiked. "Is he okay?"

"Yeah, yeah, hun. He was fine. A bit shaken, but I don't think fire hurts that boy much, or at all."

Otto interjected with a grunt, his voice dripping with disdain. "Destruction magic," he muttered, as if the term left a bad taste in his mouth.

"Not now, Otto," Izzie snapped. Surprisingly, Otto quieted down.

Izzie continued, her gaze distant. "He smothered the fire on you, but you were still out, looking grayer by the minute. He... he basically lost it then. Started screaming, bellowing like a lost soul."

Alex listened, her heart pounding.

"I'm not quite sure how to describe what happened next," Izzie said, her voice trembling slightly. "But he reached into his own chest, and when his hand came out, it was... red and drippy. Then he slammed his hand down onto your chest and told you to fucking live, 'you stupid, reckless woman.'"

Alex lay there, trying to piece together the chaotic fragments of the story, her mind racing at the thought of Lucas's desperate act to save her. The realization of how close she had come to death and the lengths Lucas had gone to bring her back was both terrifying and profoundly moving.

Alex's hands moved to check under her hospital gown, searching her chest for any sign of injury or anomaly. Her fingers shook slightly as she lifted the fabric, peering down with bated breath. To her immense relief, she found the skin unmarked. A soft, almost inaudible "Oh, thank god" escaped her lips as she let the gown fall back into place.

Looking at Izzie, Alex asked, "But he was okay? That sounds pretty risky, whatever he did."

"Oh, he passed out too, right after," Izzie replied casually, but upon noticing Alex's worried expression, she quickly added, "But he was fine by the time we got to the hospital. Just a few scrapes and spider bites." She unconsciously rubbed her arm, where a large bandage covered what was likely a spider bite wound of her own.

Alex processed this information, brows scrunching. "Oh, well, okay. Then where is he?" Her gaze flitted around the room as if expecting to find Lucas lurking in a corner or seated quietly by her bedside. The absence of his presence was suddenly more pronounced, a silent void that begged to be filled.

Otto's expression had settled into a deep frown, a clear sign of his discomfort with the situation. Izzie was fidgeting, tapping her foot nervously on the floor, while Argo let out a low, warning growl. Yet, none of them seemed willing to answer her question.

"Where is he?" Alex's voice rose, touched with both anger and panic. They had endured so much together, and the thought of being separated now was unbearable.

Glancing down, she noticed the faint outlines of the bond still present, trailing off into the unknown. A small sigh of relief escaped her lips; the connection was still there. Focusing, she could almost catch Lucas's scent, as if he were nearby. But the only emotion she could discern was a cold, iron resolve. What the hell was that man up to now?

"Izzie, I swear on the stars that I will steal and bury all of your guns all over the city in the dirtiest places I can find if you don't tell me where that fool man has gotten to right this second!"

Izzie let out a heavy sigh, her shoulders slumping slightly. "I'm sorry, hun," she said with genuine regret in her voice. Reaching into the back pocket of her jeans, she pulled out an envelope. Walking back to the front of the bed, she continued, "He gave me this yesterday after the doctors said you were going to be fine. He said to give it to you after you woke up."

With a face full of confusion and the first traces of hurt flickering in her eyes, Alex took the envelope. She held it tentatively on her lap, staring at it as if it were a puzzle she couldn't quite solve.

"I think we should give you some space," Izzie said softly, turning to Otto. She reached for him and gently guided the large man out of the room.

As Otto and Izzie left, the room fell into a quiet. Alex was alone with the envelope, the weight of its unknown contents pressing heavily on her. She took a deep breath, bracing herself for whatever message Lucas had left her.

Dear Alex,

Sorry seems like a small word for what I need to say, but it's where I have to start. Coming to Chicago, meeting you—it changed everything for me, but it also put you right in harm's way. If I hadn't shown up, you wouldn't have had to face that horror. That's on me.

Then, when I saw you dying on the ground in Mattias's lair, I thought for sure I would die with you. I didn't even know I could feel so connected to anybody after the life I've led, let alone to someone as special as you. I didn't even know I had a soul anymore, but seeing you there, I realized I would give anything, even a piece of my very heart, if it meant saving you. I hope with time, the fragment I left with you will integrate seamlessly, so you won't even notice it there. It was the only way I knew to keep your blood pumping, though I regret the violation and the imposition of carrying a part of someone like me with you forever.

I'm sorry I couldn't be there when you woke up. I knew if I had stayed, I would have taken the coward's path again and never have left. But if that had happened, I would have eventually drawn more of the many enemies I've made over the years to your doorstep, some of which make Mattias seem gentle. I couldn't do that to you and the family you've built around yourself.

I need to finally stop running and face my past. If there is even the slightest chance that what Mattias said was true, I have to find my sister and get her out before they turn her. I should have protected her from the beginning instead of believing Mattias's lies. Instead, she's had it even worse than I did. I failed her. But I have to try now. And if she can't be saved, I need to stop her from hurting more people and stop the Master once and for all. I think that's what you would do.

Please don't come looking for me. You won't find me. And it would break me if they found you. Even if the "bond" is a fairy tale, getting to meet you and be with you for even such a short time, well, it was the best week of my life. You are the bravest, strongest, kindest woman I have ever encountered. Remember, it's our choices, not our origins, that define us. You've inspired me to make the right choices, at long last.

I wish I could have stayed and loved you. But you deserve someone who already walks in the light, like you do.

Yours,

Lucas

Alex's whole body shook as she slowly lowered Lucas's letter onto her lap. Tears streamed down her cheeks in silent waves, and her grip on the letter trembled. Then, as soon as she released her grip, the letter burst into small flames that quickly consumed it until there was nothing but ash.

"That asshole!"

Argo, jumping up in surprise at the unexpected conflagration, looked at her with concern. "Boss?"

"He left, Argo. He just left. No goodbye, no chance to understand what's between us, just a letter that goes up in flames before I can even process his words."

"I'm sorry, Alex," Argo said, resting his chin on her lap, offering what comfort he could. "Some people need to walk through the darkness before they can find the light."

"I would have walked it with him!" Alex's voice rose, shrill with emotion. "We were supposed to be in this together; at least, that's what your silly prophecy said."

"Boss, I don't think Lucas believed in the prophecy. Are you saying you do?"

Alex, taking deep breaths to steady herself, was unsure how to respond. Her thoughts, though, were interrupted by Argo's next question, which seemed to read her mind.

"What happened when you killed the little... monster anyway?"

Alex pondered for a moment, the memories of the event still feeling surreal. Before confiding in Argo, she glanced around to ensure Otto wasn't within earshot.

"I'm not entirely sure, buddy. But it was like I could channel Lucas's power—the flames and the time manipulation. And the weirdest part was the blood."

"Oh?" Argo's eyes were fixed on her intently.

She could sense he was anticipating her next words. "Well, I was cut up pretty bad, and the blood was flowing. Then it was like the blood became a living weapon, an extension of my will. It solidified, forming blades in my hands that were sharper, lighter, and faster than anything I've ever wielded."

Argo inhaled sharply, his expression a mixture of concern and awe. "Well, fuck."

"Argo?" Alex said through clenched teeth. "What does it mean?"

When he looked up at her, his eyes were wide with a fear, yet there was a lift in his eyebrows and a slight, proud tilt to his chin. "It means a lot of things are about to change."

Recalling Argo's earlier comments about the prophecy before the final battle, Alex exhaled a deep sigh of trepidation. "Well, fuck," she echoed.

"But for now, you probably don't need to remember that part. It's not quite time," he said, twitching his nose.

"Remember what?" she asked, trying to recall the last few seconds of their conversation.

"Nothing boss, no big deal. Just focus on getting better."

As Alex was about to press him for more, the door opened, and Izzie re-entered the room. Her expression was a blend of concern and pity, her hands nervously wringing at her waist.

"Hun?" Izzie stepped closer to the bed, her eyes searching Alex's face. "You okay? What did the letter say?"

Exhaling deeply, Alex grappled with the storm of emotions stirred by Lucas's departure and the weight of his letter. The temptation to chase after him, fueled by their bond, was strong, yet she was torn.

"Oh, Izz," she said, a lone tear trailing down her cheek. "I'm tired, hurting, heartbroken, and terrified that the man I probably love is about to throw his life away on some harebrained suicide mission to redeem himself."

Izzie's lips pursed into a sad frown.

"Honey, he is not yours to keep or your responsibility. If he wants to try to do some good with his life, that's his choice. You need to respect it and move on."

Alex choked back a sob. "What if I can't let go? What if he dies?"

"My love, we are sometimes given burdens in this life that seem too hard to bear." Izzie spoke softly, her voice resonating with her own experiences. "But bear them we must. The only other choice is to give up. And you, my sweet girl, you do not give up. It is not in your nature. So, if the worst comes to pass, you will bear it, and you will find your way out of the pain, eventually, and you'll be stronger for it. Because that's who you are, Alex Bain. And that's what I taught you."

Alex looked at Izzie, seeing the depths of her pain and the path that she had walked to find her way once more. If Izzie had not chosen to walk that path, Alex would have never met her. She wouldn't be the person she was today. She may have become the monster she'd always feared she'd become. She owed everything to Izzie. Whatever happened, she would get through it because of and for Izzie.

"Thank you, my friend," Alex said, leaning her head against Izzie's. "I love you."

"I love you too," Izzie replied, lifting her head to plant a gentle kiss on Alex's forehead. In that moment, Alex felt a sense of resolution settle within her. No matter what lay ahead, she knew she would face it with the strength and courage Izzie had helped her find.

Alex was moments away from asking about her potential discharge from the hospital when the door suddenly flew open again. In a burst, Steve swept into the room, his usual slacks and sweater vest ensemble doing little to contain his animated demeanor. Close behind him followed Otto.

"Alex!" her boss exclaimed. "Oh, thank God. You're okay. You had me worried, Supply."

Alex and Izzie exchanged a puzzled glance as they looked over at Steve and then at Otto, who simply shrugged in response.

"When you didn't show up for work the second day, it was so unlike you. And then you didn't answer your phone! I tried your emergency contact, an Isabella Bliss, I think? No answer from her either," Steve explained, his hands gesturing expressively.

Izzie looked up, a hint of guilt in her expression. "Oh, sorry about that. Hi, I'm Sergeant Isabella Bliss, CPD. I've been here with Alex. Haven't really been checking my phone."

"Oh, Sergeant," Steve said, his voice taking on a tone of respect. "Of course, of course. I didn't mean to imply anything. I was just concerned."

"It's okay. We've all been anxious," Izzie replied smoothly.

"Then!" Steve continued, his voice rising with excitement, "I got a call from Otto of all people," he said, gesturing towards the large man, who offered another nonchalant shrug.

"He said you had been attacked by some criminal on your way home from the pharmacy the day you called in sick."

Alex blinked in surprise, processing Steve's words. The cover story was plausible. She glanced at Otto, a silent question in her eyes. Otto's presence backing up the fiction, added an unexpected layer of credibility to the tale. It seemed they had all conspired to keep the real events under wraps, a decision that left Alex grateful.

When Alex didn't respond, Izzie took over the narrative with ease. "Yes, sir. She was attacked by an unknown subject in the parking lot outside the Walgreens. We are still looking for the assailant, but no leads so far."

"My god!" Steve exclaimed, his expression one of shock.

"That is terrifying, Alex." His gaze then fell on the bandages, and his eyes widened even more. "Did they use a knife?"

Alex glanced at Izzie, who subtly nodded and then she responded with a croak, "Yeah, but I'll be fine. Just needed a refill."

"A refill?" Steve looked confused.

"Um, of blood," Alex said, trying to lighten the mood. Seeing Steve's hand fly to his mouth with a shudder, she quickly added, "Sorry, bad joke. I don't do sympathy very well."

"Oh, ha, ha," Steve responded. "Let's just keep that kind of joke out of the office, shall we?"

"Of course, boss," Alex replied.

Steve rolled his eyes. "For the hundredth time, do not call me—" He stopped mid-sentence, looked at her grinning, and then conceded, "Okay, that was an acceptable joke."

He then turned more serious. "Well, I'm glad to see you're doing okay. Please take all the time you need to recover before coming back."

Alex nodded. "I think I should be able to start working remotely by Friday. I don't want to fall too far behind, especially with the project. I know a lot of people are counting on us."

Steve shook his head. "Alex, don't worry about the project right now. Focus on your health. Besides, we're facing a slight delay anyway."

"Oh?"

"Yes, the lead consultant, Lucas, I think his name was, submitted his resignation yesterday. They'll need to find a replacement to bring up to speed before we can move forward."

Alex felt a pang of sadness at the mention of Lucas. "Oh, um, yeah, that makes sense."

"It does?" Steve asked.

"Yeah, I mean, that they'd have to replace him. I wonder

why he left," she covered quickly. "I hope the Family isn't too disappointed."

Otto, who had been silent until now, let out a small grunt. "Mr. Von Mistelweig is very pleased with the progress thus far and looks forward to continuing the project." He was clearly not talking about the Supply Chain project.

"Oh! Really? Well, that is fortuitous. You must have made quite the impression in Munich, Alex," Steve said with a hint of admiration.

"I guess so," Alex replied. The complexities of her involvement with the Von Mistelweigs weighed on her mind.

"Either way, Alex will need plenty of time to recover before she can work on any new projects!" Izzie quickly interjected, directing her statement at Otto.

Argo, from his comfortable spot under Alex's hand, gave a low, affirmative growl.

"Of course," Otto said.

"Oh my! There's a dog in the bed!" Steve suddenly exclaimed, his eyes wide with surprise. "How did I not notice there was a dog in the bed? I assume he is yours, Alex?"

"Yes, Steve. This is Argo, my number one guy," Alex said, affectionately rubbing his head as he settled back into a relaxed pose.

"Oh, well, nice to meet you, Argo. Please take good care of Alex. We need her back pronto!"

Argo responded with an eye roll as if to say, "Obviously."

"Did he just roll his eyes at me?" Steve asked, somewhat baffled.

"He's a unique dog," Alex confirmed, a small smile playing on her lips.

"Yes, well, I'm glad to see you're getting better. I need to get back to the office. We're doing the awards for the Operations

Challenge today, and I need to present the winners their trophies," Steve said, already halfway out the door.

"Of course. Wish I could be there. I'll be back soon, though."

With that, Steve left the room as quickly as he had entered.

Once he was gone, Izzie looked around the room and asked, "So, what now?"

Before Alex could respond, Otto spoke up. "I will be staying in Chicago to monitor the situation and see if the Master makes another move or sends more agents."

"Really?" Izzie asked, her mouth quirking up in a small smile.

"Yes," Otto affirmed. "Mr. Von Mistelweig is interested in continuing the partnership with you, Alex, and with you as well, Sergeant Bliss. Plus, there's a chance to intercept the Master if he ventures out."

"And that's it?" Alex asked, her tone laced with suspicion.

"And," Otto continued, "he's intrigued by how you and a single warlock managed to defeat an awake master-level vampire on your own." He paused for a moment, then added, "You know, it would be easier if you just told us. Haven't we earned your trust?"

Alex let out a heavy sigh. "How about this? As soon as I better understand it myself, and if you're still part of our team, I'll share."

Otto's expression tightened briefly in frustration, but he eventually shrugged in acceptance. "Fine. That's fair. With the warlock not being here, things are simpler anyway. And to be honest, I don't mind staying." His gaze shifted to Izzie, who responded with a slight blush.

"Okay, so we continue as usual," Alex concluded. "Keeping this city safe and seeing if we can trust each other."

Izzie laughed, her mood lightening. "You do have a way with words, Alex."

Otto grunted again.

Argo chimed in with an affirmative yip.

Despite the uncertainties and looming challenges, they had formed a rare team, each member contributing their strengths and quirks. As Alex lay there, enveloped in the support of her friends and allies, a renewed sense of purpose welled within her. She would face the future with them, keeping Chicago safe and unraveling the mysteries of her supposed powers and destiny.

Yet, amidst this resolve, Alex couldn't shake off a lingering apprehension about the prophecy. She felt there was something she should remember, playing on the edges of her mind. The words echoed, a reminder of a fate that seemed both inevitable and unfathomable.

And just as importantly, there was Lucas. His absence was a void, an unfinished chapter in her life that she couldn't leave behind. Though stretched by distance and circumstance, her connection to him remained a constant presence in her heart. She was determined to reunite with him, to explore the bond that had only just begun to reveal its true depth. Lucas had walked away to protect her, but she knew their story was far from over.

The fight against the darkness was ongoing, and Alex Bain was ready to face it head-on with her friends, her found family, and, hopefully, with Lucas by her side.

Acknowledgments

Huge thanks to the best "street team" a new author could ask for, the brave souls who endured draft after draft and never ran out of patience or insight.

Shoutout to my husband and daughter, who put up with my laser focus (read: obsession) and the madness of my writing sprints. Your support meant I never wrote alone, even if I was often lost in Alex Bain's world more than our own.

To my family—Mom, Dad, my brother, and my sisters-in-law—the original beta squad and my most enthusiastic sideline coaches: cheers for not using my manuscripts as coasters.

Kudos to my day job crew, the best damned supply chain team at the best damned candy company in the world. Your cheers kept me going, even when Mexico sugarcane was practically on fire.

And to my fellow indie authors: What a tribe! Bookstagram became my classroom, and your wisdom my curriculum. Couldn't have made it to 'The End' without you all.

Here's to late nights, endless edits, and the sweet victory of finally sharing 'Death and Sweet Temptations' with the world. You're all part of this story.

TO BE CONTINUED...

Stay sharp, readers. Alex Bain's journey through the perilous and passionate streets of Chicago is far from over. The veil between worlds has only just begun to flutter, and the next chapter promises more danger, more heartache, and temptations even sweeter and deadlier than before.

THE ADVENTURE THICKENS IN THE UPCOMING BOOK:

The tableau was like nothing Alex Bain had ever seen. And given her usual nightly encounters with the violent and bizarre, that was really saying something.

Behind her, the unmistakable sound of retching broke the night's silence. It was probably one of the newbies assigned to the perimeter, she mused. There was always at least one who hadn't seen a dead body yet. In this case, though, she couldn't blame them. Keeping her own stomach in check was proving unexpectedly difficult.

Across the alley, two detectives hovered over a laptop, their faces ghostly in the screen's glow. One gestured animatedly, pointing to a map displayed on the screen, their conversation a muted buzz in the background.

A firm grip closed on Alex's shoulder, grounding her to the moment. "You ok, hun?" The familiar voice of Sergeant Isabelle "Izzie" Bliss cut through the thick air.

The tableau was like nothing Alex Bain had ever seen and given her usual nightly encounters with the violent and bizarre, that was really saying something.

Behind her, the unmistakable sound of retching broke the night's silence. It was probably one of the newbies assigned to the perimeter, she mused. There was always at least one who hadn't seen a dead body yet. In this case, though, she couldn't blame them. Keeping her own stomach in check was proving unexpectedly difficult.

Across the alley, two detectives hovered over a laptop, their faces ghostly in the screen's glow. One gestured animatedly, pointing to a map displayed on the screen, their conversation a muted buzz in the background.

A firm grip closed on Alex's shoulder, grounding her to the moment. "You ok, hun?" The familiar voice of Sergeant Isabelle "Izzie" Bliss cut through the thick air.

A few feet away, a crime scene photographer snapped rapid-fire photos at nearby blood spatter, the camera's flash intermittently illuminating the grotesque carnival laid out before them.

"Yeah, Izzie," Alex managed, her voice steady despite the turmoil churning inside her. She motioned towards the monstrous display sprawled out in the dim light.

Exhaling, she turned to look at her oldest friend, whose olive complexion was also turning a bit green, despite over twenty years on the force and working hundreds of these less than normal cases with Alex. Whether it was from the sight or the stench of the steaming, decomposing flesh before them, she couldn't tell. Their gazes met briefly in shared disbelief.

Near the entrance of the alley, a group of uniformed officers clustered, their heads bowed in a tight circle. A sudden burst of hushed, urgent conversation drifted towards her, quickly stifled as one of them glanced over at Alex.

"Just when I thought things were calming down after last October, this happens." Her hand instinctively moved to her heart where Lucas had literally placed a piece of his own as she lay dying. Memories of her final showdown with Mattias flooded her mind.

Her friends were all down and dying, gasping in the acrid smoke from Otto's explosives. While Mattias, that horrid vampire in the skin of a child, stood before her, a sinister smile playing on his lips.

"Time to end this, little dhampir," he taunted.

Standing over this fresh kill site with Izzie at her side, her heart rate involuntarily rose. It was as if she was simultaneously in both moments – the terrifying past and the grim present.

In a swift maneuver, his hand shot out with that whip-like weapon to deliver a blow that sent Alex staggering. As pain radiated through her body, crimson droplets spilled from her arm to the soot-covered ground below.

"Hun, you ok?" she heard Izzie's voice from somewhere in the murky distance.

Alex, drawing on her last reserves of strength, feinted and then struck, her red-bladed katana, Talon, slicing into Mattias's flesh.

"Hun?" Izzie asked again, somehow closer now. Alex could feel the squeeze of Izzie's fingers on her arm.

The vampire's scream was a mix of pain and rage. But had it been Talon? Or something else? For the thousandth time, she tried to remember.

Her breathing came faster, and she could now feel Izzie shaking her in earnest. "Alex! Snap out of it, love!"

Summoning every ounce of her willpower, she sprang up, fiery blades in hand, and plunged the swords into Mattias's heart. The vampire's body stiffened, a look of disbelief on his face.

Then, Alex blinked, her vision clearing as she found herself staring into Izzie's bright emerald eyes, full of concern and just inches from her own.

"Alex!" Izzie's hands were firmly on her shoulders, grounding her. Slowly, Alex's gaze sharpened, meeting her friend's eyes, and Izzie's grip loosened. "You back with us?"

Around them, the crime scene continued its silent, grim ballet. A couple of nearby officers cast discreet glances in their direction, their expressions a mix of curiosity and wariness. One of them, a younger officer, nudged his colleague, nodding subtly towards Alex and Izzie, before turning back to his work with a shrug.

"Yeah, Izzie. I'm back," Alex nodded, her voice a soft murmur. She reached up, self-consciously adjusting her ponytail with shaking hands, a faint blush coloring her cheeks. "Um, sorry about that."

"Don't worry about it," Izzie said, letting a warmth that was just for Alex creep into her expression. "We've all been there. And this," she waved around her, "This is some shit."

"What the fuck even is this?"

"It's none of your goddamn business, is what it is." A gruff, deep voice sliced through the air from the other side of the body.

Alex and Izzie's attention snapped away from the macabre scene to a tall, uniformed man bulldozing his way to them through a cluster of crime scene analysts. His hair was cut short and practical, peppered with hints of gray that suggested more battles than he'd care to count. His sharp eyes were like cold chips of ice, surveying the scene with a clinical detachment that bordered on disinterest.

"Lieutenant Moody," Izzie acknowledged him, her voice neutral.

"I may be new here," Moody growled as he closed the distance, standing toe-to-toe with them. "But I know it's not standard procedure to allow either disgraced traffic cops or civilians into active crime scenes." His arms hung loosely at his sides, fingers twitching subtly, as if eager to draw his service weapon.

Lieutenant Moody's gaze then dropped to the body, his eyes widening ever so slightly – the only indication that it affected him. Then, his eyes lifted to Alex, sweeping over her with an overt, appraising look. A sneer curled his lips. "No matter how pretty they may be."

Alex, unfazed by the crass dismissiveness she'd often encountered from high-powered CEOs during her day job, met his gaze squarely and held it. And when he broke eye contact first, the corners of her mouth twitched upward triumphantly.

From Alex's point of view, Lieutenant Moody was a figure straight out of a cop drama, but with less charm and more grit. She wondered briefly if he had a stick hidden somewhere in the depths of his immaculate dress blues causing him to stand so straight.

"My apologies, Lieutenant, if I've overstepped," she said, her tone laced with steel. "You're new to Chicago, so let me clarify. I have a longstanding relationship with the CPD as a consultant for," she paused, pressing her lips together, "let's say, the more difficult to classify cases. And Sergeant Bliss here, despite the shift in her duties since leading Special Investigations, remains my liaison."

As she sized him up, Alex couldn't help but pity Lieutenant Moody. He was a textbook cop thrown into a story that defied the conventional plot, facing a chapter where the rules no longer applied.

Lieutenant Moody's stance shifted as he folded his arms, reassessing Alex with a new wariness. He seemed to recalibrate his opinion of her, recognizing perhaps that she was not someone to be written off lightly. "Be that as it may, Miss Bain—"

"Ms. Bain," she corrected him.

"Ms. Bain," he amended begrudgingly. "Regardless, the CPD does not require your services. Neither of you. And you can consider that as standing for future cases now that I'm in charge."

"Lieutenant!" Izzie interjected, her voice strained with frustration.

"No. Sergeant Bliss, Ms. Bain," he insisted, his voice rising. "Leave the premises now."

Izzie's hands balled into fists at her sides, her body taut with contained anger as she remained rooted with her gaze locked in a silent standoff with the Lieutenant.

"Now!" he barked, his authority unwavering. "Or I'll charge you both with obstruction of justice."

Alex gently squeezed Izzie's arm, giving her a nod towards the exit. "Let's go, Izzie," she said calmly. "They'll be knocking on our door for help soon enough, especially with this one."

She flashed the Lieutenant a cheeky wink and spun on her heel, long blonde ponytail bouncing behind her as she strode confidently out of the alleyway with Izzie close on her heels.

The scene of untold violence now behind her, Izzie muttered a string of curses under her breath, "Maldita sea, ese estúpido imbécil!"

Alex couldn't help but smile, her chuckle barely audible. She knew well enough the storm that Lieutenant Moody had called down upon himself.

Reaching her well-worn Jeep, Alex popped the trunk and carefully stowed away the Twins, her two sheathed short swords, that had been her stealthy companions under the long winter coat.

"That was quick," Otto's voice emerged from the shadows.

"That. Fucking. Asshole!" Izzie's voice was a low, menacing growl, her fist coming down hard on the hood of the Jeep.

"Hey, watch the paint, Izz!" Alex exclaimed from the back of the Jeep.

Otto sighed, "Oh boy. What happened, putzi?" He couldn't hide a small smile. Izzie's fiery moods always seemed to amuse him, and Alex thought to herself for the millionth time that Germans were freakin' weird.

"Do not call me that!" Izzie's voice hit a near shriek.

"But putzi, you're just so cute when you're angry," he said, making an exaggerated motion as if to hug her.

Alex slammed the trunk shut, hoping it would mask her laughter. Only Otto, the enigmatic vampire hunter from the Von Mistelweig family – the owners of Sweet Temptations – had the unique privilege of teasing Izzie in such a manner.

Izzie and Otto's bickering, or was it flirting, continued unabated. Alex circled to the driver's side and slid into the Jeep, still wearing a smile. The past six months had been an unrelenting storm. Recovering from her injuries after the nightmarish battle with the spider shifter and Mattias had been tough enough. But then Lucas had left, chasing some hairbrained mission alone on the misguided assumption that he wasn't good enough for her.

The ache of his absence was a dull persistent throb. She glanced down at her chest, where the golden threads of the mystical bond that tied them together shimmered faintly. The strands were growing thinner, less vibrant, with each passing day. And despite the fragment of Lucas that pulsed in her heart, she could barely feel him anymore. Her breath hitched, unsteady and shallow.

Before Lucas, she had resigned herself to being alone, minus Argo and Izzie, content in her own darkness, but he had changed all that. Then he left. And life just kept moving forward, despite her desperate cries for it to slow down so she could figure her shit out. The monsters kept coming to prey on

Chicago, and her job at Sweet Temptations was going better than ever, largely due to her efforts to get low-cost, reliable raw materials when nobody else could.

The slamming of the Jeep's doors shook her out of her reveries as Izzie climbed into the front seat and Otto into the back, ducking his head to fit.

As the Jeep's engine rumbled to life, the comforting hum did little to soothe the churn of Alex's thoughts. The glow of streetlights cast a flickering light across her face with each passing block.

"I can't believe that guy," Izzie huffed, her breath fogging up the window.

Alex glanced over, seeing the frustration etched in Izzie's features, a stark contrast to her usual composed demeanor. "Moody's got a lot to learn about how things work around here," she said, navigating the Jeep through the winding streets of Chicago. "But don't let him get to you, Izzie. We've dealt with worse."

Izzie nodded, but the tightness in her jaw didn't ease. "It's not just Moody. Something's off at the CPD," she said through clenched teeth. "They're acting like they don't see what's right in front of them. They've never liked it, but they never completely ignored the supernatural. They've always been more than happy to let me do the job. Too many people would die if they didn't."

The city lights blurred as they drove, each one a reminder of the endless fight against the darkness that lurked in the corners of Chicago. The silence in the car was heavy. This case felt different. Like it wasn't just another rogue vamp or shifter preying on humanity. It felt like last October.

In the rearview mirror, Otto's figure loomed, his presence more pragmatic than comforting. "So, what did you see at the crime scene?" he demanded.

Alex's grip tightened on the steering wheel as she recounted the grotesque details, the words feeling heavy in her mouth.

"It was like nothing I've ever seen before," she began, her voice steady but laced with unease. "Izzie?" she prompted, glancing at her friend for her take on the gruesome spectacle.

Izzie looked nauseous, her complexion pale. "Yeah, me either. I don't even know how to describe it," she admitted, her voice barely above a whisper.

Alex continued, "It wasn't like with a crazed shifter, where the body is torn to pieces, with signs of eating. It was worse. It was like the body had been disassembled in a frenzy by something with superhuman strength and then left in a..." Alex paused, struggling to suppress the bile rising in her throat, "...left in a, like pile."

Izzie's voice took on a grave tone. "No signs of consumption, or even claw marks. No signs that the victim fought back, though it would be hard to tell if they had. I have no idea what could have done that."

Otto looked thoughtful in the backseat, his brow creased in concentration. "Notice anything the regular cops missed, Alex?"

She let out a weary sigh. The truth about her, that edge of dark wildness, her half-vampire nature, was still fresh news to Otto. He was grappling with it, irked about being kept out of the loop and, probably, about having unknowingly fought alongside one of the monsters, she thought gloomily.

"Yes," Alex replied, shooting a quick glance at Izzie, "there was a detail I couldn't exactly share with our dear Lieutenant."

Izzie raised an eyebrow.

"I caught a nonhuman scent," she said, wrinkling her nose in distaste, "either on or within the body."

Otto didn't look surprised, "so, you know what did this." A grunt of satisfaction escaping him.

Alex rolled her eyes, a flicker of irritation crossing her face. Trust Otto to be prickly about secrets but all too ready to leverage her unusual abilities. She paused, refocusing on the matter at hand. "Actually, no," she corrected with a hesitant tone. "I know what the victim was, not what killed them."

The Jeep's engine hummed a low, steady rhythm as the trio navigated the dark streets, entering the quiet town of Evanston.

"Fuck," Izzie cursed under her breath. "A supernatural was killed?" She knew the implications were dangerous if it was true.

"So, not our problem, then," Otto said, his words hanging in the air.

Both Alex and Izzie turned to glare at him through the rearview mirror. Izzie's eyes were sharp, her lips pressed into a thin line. "Otto, you know that's not how we do things in this city," she retorted. It was a long-standing argument.

"Just because you're not 100% human doesn't mean you're not a person. Everyone deserves someone looking out for them, fighting for justice." She gave Alex a side-long glance.

Alex's lips curved into a grin. That unwavering determination to do what was right was how her completely mundane, vanilla human friend had become the cornerstone of justice for the supernatural community in Chicago. She always cared and always fought for those who couldn't do it themselves, no matter the danger to herself. In her opinion, Izzie was a goddamn hero.

Otto, knowing defeat was inevitable, raised his arms in acquiescence. "Fine, fine. We will help all the bloodthirsty monsters, too. Why not?"

Izzie's glare lingered on him for a beat longer before she pivoted towards Alex. "So, what was it then?" Her voice held a mix of skepticism and curiosity. "Maybe something easily mistaken for human or something weak? A butterfly shifter, or maybe a newly dead vamp?"

Alex's response came with a noticeable gulp, her throat bobbing as she struggled to articulate the truth. "No, Izz," she said, her voice barely steady. "Unless I've completely lost it, it was a werewolf. And a powerful one at that. I could smell its musk" She paused, swallowing again. "Plus the fear. I could smell how terrified it must have been when whatever happened, happened."

Izzie just blinked and Otto's voice cut through the tension from the backseat. "Well, fuck," he muttered, while Izzie and Alex exchanged a look. A werewolf being reduced to prey was disturbing, to say the least.

The silence that enveloped the Jeep was dense, almost suffocating. The mental image of a werewolf, a creature usually at the apex of the predatory chain, being hunted and killed so thoroughly was not just alarming; it was unprecedented. Alex's mind raced, yet she found herself at a loss. The list of beings capable of such an act was almost non-existent, and none of the options boded well for them.

The Jeep's engine groaned as they reached Alex's driveway, the familiar sight of her home cutting through the night like a beacon. Alex's hands stayed on the steering wheel for a moment longer than necessary, her shoulders finally relaxing under the weight of the night's revelations. As she engaged the Park gear with a decisive flick, she closed her eyes for a moment, enjoying the brief respite. There was indeed no place like home.

Alex turned to face her companions. "No matter what the CPD chooses to believe, we know that whatever's out there isn't human." A fire seemed to flicker in her gaze. "And it's not likely to stop, unless someone intervenes, violently."

Izzie's response was subtle, a small nod, but her brows were furrowed and her jaw set.

Otto, ever the man of few words, offered a grunt from the backseat.

Once out of the Jeep, Izzie's stomach rumbled, seemingly forgetting the horrors they had just left behind. "I couldn't even think about food a second ago," she said, voice rising in excitement as she inhaled deeply and gestured towards the house. "But whatever Argo has cooking, I'm suddenly famished, pile of flesh or no."

Alex grimaced, retrieving the Twins from the trunk. "Gross, Izzie," she teased, her mouth quirked up in a half-smile.

As they walked up to her small, ranch-style house, nestled in the quiet neighborhood of Evanston, Alex's eyes traced the faint impressions of blood on the stone path – remnants of a hunt from six months ago, before her world had been turned upside down. She sighed, a mix of nostalgia and acceptance. Izzie was right; despite everything, life had a way of moving forward.

She was also right about the food. The enticing aroma of something undeniably delicious wafted from the house, momentarily pushing aside the memories of the night's grim discoveries.

From behind, Otto's voice cut through the night. "Are you ever going to tell me how the corgi cooks the food?"

"Don't overthink it, big guy," Izzie teased, squeezing his forearm.

Otto's frown was almost audible. "Truly, it defies all sense of logic. He lacks opposable thumbs and the height required to reach the top of the counters."

Still listening to Izzie and Otto discuss the mysteries of corgi fine dining, Alex inserted her key into the door, the familiar sound of the lock clicking a subtle reminder of safety and her version of normalcy that awaited them.

Stepping into the dimly lit hallway, she barely had time to shrug off her long winter jacket before a flurry of fur barreled towards her.

"Hey boss!" The deep, unearthly voice of her furry best friend greeted her as he skidded to a halt at her feet, nails slipping on the polished floor.

"Hey, Argo," she grinned, kneeling to embrace the enthusiastic corgi. His small, stout body wiggled with delight as he licked her face, his tail beating a rapid rhythm of joy. "Missed you too, buddy."

Argo paused, his large eyes locking with hers, revealing a flicker of his infernal origins. "Rough night?"

Ruffling his fur, Alex chuckled, "You could say that. But let's not talk shop now."

The moment was broken by the sound of the front door closing again. Otto entered, familiar with the house after six months of partnering with Alex and Izzie in the city's monster management. Tall and broad-shouldered, he seemed to barely fit in the hallway as he hung his coat by the door and headed straight to the fridge.

Izzie followed close behind, her movements flowing with fluid grace. She slipped off her jacket, revealing her generous curves usually hidden under her stocky police uniform. Looking in a nearby mirror she attempted to smooth some of her brown curls escaping from her bun, her gaze casually following Otto. The corners of her mouth curved into a faint, knowing smile as she took in the snug fit of his jeans.

From her position on the bench facing the hallway and kitchen, Alex beamed at Izzie, cocking an eyebrow.

Caught ogling the wall of muscle at the fridge, Izzie flipped a rude gesture and took off towards what Alex knew was her favorite place in the house.

"Hope you don't mind, Alex," Izzie called over her shoulder, a playful tone in her voice as she uncorked the bottle.

"Make yourselves at home, why don't you?" Alex retorted with mock annoyance, standing up from the bench.

Argo trotted beside her, eyeing Izzie and Otto. "They really think they own the place, don't they, boss?"

Alex swept Argo into a warm embrace, playfully ignoring his wriggling attempts to escape. "Don't worry, buddy, we all know who's really in charge here," she said with a laugh, planting an affectionate kiss atop his head before gently setting him back on the ground.

Argo quickly composed himself, shaking his body from nose to tail in a swift, dignified manner. "Yes, well, obviously," he said, and proceeded to straighten his fur with a few deliberate licks to his paws. Once satisfied, he sat up straight, holding his head high, and raised one small arm to point at the oven, "Dinner is ready."

Otto cracked open a beer, taking a long swig before glancing over at Argo. "I hope I selected a good pairing for whatever you made, Argo."

Maybe it was the horror of the night and its dreadful implications. Maybe it was the relief at making it six months past last October, an encounter that should have killed them all. Maybe it was the accumulation of insanity in that one little comment. But the room erupted in laughter. Even Otto and Argo were chuckling lightly.

"Oh my god. You are all ridiculous. Let's eat already. I'm starving." She took a step towards the kitchen, "And Izzie! Pour me one too. You are not drinking my best red all on your own."

The rich aroma of a pasta dish filled the air as the group converged around the stove. Argo, with his unique culinary talents, had prepared a sumptuous spaghetti carbonara, the creamy sauce perfectly coating each strand, topped with crisped pancetta and a sprinkle of fresh parsley.

Izzie, with a flourish, poured wine into another glass. Otto, his interest clearly piqued by the scent of the meal, carefully dished out generous portions onto plates, his movements precise and methodical. Watching her friends with affection, Alex leaned against the counter, waiting for Otto to hand her a plate.

As they gathered at the dining table, Argo settled into his usual spot in a dog bed by Alex's chair, his eyes following the food with a hint of pride. The group began to eat, the comforting clink of cutlery mingling with the soft background hum of the house.

Otto, fork midway to his mouth, looked at Alex, "So, about the case..."

Alex raised a hand. "No monster business until we're done. House rules."

Izzie nodded in agreement, sipping her wine, and asked, "How's the day job? Still making the world sweeter one cake and chocolate at a time?"

Alex nodded, a genuine smile crossing her face. "It's going really well. Last year was our best year ever." She paused, glancing at Otto. "And now they want me to build a specialized supply chain for our new international product."

Otto, catching her pointed look, raised his hands defensively. "I have no idea if this is from the Patriarch or not."

Izzie chuckled, "It's so weird that Alex's boss is basically a Batman for vampires. Mysterious billionaire fights monsters at night. Practically stalks pretty young supply chain executives across the world."

Otto snorted in response.

Alex, ignoring Izzie, turned to Otto. "Have you told him about me? That I'm a dhampir?"

Otto met her gaze, his tone serious. "No, you have my word. I have omitted that piece of information from my reports... But it might be wise to inform him. The amount of knowledge the Family has access to might help you."

Izzie interjected sharply, "There's nothing wrong with Alex, nothing to fix!"

Alex sighed, "It's fine, Izz. And I don't know if there's nothing wrong with me." She looked back at Otto, "Thank you. But I'm not ready to share that with anyone else yet."

Otto nodded, pasta hanging from his fork. "Thank you for trusting me."

Under the table, Izzie's hand found Otto's, giving it a gentle, reassuring squeeze. Alex observed them discreetly, noting a tenderness in Izzie's actions that she had never seen before. Izzie, always so guarded, especially with men, was opening up in a way that was both surprising and heartening.

Alex's mind wandered briefly to the Patriarch, the enigmatic head of the family that owned Sweet Temptations and his unusual vampire-hunting operations. Despite the complexities and dangers it brought, she couldn't help but feel a sense of gratitude towards him for bringing Otto into their lives. The events of October had left Izzie shattered. Mattias, that sick fuck, had dredged up all her old pain and wounds from the trauma of losing her only child and husband to a vengeful vampire before she had met Alex. Unfortunately, Alex had been too consumed by her own turmoil to offer the support Izzie needed.

Thankfully, Otto had been there. His stoic, unwavering presence had been a beacon for Izzie in her darkest hours. He had been the one to guide her back, to offer a shoulder when Alex couldn't. And now, their relationship had evolved into something deeper, something more. The subtle blush on Izzie's cheeks whenever Otto was near, and his instinctive protective stance; always positioning himself between her and any perceived threat. Given Alex's lack of anyone special, she practically soaked in the glow of their blossoming love.

Izzie caught her watching and smiled. Setting down her wine, a small smirk played on her lips. "So, Alex, it looks like you will have some investigating to do."

"Oh, I see. You are the one to decide when we can and cannot talk about the case," Otto grumbled.

"Investigating?" Alex raised her eyebrows.

"Yes, hun. Investigating only you can do," she practically purred.

"Huh?"

"Well, if the victim was a shifter, then you know the place, and," her grin became practically feral, "the best person to ask for information."

Alex's eyebrows scrunched as she swirled her wine, trying to follow Izzie's train of thought, then her eyes widened and her jaw dropped. She practically hissed, "Izzie!"

Otto looked between the two of them in confusion, beer bottle hanging from his lips.

Izzie batted her eyelashes, "Oh Finn, please, please tell me everything you know about werewolves in the city."

Alex threw a noodle at her, creamy white sauce splashing. "Oh my god! Izzie. It's not like that, and you know it, you asshat."

"The bartender at that monster hangout?" Otto asked.

"The sexy bartender," Argo woofed from under the table.

"What! Argo! You traitor! I've never said anything like that," Alex shrieked.

"Oh, Alex," Izzie cooed, "You don't have to. There's obviously something there. And he's cute enough for something fun." Otto grumbled, probably not liking Izzie's talk about another man's good looks.

Alex could feel her panic rising. This was not what she wanted to talk to them about, talk to anybody about. Her pulse quickened, the steady beat escalating into a frantic rhythm. Each breath felt shorter, sharper, as if the air itself was thinning. *I couldn't possibly. Lucas, Lucas is still out there. And probably in danger. If anything, I should be trying to find him. Not hanging out with an arguably good looking, though incredibly aggravating, bartender who is not my type at all. Case or no!* She thought.

Her thoughts spiraled – the haunting image of Lucas, still out there, fighting for his life, consumed her. The guilt was suffocating; guilt over her own nature, guilt for surviving while Lucas suffered, guilt for not pursuing him, and the gnawing guilt of wanting to move on, though definitely NOT with Mr. "Thinks he's so cool and mysterious" Finn.

Note From The Author

Thank you so much for spending time reading my book.

I would really appreciate if you could:

Review this. Reviews, even brief ones, are huge help to new authors. If you enjoyed this story and don't mind sharing your opinion, please consider leaving a review on Amazon.

Share this: When you share this book on social media, you're letting more people discover this story. And word-of-mouth is the nest marketing for a budding author.

Connect with me. I'd love to hear from you. Stop by my webpage linktr.ee/kristencoar to connect, sign up for my newsletter and ARCs for upcoming releases.

About the Author

Meet Kristen Coar. Like Alex Bain, she's a supply chain professional by day and a warrior by night. Post commute, her living room transforms into the ultimate fantasy arena and, with her tiny tot of terror, she wages war against the forces of evil. Together they become fearless guardians of hearth, home, and, most importantly, the elusive TV remote.

When she's not fighting for her life in her toddler's imagination, Kristen trades spreadsheets for storyboards. With a glass of wine in hand and a corgi or two curled at her feet, she plots out Alex's next adventure while nibbling on whatever culinary delight her husband pulled together. Because lord knows, she's no chef.

Kristen's prose invites readers behind the veil where everyday life meets raw, shadowy magic. Her inaugural novel lures us into a world steeped in enchantment and ethical enigmas, introducing us to characters as complex as they are compelling. Dive into Kristen's universe, where the allure of darkness is just a heartbeat away from the mundane.